No Place Like

ANNA BOORSTIN

For my sons, Nico, Jakob and Jurriaan Brugge, who make me proud every day.

For my mother, Hannah C. Pakula, who inspired me to write.

And, in memory of my real life Ben, Jonas Livingston, and of my fathers, Robert L. Boorstin and Alan J. Pakula — I miss you every day.

No Place Like

CHAPTER ONE

One morning, not so long ago, I awoke to find an extra room in my apartment.

I walked right by. My conscious mind registered something off, but not until after I passed it. I stopped and turned around, questioning what my brain told me I had seen.

There it was—a new door off my hallway, complete with a doorknob, hinges and mouldings that seemed to match all the other doors in the apartment. It had not been there the day before.

It wasn't just a new door. I could hear a sound too, coming from behind the door. I could hear the voice of a newscaster. It sounded like bad news coming from a television that couldn't exist, in a room that never existed before.

My adrenaline surged as I tentatively turned the doorknob and pushed it open. Inside, there was an office—an office that looked a lot like my late husband Simon's office in our old house. I took a few steps in. I recognized the furniture: Simon's Eames chair with the duct tape covering a never-repaired tear in the seat back, and the desk Simon had purchased from a garage sale. He had sanded and refinished it with a lovely buttery shellac. There could only be one like it in the whole world.

Incredibly—standing in a space that I knew could not exist—what was on the television was even stranger. Bad news, indeed. It seemed that some unknown protestors had set off a dirty bomb on Ellis

Island. Television reporters wearing hazmat suits stood with microphones in front of the harbor. Smoke rose over the sounds and images of disaster—sirens, ambulances, crying children.

My dog Gretel barked from the hall, startling me. It was her distress bark, the one that brooked no avoidance. Plus she's a Great Dane so when she barks, it's loud. Gretel stood at the doorway with the fur standing up on her neck and back. I took the few steps through the door into the hall to calm her. When I turned around again, the door was gone. The wall was solid. I heard no television.

Gretel licked my hand, mollified now that I was by her side. But my heart still thumped way too quickly. I tried to breathe it back to a normal rhythm.

What about the news story? A terrorist attack?

In the living room, I grabbed the remote and found a news channel. Then another and another. There was nothing; not a single disaster today. Business as usual.

I collapsed onto the couch. Gretel stood guard, and I didn't quite know what she was guarding me from. Myself? Had my own brain gone awry?

CHAPTER TWO

Something had been wrong for a month or so already, I had to admit it. This new room off the hall was the most egregious of the many things I had seen and heard, though there were a lot of contenders—half-seen visions and half-heard voices that logically could not exist. After breezing through recent years enjoying my retirement (I had owned a landscape design company), my grandchildren (I have four), and the company of my dog (the aforementioned Gretel), my life had gotten, um, weird. Sitting on the couch, I totted up the incidents—I had heard my dead husband's voice, seen impossible photos, and more than once, on the table by my bed, I found a book I did not own and was not reading.

All this had begun with what felt like ordinary optical illusions. I'd see a shadow at the periphery of my vision and I'd turn my head toward it wondering, intruder? spider? (or worse) rodent? But it was always a trick of the light, a change in perspective. Shapes appeared in the corner of my eye—a cup of tea steaming on the kitchen counter, a ring of moisture from a glass that wasn't there, an apparition that looked like my dead husband. As soon as I turned my head toward the phantom person or object, it was gone.

Then one morning, a bottle of perfume caught the light on my bathroom counter. The cut glass gleamed with the tiniest remnant of the perfume's gold—as if lit for its Hollywood close-up. I opened the stopper and sniffed. Barely there, the scent of my mother, my childhood. It had been years since I last inhaled its aroma.

The scent took me back. I was different, once. I had parents and a twin brother and a little sister. It's only Lily and me now, both of us in our seventies, but two peas in a pod we are not. My twin brother Ben—we were those two peas and more. He had been my other half. We were always "Ben and Lexie" or "the twins." We got along so well that in third grade, when our mother arranged for us to be in different classes, I refused to go to school. Ben finally convinced me. He walked me into my classroom and promised to have lunch with me every single day.

I sat down on the edge of the tub and allowed myself to remember. Ben so clever, Ben so kind. Gone for more than forty years, but still he lingers in my soul. He, too, would be old now. He might have had his own family, a little girl of his own, a little boy he'd have taught to make the model airplanes he hung carefully from his ceiling when we were young.

I smiled, but tears filled my eyes. As I tried to stop them—because what good are they anyway?—I blinked, and my bathroom, well, it changed. I could see the perfume bottle, but now there were twice as many items on the counter. A navy washcloth, a vase with a beaded flower, and even the brand of aftershave my late husband Simon had used. I felt my heart pound, I blinked again, and my own bathroom counter was back, in all its mundane glory.

But that night I dreamed of Ben—Ben alive, Ben with me and Simon, Ben supposed-to-be-dead but alive. Simon supposed-to-be-dead but alive, too. The three of us laughing at some dumb joke.

I woke up crying, Gretel's slobber replacing the tears as fast as they appeared.

The next morning, when I reached over to turn on the light, I saw one of those books I was definitely not reading. I had never before seen it, this large hard-bound biography of a Russian empress. Where was my mystery, the one I'd stayed up reading the night before, the comfy predictable story set in the sweet British town with its charming eccentric detective? Other than books about plants, I diligently avoid reading non-fiction.

Gretel was whining—I'd slept later than usual, and I had to take her out before I did anything else. There was no time to even investigate the book. I threw on some clothes, grabbed the plastic bags, and told myself I'd figure out what was happening when I got back home. A logical explanation would absolutely exist.

I walked Gretel around our block trying to calm myself. *Everything is normal*, I repeated, like a mantra. My neighborhood, my dog, it was all as it should have been. Maybe I'd been asleep and that book had been part of a dream. I laughed, thinking that I might be the only person on the planet for whom it would be a nightmare to read a biography. Everyone else loves biographies.

I didn't notice until I was almost home that the beige apartment building across the street was painted blue. I was curious why I hadn't noticed the process, occurring as it would have right across the street, with workers and scaffolds and the smell of paint. I took the dog out at least twice, usually three times a day. How could I miss them painting an entire building? But I shrugged it off, assuming I was getting less observant in my old age.

When we got back to the apartment I went down the hall to check the book on my bedside table right away. And thank goodness—my cozy mystery was back. What a relief. I settled myself on the couch, feet snuggled into Gretel's warm body, and finished reading the mystery, reveling in each expectation the book fulfilled.

When Gretel and I went out later, the color of the building across the street was back to tan. Had the blue paint I'd seen been a trick of the light? A tangling of the rods or cones in my aging eyes?

A couple days after that, I saw the Russian biography on my bedside table again. I assured myself it was nothing more sinister than a recurring dream. I noted that the bookmark had moved along, though. I thought, *dream-me, the biography-reader, is making progress through the book.*

More minor weirdnesses occurred:

New dangly silver earrings I'd never seen before hung on my earring tree. And then they didn't.

My extensive stash of tea canisters sported fancy calligraphed labels, rather than my handwritten (more like scrawled) ones. And then they didn't.

I suspected at the time—at least subconsciously—that I ought to take all these strange visions more seriously, investigate, maybe even see a few doctors.

Instead, I went right along pretending my life was normal.

As a rule, I don't need an explainable universe. Mostly I can handle the idea that I'm not smart enough to understand life's complexities—quantum physics, abnormal psychology, city planning, man's inhumanity to man—all the rest. Normally I do pretty well with uncertainty. If there was a person who had "lived in the moment," it was me with my hands in the soil, relishing my garden, my children, and now grandchildren, and all that goes with living the privileged and comfortable life of an educated woman in America.

And yet.

The first "final straw" occurred on a night when I fell asleep watching television. I had wanted a laugh and must have been about halfway through the third episode of a popular sit-com. I don't know if I was too tired or stressed for the humor to do its job, but I closed my eyes. When I opened them, who-knows-how-much-time-later, the television spouted news. Bad news.

I knew I hadn't changed the channel.

I picked up the remote and pushed "pause." Nothing happened. Whatever was playing wasn't streaming, it was live.

Another disaster on the news, this time in Chicago, at some tall building—a big tourist attraction. It was late at night, so the view was punctuated by the lights of emergency vehicles and circling helicopters. The reporter in a hazmat suit alternated between listening to her earpiece and trying to speak loudly enough into her microphone to be heard over the sirens. Confused as I was, I sat back to listen.

The dog at my feet stood, nudged my knee, and barked. I looked down. The dog was not Gretel.

CHAPTER THREE

The dog was a Dane, too, but male, and brindle-coated. I cringed as he barked too loudly for an apartment building at that time of night. Adrenaline cut through what was left of my sleepiness and confusion, but I shushed him and scratched his silky ear with no fear—really, I was not thinking at all clearly. I couldn't even determine what disturbed me most—the attacks on TV were of course extraordinary, but a dog I'd never seen before? I couldn't process either one.

Unfamiliar items surrounded me. On one wall was a botanical print I did not recognize. A windowsill held a succulent-filled planter shaped like a Ferris wheel. It was absolutely not mine. I was beginning to take stock of all the differences in the room when the not-Gretel dog tried to push his way out from behind the coffee table and knocked me backwards onto the couch.

I struggled my way back to sitting up. Gretel gazed at me placidly from the other side of the room. The botanical print and the planter were gone. The sitcom I'd been watching when I'd fallen asleep spouted its laugh track as if there'd been no interruption.

So much for my relaxing evening.

The next morning I decided—finally—to investigate all the recent craziness (in my brain?). I came up with a few internet search terms:

"possible hallucinations," "vivid dreams," and (especially cheery) "brain tumor symptoms." As the results loaded, I glanced up.

My bulletin board was wrong, all wrong. It no longer displayed the carefully curated mementos of my life with my late husband, my children, and grandchildren. Now it was covered with glossy photographs of rare plants and succulents, botanical information, pages ripped from catalogs. Years ago I'd had a bulletin board like it, but at my office. I didn't even have a cactus on my windowsill anymore. I blinked, disbelieving.

Was this a prank? Was I in the wrong apartment somehow?

As yet another wave of panic roiled my belly, I heard a voice I recognized—my husband Simon calling from down the hall. "Lexie?"

Simon had been dead for over ten years.

Though I knew my husband's voice had to be some kind of brain misfire from the depths of my memory, Gretel and I walked through the entire apartment checking for an intruder. There was no one. No one but me and my dog.

When I returned to my office, the bulletin board was back as it had been before. No plants. The usual photos of my children when they were small, funny notes from Simon, tokens of our anniversaries and birthdays—it was all back, exactly as it had been since I'd moved in after Simon died and I sold our family home. I tried to think.

Was I descending into dementia?

But my words were almost always where I could find them, I still knew how to drive a car, I didn't get lost on regular outings and I hadn't ever put my keys in the toaster oven. I could identify myself in the mirror. I knew what year it was, I could name the president and a surprising number of congresspeople.

Nevertheless, it felt like I had reached a threshold.

It was time to make an appointment with my neurologist.

I already have a neurologist, actually. In the first world, in affluent Santa Monica where I live, frequent migraines will get you a neurologist. Over the years, Dr. Graham had demonstrated genuine kindness, along with what turned out to be a rare unwillingness to blame the migraine victim. You'd be surprised at the number of emergency room reprimands from wannabe experts I've received while aiming my vomit toward a bedpan. Dos and don'ts, try-this's, watch out for sugar, chocolate, cheese… How's your calcium? Your magnesium? Have you tried meditating?

Dr. Graham understood. He didn't lecture.

I made an appointment, grateful he was still in business. I calculated that he wasn't a lot younger than I was.

I went to his office and told him my story, though I may have downplayed the "hallucination vs. dream" factor. He did an exam and ordered some tests, including an MRI, "to be on the safe side." After I stewed for two days about my possible-but-unlikely brain tumor (Dr. Graham said it was *very* unlikely) he called to report my results as "perfectly healthy."

So, in spite of the nagging sense that all was not as it seemed, I felt justified in my decision to let it all go, not worry, and not say anything to anyone.

Another week went by while I pretended there was nothing wrong.

I spent a night with my friend Bill. I didn't mention anything.

I saw a few friends for lunch. I didn't tell them either.

I talked to my kids on the phone and said absolutely zilch about either visions or hallucinations. My daughter Nora would be down from Santa Barbara the next week, and my son Tom and I were already planning to get together a few days after that. Anton, my youngest, and his wife had had a baby girl earlier in the year whom I hadn't seen since right after she was born. I planned to go up to Seattle in a few weeks to see her again and spend her first Halloween with them.

I said nothing to any of them. Why should I bother them when the doctor—the neurologist no less!—had given me a clean bill of health?

That was—of course—when I saw the new room in my apartment.

CHAPTER FOUR

Then I tripped over Gretel.

I have to say that it wasn't her fault. It's not that she doesn't get in the way sometimes, she does, but I'm used to having an enormous obstacle somewhere near my feet most of the time. And she's a Harlequin Dane with the black and white blotches, so unless it's pitch dark I can usually see her.

The truth is, I fell because in spite of every assurance Dr. Graham gave me, I finally freaked out.

I had been sitting at my desk, checking my landscaping blog. Though I sold my company and retired, I keep the site up as a source for people who want to create or maintain a water-wise garden. The use of drought tolerant plants, as far as I am concerned, is more than a decorative option here in Southern California—it's an ethical responsibility. My site, replete as it is with plant recommendations and tips on care, makes me feel as if I am still contributing to the health of the planet.

As I waited for a page to load, I noticed a framed photo on my cluttered desk, just to the right of my monitor. I knew I had never seen it before, this image of me between my brother Ben and my husband Simon, my arms around both their shoulders, smiles on all our faces. The catch—and it's a big one—was that we were all old in the photograph. At first I didn't recognize Ben, who had been in his thirties when he died. Simon lived to the grand old age of sixty-two and he had been gone for more than ten years. This photograph could not exist—two of the people in it no longer existed, at least on this mortal plane.

I picked it up, sure I had mistaken what I'd seen. At the same moment, my peripheral vision caught a person standing in my office doorway. This was no optical illusion. It didn't disappear when I looked straight on.

It was Simon.

I dropped the photo, tried not to scream, and stood up so quickly I lost my balance. In my attempt to not land on Gretel—naturally, she had parked herself between my chair and the office door—I fell. On the way down, I banged my forehead on the edge of the file cabinet. Luckily, I missed the corner. Big ouch, though I didn't lose consciousness.

Gretel, as you can imagine, was very sorry. She whined and licked me until I sat up.

By then, both the impossible photo and the equally impossible apparition of my dead husband, had disappeared.

It took me a very long time to calm down.

Upsetting, extremely; painful, definitely. Worse, the next day I was meeting my daughter Nora for dinner. There would be a bump on my forehead and Nora would lecture me about being careful, and about Gretel.

My kids couldn't believe I got another Dane after Alfred died. I'd always wanted a Dane, but getting Alfred was a fluke, a fabulous stroke of serendipity in the wake of Simon's death. I was learning to live alone after all those inundated years of husband, children, dogs, hamsters, goldfish, the occasional cat. My house felt huge, empty, and sad.

Alfred was an older rescue a friend had decided was meant for me. I used to say that Alfred's best quality was that he would never go to college. He could be wild, and he did not play well with others—dogs,

I mean—which meant walking could be a chore. He also adored all human beings, even (especially?) when they didn't adore him back, which also could make walking a chore. He certainly entertained me for the few years we had together. After he died, when I chose Gretel, my children fussed at me—Anton especially. Anton had been there when we had to put Alfred down, and I was in terrible shape. Too much loss, I said. But it turns out, I am a person who needs a dog.

Gretel is a good girl, really a much better dog than Alfred. She likes other dogs, keeps her nose (mostly) out of people's crotches, doesn't steal food off the counter, and never chews her bedding, which is why I allow her on my bed, which I never did with Alfred. (I let her up there only when Bill isn't staying over, but that's another story.) She can't help it if she gets in the way sometimes.

I went into the bathroom to survey the burgeoning bump on my head in the mirror. It was too blurry. I needed my reading glasses. Once I found them and looked again, I knew that there was no way to hide the bump with either my hair or with makeup. (Artfully applying makeup, to be honest, is not in my skill set.)

Nora would definitely notice.

CHAPTER FIVE

Nora came in from Santa Barbara once a year for a check-up with Dr. Graham. She began seeing him in her early teens, when she started having migraines, too. Whenever she came down to L.A. we scheduled an early dinner at a favorite bistro, one of the few remaining family-owned Italian restaurants near me.

Nora was already seated when I arrived. We hugged, then I held her at arm's length and appraised her. My beautiful daughter seemed calm, her skin looked healthy, and now that her daughters were older, she looked fairly well-rested.

"You look good," I said. "How was Dr. Graham?"

"The usual." She shook her head. "There's a bunch of new treatments but the one he gave me last time seems to be working. I guess they've actually made some progress."

My own migraines had almost stopped after I had my kids, then disappeared completely at menopause. It's terrible when you experience a relief that your children don't, especially when you're the source of the flawed genetic material.

Our drinks came and we clinked glasses.

"Mom, is that a bruise on your head?" Nora asked. She inspected me, and guiltily, I looked down at my plate.

Nora ran her fingers gently over the bump. "What *is* that?"

"To tell you the truth, sweetie, I tripped," I said.

"Was it Gretel?" Nora was forever waiting for the dog to knock me over.

"I got startled," I said. "I wasn't thinking. But I definitely didn't lose consciousness, and it doesn't hurt anymore."

Nora shook her head.

"And, before you blame Gretel," I added, "it absolutely was not her fault. It's fine now. I'm fine." I looked down at the breadbasket as if finished with that story and on to my next dilemma—bread or no bread? "And how are those grandbabies of mine?"

"You're changing the subject." Nora looked stern. "You should go see Dr. Graham."

I shook my head. I didn't want to admit I'd already seen him but for a different (and way more worrisome) reason. I said, "It's fine, I promise. The bump will go down in a few days." I looked at my daughter's concerned face and tried to imagine how I would have felt if my mother told me a similar story. I reached over and patted her hand. "If anything like this happens again, I promise I'll go see a doctor."

"Okay," Nora sighed, not thoroughly assuaged, but apparently willing to indulge me. "If you promise."

I nodded. "Then catch me up on the kids."

Nora and Jack's daughters, Audrey and Ruby, were nine and seven. They were great and easy kids, and the hardest thing about being their parents seemed to be getting them to all their activities. The complexities of middle and high school were still in their future, but I looked forward to the Circle of Life moment when they'd be teenagers and come to me and complain about their parents.

Our dinner came and, without giving me a moment to change gears, Nora asked if I was still seeing Bill.

"Why don't you bring him along sometime so I can meet him?" she asked. "Or bring him up to Santa Barbara the next time you visit?"

16

I had to think about my answer. "I guess I don't think it's that important."

Nora bristled. "Of course it's important."

"I mean for me," I laughed.

I hadn't ever said it out loud before. What was I doing with Bill if I didn't think our relationship was important?

I mumbled something along the lines of, "It's not a big deal. We have a nice time together, but..."

"But what?" Nora was gearing up for a real interrogation. Who was the mother and who was the daughter here?

I grimaced. "You don't need to grill me about my love life."

"I'm not," said Nora. "I just want you to be happy."

"Really, sweetie, our relationship is totally what it should be. I like him, and it's nice to have someone to go to the movies with, or dinner, but it's not a big deal."

"I know you've said you don't love him, Mom, but if you won't let yourself—"

I cut her off. I had to. "It doesn't measure up. And that's fine. It's appropriate, even."

"You mean compared to Dad."

"Yes," I said. "Your dad was it for me. You could call this gravy."

I watched Nora try to decide if it was worth arguing about. Finally, she asked, "What if that gravy is great and you won't let yourself enjoy it? What if you're not letting yourself feel something for him?"

I shook my head, wanting to bring this conversation to a close, "If something changes, I'll let you know."

"Okay, Mom." Nora's eyes filled with tears. She added, "But you deserve to be happy. And we'd all love to meet him whenever you're ready."

On the way home, I chided myself for being so dismissive. Nora's life was full—kids, husband, work—of course, it was difficult for her to imagine that I could be happy with only my large dog and occasional sex with a man I liked but didn't love. How could I explain the relief of being accountable to no one but myself, after all those years taking care of my family and my business?

After dinner, I took Gretel around the block, thinking intently about whether I should still be seeing Bill when my feelings about him were lukewarm. My reward for this introspection (a.k.a. not paying attention) was to slam my toe into a piece of the sidewalk pushed up by a tree root.

I swore and limped onward. Who would walk Gretel if I hurt myself? The kids were too far away and the dog walker was expensive. Bill wouldn't do it. He wasn't too fond of Gretel and she wasn't too fond of him either. There was a rivalry there from the moment they met when Bill came to pick me up for our second date. Gretel got between us as soon as he came to the door and growled when he kissed me on the cheek. She was nicer to random delivery people! I had admonished her right away.

Bill was a retired entertainment lawyer originally from New York. He'd been divorced for more than twenty years, and funnily enough, he had known my late husband Simon through work—though, since I use my maiden name, it took us a while to make that connection.

A few years after he retired, Bill moved to Sherman Oaks to be near his grandchildren. When he decided to put some plants in the little patch of land outside his ground-floor condo, a mutual friend set us up for coffee.

The thing is, when you've lost your beloved mate, you don't want just anyone. You want *that* person back.

Bill was not that person. But he was an interesting guy, a big reader, and, as it happened, we liked the same food. He was also devoted to his grandkids, which was admittedly a turn-on for me. On the days his daughter worked, he picked the kids up from their pre-schools and babysat. It spoke to good character. Though I was certainly nervous about becoming intimate with someone after Simon died, it had been an easy relationship to fall into.

I sighed, prompting a sweet look from Gretel, whose attention and sensitivity to my moods sometimes seemed preternatural.

I was grateful for a good night's sleep. By morning my foot felt fine. It was a lovely fall day, and I took Gretel on a hike, then updated my blog, adding several photos of the plants I'd seen that morning. I wrote a few paragraphs about the beauty of California natives and offered suggestions for a follower's recently planted succulents.

Ever since I'd seen that impossible photo of me with my dead brother and husband, I'd wondered why I didn't have any photos of my brother displayed in my apartment. I had plenty of Simon, the kids and the rest of my family, but none of Ben.

Lily and I had digitized all the family photos when we moved our elderly parents into assisted living. I pulled out the first CD and scrolled through it. Within an hour, I had some good candidates—one from a toddler birthday party, another from our first day of kindergarten, and the last one professionally taken at a department store when we were about eight. I put photo paper in the printer and it whirred into action. While the printer worked, I perused other photos, and thought about everything from the silly Halloween costumes I'd worn over the years to how much Lily now looked like my mother. And then a shot of Ben and me in fifth grade, one I had completely forgotten.

Ben and I were mid-June babies—yes, for all the astrology fans, Geminis *and* twins. Since it was the end of the school year, our separate classes had merged for a joint birthday party. I recognized a couple of my elementary school classmates in the background, and I could see my mother standing near the door talking to Ben's teacher. Ben and I wore our obligatory birthday crowns—construction paper bands (pink for me, blue for Ben) with eleven paper candles glued onto each. Ben had purple birthday cake icing around his mouth and I stood at his side, my own birthday crown somewhat askew, gazing at him with amusement and adoration. It was a great photo. It brought back memories.

Oh, Ben. Ben. My beloved brother, so many years gone now. I examined his happy boy's face from before he lost his bearings, and all the tears that I'd held back flooded out. There was loneliness and there was regret, no matter how many times I told myself it wasn't my fault. Logic notwithstanding, I continued to berate myself. How could I have not seen it in time?

When I ran out of tears, I splashed my face with cold water. I examined myself in the mirror. Still blotchy but the bump on my forehead had gone down a little. I decided—optimistically—that it was a sign, to put all the strange events of the past few weeks behind me. I had simply needed a good cry, that was all.

Bill called after lunch

We got together maybe once a week, and he was the one who usually called to set up dates. I didn't like to leave Gretel alone overnight so Bill usually came to my place. Sherman Oaks is about 20 minutes away from Santa Monica by freeway—but only in the dead of night. The rest of the time it can take anywhere from forty-five minutes to forever. Not particularly convenient, but the distance suited me more than I wanted to let on.

When Bill spent the night, it was under Gretel's little-too-watchful gaze. It wasn't completely awkward, but it wasn't ideal. In truth, over time Bill and Gretel had somewhat warmed to each other. At least she didn't growl at him anymore. And, though I was glad—and relieved—about that, I knew I wasn't "all in" either, which might be what Gretel sensed.

In spite of Nora's prompting, I hadn't (yet?) introduced Bill to any of my kids. I'd met his daughter a few times when I was just the garden lady and she had dropped by, but lately I'd sensed that Bill wanted to be included more in my family. I was also beginning to realize—as someone in the kinda-sweet spot between friend-with-benefits and girlfriend—that I had no interest in defining our relationship further, and even less in including him in my family gatherings.

I did *like* Bill. I also liked not always relying on friends to see movies, try new restaurants, or get out of the house for an evening. Bill seemed to have only one character flaw—a bit of a temper. It certainly wasn't dangerous, or even notable for a guy of his generation, and he'd never directed it at me, but I had heard him lose it a few times on the phone, and once with a waiter who wasn't paying proper attention to our table.

All of which made me feel a certain amount of guilt about our relationship—and also explained my hesitation talking about it with Nora. So, that day, when Bill volunteered to drive over and take me out to dinner, I said yes, and hoped like heck I wouldn't have any of my weird spells in his presence. If I'd felt genuinely close to him, I might have confided my embarrassing secret about seeing and hearing things that weren't there, but I wasn't ready to talk to anyone about it yet. It had been hard enough to tell Dr. Graham—and even for him, I had skimmed over most of the details.

Bill picked me up and at dinner we had a lovely time discussing the abysmal political situation—making grand statements about how wrong everything was, and cheering each other on—but afterwards, as we drove back to my apartment, I realized that I was not in the mood to keep talking. I was tired and wanted to be alone. At least the traffic was dying down. I wouldn't have to feel too bad about sending Bill back to the freeway.

As we approached my block, I said, "Bill?"

"Hmm?" We were at the stop sign.

"Would it be terrible if I didn't invite you in?"

He looked over at me and asked, "Are you feeling okay?"

The perfect excuse. I could work with that.

A car in back of us honked. We'd been sitting at the stop sign a few seconds too long. Bill drove forward.

"Um, not really," I said. "I think the wine might have had those sulfite things. I may be getting a migraine," (not even remotely true) "and if I am, it won't be pretty."

His forehead creased in concern. "I'm sorry," he said. "Do you want me to take Gretel out for you before I leave?"

I tried not to wince at his kindness. He didn't know I was lying, but still. "No, but that's very sweet of you." I tried out a pained smile. "The night air sometimes helps."

We chastely kissed good night in the car, and gentleman that he was, Bill made sure I got inside before he drove on. I felt guilty again—he was such a nice guy—but I also felt relieved.

CHAPTER SIX

A few uneventful days allowed me to relax. I met a friend for lunch. I noodled with my website and looked through more photos from my past. My dreams were full of activity and intrigue, but at least I woke in the morning with the right book on my bedside table. I almost felt like myself again.

Tom, my eldest, came up from Orange County for a visit. We took Gretel for a walk in the park and sat on a bench overlooking the ocean. Tom talked about his loopy ex and her loopy childrearing methods. I wished there was something I could do, but it would only make the situation worse. Denise was a slave to the New Age Panic of the Week. Poor Matt had a ridiculously limited diet—no dairy, wheat, eggs, eggplant, tomatoes (I couldn't keep track of the whole list)—and she took him to a doctor I wasn't sure had an actual M.D. But expressing my opinion to Tom for the umpteenth time would only make him feel worse. So I didn't.

I could see Tom was gearing up to ask me a question. I waited. He'd get to it. We sat silently watching the walkers, runners, strollers, dogs, and families, all out on a pleasant autumn day.

"How old was your brother when he started doing drugs?"

Ah.

"We were both about thirteen," I answered. "I thought you knew that. It wasn't much at first, just pot, which wasn't very strong then anyway."

"Yeah," said Tom, scratching Gretel under her chin. "I think Matt's friends may be smoking."

I listened and decided that I shouldn't pile fuel on any potential fires. For me and lots of my friends, smoking pot was a rite of passage, a way of saying *We aren't like you!* to the adults. Fairly harmless. But there are always a few kids who, for whatever reason—genetics? environment?—begin to prefer life in an altered state of consciousness. Ben was pure proof that there is no telling who will go which way, or how serious it might become.

"We were raised in the same house, we were the same age, and for a long time we had a lot of friends in common," I said. "He fell into drugs and I didn't, and I have a few cobbled-together theories, but I don't really know why it was him and not me. Or if there even was a why." Tom seemed subdued, stroking Gretel's big head, which she'd kindly placed in his lap. "Are you worried?"

"I don't know," he answered. "I don't know if anything's going on at all."

"Why do you think his friends are smoking?"

"I picked him and some friends up at a birthday party. One of those big OC houses, you know?"

I nodded.

"It's not like I don't know the smell," he said, shaking his head ruefully. "I had three of them in the car, and who knows who did what?—-if anything? I debated talking to Matt about it after we dropped off the other kids."

Gretel nosed further onto Tom's lap and he heaved her head off, got up, and leaned back on the concrete fence, looking at me. "I hate not saying what's on my mind with him, but he's gotten touchy, and if he complains to his mom…"

"I know, sweetie." I stood up too, pulling Gretel over with us. "It's important that you bring it up, though."

"Yeah," Tom said. We stood in silence, looking out over the almost empty autumn beach.

I debated what advice to give, if any. These decisions never get easier. I had the same debates with Simon when Tom and his brother and sister were young—what amount of what to say? Would they do Y because I said X? How much of my own experience to disclose? And I'd had Simon to bounce my fears off of. Denise was the last person with whom Tom could discuss any concerns.

"It won't hurt to talk to him about Ben," I said. "It happened, it's a fact. Family history."

"It made a big difference for me," Tom said. "I remember his funeral and how you cried like a crazy person. I'd never seen that before."

"I'm sorry," I said. "I knew it scared you."

"It did." Tom put his arm around my shoulder to let me know it was all water under the bridge. Tom was such a good guy. He couldn't even blame me for something I did.

Nora and Anton had been too young to go to the funeral but Tom was seven. He loved his glamorous uncle and had lobbied hard to go. I took the easy way out and let him come along. Simon didn't think it was a bad idea, either.

Then, during the burial, standing in front of the coffin that rainy morning, I collapsed, unable to stop crying or catch my breath. How could my twin, the boy who had shared my life from the beginning, be lowered into the cold muddy ground without me? My parents, who I should have "been there for," were a mess, but Simon and my father helped me up and held me for the rest of the service. When my vision finally cleared, I saw my little Tom leaning on Simon's other side, and I saw how my emotion had frightened him. My sweet boy.

"You're a good soul," I said.

Tom laughed ruefully. "If only it would help me talk to my kid!"

I thought about Tom's predicament after he headed back home. I wouldn't wish parenting with a neurotic ex on anyone, least of all my son. He seemed to have inherited my sense of responsibility for everyone and everything—from the care he took of his son all the way through issues like the plight of the rainforest, Monarch butterflies, and the ozone layer. Was it genetic? Nora and Anton certainly didn't take on the world with such seriousness.

Something in me changed at Ben's funeral all those years ago. I decided that I couldn't collapse and still be a good mother. Number One on the list of top parenting tips: *Don't scare the kids.* Hell, I had scared myself. I had never experienced such a physical outpouring of grief before, and I haven't since. My parents died in their eighties, so we knew it was coming, and we all could guess Simon wasn't going to make it after the initial treatments failed. But Ben—it had felt like my entire world turned inside out. I still carried a strangely palpable sense of lack, a part of me gone forever.

That day at Ben's funeral, Tom—young as he was—saw first-hand the effects of drug addiction on the family left behind. It made sense that Tom would fret. Thinking back, I realized I had no idea if Tom had ever dabbled in drugs in high school or college. He did tell me—appalled—that a huge number of his architecture school classmates used prescription stimulants bought from friends.

Nora and Anton had been different. No real crises, but I knew they experimented. And in spite of what happened to Ben, I had no such fears about Nora and Anton. I could see they were fine. I knew what to look for, possibly because of Ben. My parents wouldn't have had any idea. It was a different time; rehab wasn't a thing.

That night I dreamed that Ben, Simon, and I were on a hike with Mabel, our childhood beagle. The day was drizzly, the trail muddy, slick, and steep. Unaccountably, I wore sandals. Mud clung to my feet and slowed me down. I stopped to try to take off the sandals, but mud glued the buckles in place. Mabel, always eager, strained at her leash. My feet got heavier. I stopped again, this time to try to kick the mud off. Simon took Mabel's leash from me and he and Ben moved farther up the hill. They disappeared around a turn in the trail. When I got to the turn myself, they were already gone. I tried to hurry, but now each footstep slid backwards. I could see something on the trail ahead, a little bundle of red, brown, black, and white. I struggled forward and looked down to see what was left of Mabel, her empty skin, blood pooled in the mud puddles around her. I screamed and woke up.

I was drenched in sweat and my heart was racing. The meaning of the dream was obvious but frightening anyway—death took my loved ones and left me behind. I knew that already. I also knew that my conversation with Tom had sparked the dream. Neither of those choice bits of insight helped calm me down, though; I was thoroughly awake. I turned on the light and picked up my book, and read until it was light outside.

Lily called the next morning from her car. She almost never called me, so I was suspicious. Suspicious but curious, too.

"I'm headed to the club," Lily said.

Lily practically ran her local country club. She played tennis. We were so very different.

She said, "The tennis pro is retiring. I need to do the seating for the dinner. Hang on a second."

I heard the rhythmic click of her turn signal.

"Sorry about that," she said. "It's a tough corner and I needed to concentrate. I think my eyes are getting worse."

"You and me both," I said.

"Nora called me."

"Oh, I know what this is about!" I chuckled. When Nora was worried she consulted her Aunt Lily. "I had a teensy fall. No big deal, not Gretel's fault, not a sign of catastrophe, just a regular accident."

I heard Lily snort. She continued, "But due diligence here, are you sure you're okay? Did that big dog of yours knock you over? Nora seemed to think you were covering for her."

"No. Maybe." I had to laugh again. "I got startled and fell right over her, poor girl. I couldn't fool Nora—my hair's too thin to cover the bruise."

"Yeah, she told me," Lily said. "Remember how Mom used to tell us we should be grateful our hair wasn't as thick as hers? Like it was some burden to have that mass of gorgeous hair. It's all I can do to keep my scalp from getting sunburned with a hat on. I'm waiting for them to make shampoo with sunscreen in it!"

This was familiar and comfortable territory for Lily and me. The annoyances of getting old and the memories of our parents. Taking care of them in their last years had brought us together. Even Ben's death hadn't been a powerful enough magnet for such different sisters, but we'd been younger then, full of our own lives—when Ben died, I'd had three small children, and Lily had recently been promoted to partner in her firm. Sharing a room as children, it turned out, had done nothing to help us get along. We were too different.

"You're alright?" she asked. "Not keeping any secrets from the kids?"

It was a little too close to the truth, but I laughed it off.

"And that guy you're seeing? What's his name?" she asked.

"Bill," I answered.

"You still seeing him?"

I harrumphed. "Inquiring minds want to know?"

"Of course!" Lily said. "I take my Aunt Lily responsibilities very seriously. Prying into your life is one of those responsibilities."

"You can tell Nora that I'm fine. Really."

I heard the car motor slow and shift. Lily said, "Well, Lex, I'm here. I've gotta go." I heard her window roll down and she said something to someone, presumably one of the valets at her club.

"No problem," I said. "Talk soon."

"Sure," she answered. "You're okay, though, right? Are your pupils the same size and everything?"

"Yes, they are," I said. "And thank you Nurse Lilybelle."

"Love you, too," she answered, laughing.

I desperately needed a nap. After I ate my lunch, I lay down and conked out almost immediately.

When I woke up I did not know where I was. I had to concentrate to recognize that I was in my own room, on my own bed. I looked at my phone. It said 4:06 p.m., which meant that I'd slept for more than three hours, enough time in a deep sleep to thoroughly disorient me.

I wondered why Gretel wasn't with me in the bedroom. I walked to the living room to find her. There she sat contentedly, on the floor between my long-dead brother Ben, and my dead husband Simon.

CHAPTER SEVEN

I stopped short, as if I'd walked into an invisible wall. *I must be dreaming. Obviously, any vision that includes dead people is a dream.* But the details were remarkably vivid—my living room, my dog, my dead brother, and my dead husband chatting comfortably.

But this has to be a dream.

I forced myself to breathe, to be conscious of my lungs filling with air, pushing it out again.

When had I ever been aware of my breathing in a dream?

Ben and Simon were both appropriately aged, but recognizable, especially because I'd recently seen that impossible photo of the three of us. Undoubtedly these were the same men as their younger selves, but weathered, grayed. Simon was as thin as ever, his head shaven, more white now in his short beard. He wore his life-long uniform—jeans and a blue dress shirt. Ben was still lanky but with a slight paunch, and his brown eyes looked up at me as if sitting on my couch talking with my husband were entirely normal. The last time I'd seen Ben before he died, his face had been patchy, his bad skin a visible result of his habit. Here his skin was clear, and his five-o'clock-shadow silvered. He was dressed in black pants, and over them, not tucked in, a stylish button-down shirt. It was a thing of beauty. Black, with tiny silver threads striped vertically, buttons of red and silver, and a Nehru collar.

Gretel—who had paid zero attention when I appeared in the room—seemed to be trying to climb into his lap.

Ben was alive in this dream. Simon too. I felt the blood drain to my feet like I'd stood up way too fast. My legs felt wobbly.

"Did you have a good nap?" Simon asked.

"Uh huh," I think I gasped. *How did he know I'd taken a nap? He was dead.*

I reminded myself that I was dreaming.

"Ben stopped by on his way to dinner," Simon added, his head dipping in Ben's direction as my brain whirled. "Are you okay?"

"Kind of," I managed. "I guess I slept too long. I'm not sure where I am yet."

"Hey, Sis," said Ben, wrestling Gretel out of the way. As I faltered toward him, he got up to give me a hug.

I stood there, too flabbergasted to speak. His warmth, his smell—some expensive cologne or after-shave, I could tell, over the boy-smell that sparked memories in my brain. *Why can I smell in my dream?* Ben let me go and looked at me quizzically.

"That is a stunning shirt," I said. It was all I could get out of my mouth.

I must be in shock. Could you go into shock in a dream?

Ben raised his eyebrows at Simon, who shrugged and asked me if I'd like a cup of tea. I nodded gratefully. As Simon walked past me toward the kitchen I reached out to him—and found myself in another hug, this one so well-worn and comfortable that I sank in without a thought. Amazement and gratitude raced through my brain. Happiness, too, of an intensity I had not felt in years.

"Thanks," I said, as we separated. He too gave me an odd look.

I had to be in shock.

I continued unsteadily to our old armchair, now covered in a dark green chenille—I didn't recognize this slipcover at all. My brain got stuck enumerating the three or four slipcovers that had preceded it, and I thought, *but wait, this was a red floral yesterday.* Absurd. My mind raced with questions and I tried to fill in answers. I sat—dropped, more like—and asked, "What on earth is going on?"

"Sorry?" Ben asked. Gretel had now succeeded in climbing on the couch next to him. It looked different too. A subtle dotted pattern in reds, blues, and a dark forest green.

I shook my head hard, as if trying to dislodge what I saw. "I don't know what to say."

Ben knit his brows. "Oh-kaay." He drew out the second syllable. "Is there something you were supposed to say?"

I realized I probably shouldn't have spoken at all. I should just be still. This was a literal dream come true and I was in it. The people I lost—here they were, like nothing had ever happened. Ben had not overdosed; Simon had not died of cancer. I felt tears well up. They were here, I was here with them. Dream or not, it was the future I'd been meant to have, my brother, my husband and me hanging out, shooting the shit in our old age.

Did I want to mess with this?

Question it?

No. I did not. Even if it was a dream, I was going right along with it.

I said, "Wait, you're on your way where?"

Ben told me he had to be somewhere in Malibu and couldn't stay long. "I didn't know you'd be asleep," he continued, "but Simon and I had a nice conversation about your shortcomings while you were out." He put air quotes around "out." He still had the same wicked grin. His eyes crinkled when he teased me.

I felt like I was on stage in a play but didn't know my lines. It was ironically comforting, because the "on stage and don't remember my lines" bad dream is so typical, so normal. *Calm down, relax, go with the flow*—I repeated these phrases in a loop in my head. Somehow, I managed to ask Ben about the dinner he was going to. His answer revealed no backstory, only that he would meet people he knew from work, which was apparently some tech job.

Simon brought me my tea and shooed Gretel off the couch where she had parked herself next to Ben. She came over and put her head in my lap, snuffling at my tea. It was Gretel all right. My same dog. All her spots were in the same places – at least that's what it looked like. Ben called her over to allow me to drink my tea without spilling. She abandoned me instantly. He picked up the flap of one of her big ears and stage whispered, "Ursula and Wallace are going to be jealous." It was hard to keep from smiling. Ben had always had a way with dogs.

And there was a clue—Ben had dogs—and he had always named his dogs after favorite writers; when he died we took in his Melville, a then-elderly stray he'd adopted. Heartbroken too, Melville died within a few months. Had none of that happened now?

But at least it gave me a specific question to ask. "How are those beasts?"

Many more questions flew through my head. Small jolts of adrenaline accompanied each one, and I tried to tamp them down and act normal.

"The dogs are fine. Annoying. Funny. You know. Ursula bullies Wallace."

"Any new photos?" As questions go, this was a safe bet. My brother had carried around photos of his dogs even before there were cell phones. Ben pulled out his phone and clicked through. He handed it to me. I couldn't help it. I laughed out loud at the first image. A French Bulldog stood with her front paws resting on the neck of a pit mix lying literally under her paws. Poor Wallace—he had a long-suffering air about him. I felt some of my tension ease.

"Can I look?" I was hoping to see more than his dog photos and find out more about this dream world I had wandered into.

"'Course," said Ben. "You don't need to ask. You must not be awake yet."

I swiped through the photos, trying to keep my facial reactions minimal while Ben and Simon continued a conversation about politics they must have started before I woke up. The world was a mess. That didn't sound any different than non-dream reality.

Photos of Ben's dogs were interspersed with photos of his house, which looked to be in the hills above Hollywood and very snazzy. No surprise there. As- a child, he had to arrange his possessions just so. I swiped through shots of artworks, buildings, a few documents, some friends I didn't know, and a shot of a classic sunset from the Hollywood Hills. No children. No girlfriend or wife. But as I kept on, I found a shot of a smiling dark-haired woman about our age, taken at a bar with low light, but recognizable as one of Ben's girlfriends before he died.

"Is that Sharon?" I asked, turning the phone to Ben.

He squinted. "Yep."

"I didn't know you see her."

"I wouldn't say I see her. But she found me and got in touch and I met up with her at a bar. Unfortunately, she's still incredibly needy. I'm glad I worked that out a long time ago."

"Why didn't you tell me you saw her?" I asked. I was getting caught up in the moment, dream or not. "You know how I felt about her."

Simon rolled his eyes. "Lexie, your brother is entitled to a private life. Even from you."

Ben laughed and shook his head. "You know she'll still be cross-examining me when we're ninety!"

"Sorry," I said. This seemed like a subject that had been talked about a lot. But I couldn't help my curiosity, "Anyone on the horizon?" I asked.

More eye-rolling from both men. Then Simon asked, "How's Tasha?"

Tasha???

"She's good," said Ben with a big smile. "I think she might even graduate on time."

I could feel my heart speed up. Who was Tasha? If she was going to graduate, she must be young, right? Could it be…? I had an idea. "Any new photos?" I asked, as if I knew who we were talking about.

I handed back the phone. He poked at the screen a few times and returned it.

I scrolled through photo after photo of a tall girl with Ben's features in various cold weather outfits in front of Gothic buildings. Tasha must be at college. Understanding began to percolate. I could see a bit of me in Tasha, a bit of Nora. After all, they would be cousins. Tasha had to be around twenty, about fifteen years younger than Nora, but the family resemblance was there. "Great shots," I said, hoping my smile didn't give away how overjoyed this had made me. *Ben has a daughter!* Next came a series of photos in what must be her house, demonstrating, à la Vanna White, the motley pieces of furniture she and her friends had accumulated. It was kind of messy, which was precisely how it should have been.

"She looks happy," I said. It took every bit of concentration and energy I had to not break down in tears while I thought, *This is the best dream ever!*

"I know," said Ben with a huge grin. "The love of my life is happy." He looked down. "Sorry, Gretel, it's not you. But you're about fourth on that list." He stood up and brushed himself off. I gave him his phone, smiling so broadly that I thought I must look like a loon. My brother had a child! What could be better? It was hard work tamping down my inner turmoil and keeping my face expressionless.

Gretel moped when she saw Ben heading for the door.

After Ben left, I moved over to the couch to sit next to Simon, determined to make the most of my husband's return to me. Dream or not, I couldn't remember feeling this elated in too many years to count. I stuffed down my tears, my panic, my questions about my sanity—even having a dream like this seemed like a red flag—and snuggled into Simon's shoulder. "Thanks for the tea," I said. He put his arm around me. We sat quietly for a few minutes while questions ran through my brain. How were our kids? Were they okay? Leading the same or similar lives? How could I ask? Would it matter *how* I asked if this was indeed a dream? I should go for it. I needed to know if this was my happy place.

I said, "I'm lucky to have Ben in my life. And you obviously." My laugh sounded a little too shrill to me. "You are excellent men."

"Our sons are, too," mused Simon. "And Nora is great. We are damned lucky."

Thank goodness. I exhaled in relief. I could relax now. All was right with this world. I was going to enjoy it and be thankful for it. Maybe my other life was the dream and all those bad things—drugs, cancer, loneliness—never occurred. It didn't strike me as a remotely absurd speculation in the moment because I was so happy.

"And don't forget Lily," I said. I felt Simon instantly tense up beside me. What did I say wrong? I should backtrack. "I mean we're super different—much more different than me and Ben…" I trailed off.

Simon's mouth had opened in a still-familiar expression of disappointment, the one he used to level at our kids when he thought they'd broken an important rule.

I tried to assuage him. "I mean, I know you never quite got along…"

"That's not the point," he said. "What happened to Lily… You know I wouldn't wish that on my worst enemy."

Oh no.

CHAPTER EIGHT

Simon clammed up. He pulled his arm from around my shoulder and hunched forward, concentrating on pushing back his cuticles, a little habit he had when he was bored or anxious and had to sit still.

Whatever occurred had clearly been awful. How was I going to find out what it was?

"I'm sorry, sweetie," I said, not knowing exactly what I was sorry for.

"It's okay."

I sipped my tea and thought. What had happened to my little sister? My heart sped up. I decided to assume the worst. "I do miss her, you know."

"Of course you do."

He wasn't going to make this easy. Could there be a clue in this dream apartment that would help me figure out what I'd done wrong? Maybe I had an office full of information that would help me navigate this dream. I started to get up.

Simon stopped me. "Where are you going?"

"Office," I said.

He shook his head. "We agreed not to let conversations like this just go away. We need to talk about it."

Oh.

At least he seemed to think my reluctance originated in some emotional reaction, rather than the not-knowing blankness in my brain. I sat back down and said, "Then sweetie, you should go first. Tell me what's on your mind."

Simon swallowed. "Whenever we're feeling good, feeling grateful, you bring up Lily."

"I do?"

"Yes, you do. It's like you can't accept the good moments without... It's like I'm sitting in a nice warm king-size bathtub and for no apparent reason you pour ice cubes down my back."

"Oh dear. I'm sorry." I said. What else could I say?

"You have to stop doing that," he said.

I looked into Simon's beautiful light grey eyes—and put my hand to his cheek. I didn't know what I was doing, but if he needed something, I'd agree. "I know," I said. "It's a bad habit. I will try harder."

Simon exhaled and leaned back on the couch. The muscles in his face, in his hands, I could see them unwinding. I leaned back myself and sighed my own sigh of relief. I must have said the right thing. He pulled me closer, I turned and he kissed me.

I had loved Simon from our first kiss in the parking lot of a storied gay bar in Venice. I was there with my friend Geoff, and when Simon came in with a friend—blinking, as everyone did who entered the dim space from the bright sun outside—I assumed they were a couple. Both of them were handsome and well-dressed for people our age. I was twenty-two. I wore overalls and no makeup. Most of my male friends wore faded jeans with ironic t-shirts. Simon, even then, wore a crisply ironed, long-sleeved, button-down shirt. I thought he was cute, but I didn't think about it too much.

Simon's friend approached Geoff, leaving Simon and me to talk, which we did, mostly about films we loved—an easy topic, and, as it happened, the area Simon wanted to work in. When we looked over, our friends had moved down the bar and were clearly flirting. Simon saw too but didn't seem remotely disturbed that his boyfriend was hitting on Geoff. When we got to the parking lot—squinting in the sunlight again—and he asked me to the movies for the next night, I finally figured it out. He wasn't gay. His friend was gay.

The sun was beginning to set behind me, throwing light on Simon's face. I remember how beautiful he was. We kissed. And, corny as it sounds, as our years together went on, I never fell out of love with him. He was a gift—unexpected, unsought, and utterly right for me.

In my dream, here, sitting next to me on our familiar yet unfamiliar couch, Simon was still right for me. It felt like no time at all had passed since we'd been young and newly in love.

There's such comfort in familiarity. Skin that smells and tastes like home. I read somewhere that many people need to experience the endorphin charge of falling in love (or lust) over and over—that it's what people seek when they cheat, especially as middle age approaches. Not me. I never felt anything but grateful to be with this wonderful man who knew my body as well as I knew his.

During the years it took the cancer to kill him—the real Simon, I mean, not this dream-Simon—every time we had sex I asked myself if this would be the last time. Then, as he got sicker, I wondered whether I would ever again experience physical intimacy after he was gone. When I decided to have sex with Bill—to go through with it, I mean—it felt experimental, like I was trying some new combination of movements and feelings for the first time. The fact that the parts fit and it all worked had been almost a surprise to me. The fact that I'd had fun had definitely been a surprise. (Maybe things work more slowly at our age, but they do work.)

Sex on the couch with my husband!

I lay back afterward, adjusted the cushions, and looked at the space where Simon had been. He'd gone to take a shower as if this were a normal evening.

Yet it was curious—sex had never worked before in my dreams. I could get aroused, but never satisfied and this had been more than satisfying. Did other people have orgasms in dreams? I knew adolescent boys did all the time, but women in their seventies?

It was the first moment I suspected I might not be dreaming. At the same time, I was a little afraid to doze off. What if the dream ended, leaving me alone again without Ben and Simon? I got up, determined to explore my new dream world.

I walked toward my office and was confused to see an extra door off the hallway to my right. I still wasn't putting anything together. I peered in. It looked like it must be Simon's office. Movie posters on the walls, some for films Simon had worked on, some classic favorites. Photos of me and the kids on his desk. A stationary bike. Huh. I had seen something similar before and assumed I was hallucinating. Or was that some kind of premonition?

The room on the left was the same as in my non-dream apartment, a bedroom with its own ensuite bathroom. I heard the shower and the sound of Simon's tuneless humming. Across the hall from the bedroom was my office—also where it was in my waking world, and set up almost identically—a desk with a computer, bulletin board in the back of the desk, and bookshelves over file cabinets on one wall. Curiously, the bulletin board looked familiar, too—lots of photos of plants and landscaping information. It made sense to me in the moment, I figured my brain had hung on to the image and reproduced it here, in this dream.

Thoughts of Lily nagged at me. From the way Simon reacted when I mentioned her name, it seemed like whatever happened to her might put a substantial snag in my dream-happiness. Why had Simon been so upset? I could already tell that asking would get me nowhere. I'd have to find out for myself.

I sat down in the desk chair, the same kind I was used to, but blue instead of black. I turned on the computer, the same kind I had in my non-dream life. Would I need a password to log on? I pictured myself in one of my regular dream ruts, trying to enter a password over and over and never getting it right. My dreams often feature mundane tasks I cannot complete, easy goals that slip from my grasp. I try to dial a phone, place a key in a lock. Sisyphus had nothing on dream-me when it came to preordained failure. In this case, I was lucky. No password necessary. Like my real-life computer, this computer-in-my-dream had no provisions for a user less trusted than me.

Would there be anything about Lily on the internet? If not, how would I figure out what had happened? I didn't even know how long ago whatever-it-was had occurred.

Here I was, in an almost familiar place, in a dream I wholeheartedly wanted to embrace. Would I be allowed to stay in this dream? Or would my foolish skepticism, self-doubt and common sense override my happiness and wake me up?

The word "hallucination" flitted across my brain. What if Dr. Graham had lied, and I did have a brain tumor, and he didn't want to tell me for fear I'd give up and die faster? What if I was in a coma and all of this was imaginary?

I did a test. I pinched myself. It hurt. Then I counted out the things my body—not my brain—had experienced since I'd woken from my nap. Hugged two (dead) people. Had a big dog's head in my lap. Drank tea. Had great sex (with my dead husband). Felt drowsy. Walked down the hall. Pinched myself.

Okay, I had proved that in this dream, my body reacted as it would in real life. It was not particularly helpful.

Simon stuck his head around my office door about half an hour later to discuss dinner. He had always been a good cook; in fact, he was a much better cook than I was. But it was hard for me to be all breezy about the menu for dinner because by then I had Googled my sister's name. That's all it took—her name. I don't know why I assumed that Google would exist in this dream, but I never thought to question it.

There was an extraordinary amount of information about something that happened so long ago, probably because it was sensational—bad sensational, the stuff of tabloids and hours of cable news coverage every week. There was even a link to a podcast—one of those "how past crimes were solved" programs. Also, plenty of newspaper articles were conveniently digitized from that time.

Lily had come over to our apartment in Hollywood for dinner soon after Simon and I had moved in together. It was fifty years ago – we were all in our twenties. By all accounts, it had been a normal evening, but of course, since this was a dream, and it hadn't actually happened, I remembered none of it. Simon, Lily, and I had finished dinner around 10, not that late, really, and Simon had insisted on walking Lily to her car, but she had laughed at him and said it was silly, she was parked right across the street from our building. Simon declared he would watch her out the window as she made her way from the apartment's front door to her car. She couldn't object to that. And he did, he watched. But at the moment Lily stepped into the road, a mere few yards from her beat-up blue Impala, I called to him from the kitchen and asked about leftovers. He looked around for just a second. When he looked back, Lily was already in her car, and he saw her back up to maneuver out of the tight space. He watched her drive away, but he didn't see the guy in the back seat, the guy who had been hiding behind the car while she unlocked it. He didn't see that the guy held a gun to my poor little sister's head.

The guy made her drive to a deserted place, raped and stabbed her, and put her in her own trunk where she bled to death. He did the same thing to a few other women before he was caught, tried, and put on death row, where he remained until he died of cancer in the early 1990s.

CHAPTER NINE

I felt sick to my stomach. My dream had become a nightmare. I couldn't get the pictures out of my head—one of the papers posted an image of the car where it was found, surrounded by yellow police tape. There were shots of me and Simon and Ben and my parents. I couldn't stop thinking about poor Lily, feeling the gun on her neck, praying for a way out.

I wasn't happy with my dream anymore. Having Ben and Simon alive here, how could it make up for something this awful? Yes, in reality Ben was gone, but he had done it to himself. That sounds harsh, I know, but it is true. Simon had died of cancer and there had been bad, bad pain at the end. But it couldn't be compared with Lily's horrendous murder. Simon had lived long enough to have what you'd call a full life—he'd loved his work, he loved me and his children, and we could care for him as he left this world.

No wonder Simon had reacted the way he did. It was obvious from the newspaper archives that he had been left with horrendous guilt. One pseudo-news organization had written a whole editorial about it. How walking "our women" to their cars at night shouldn't be a necessity. They had interviewed my parents, who had somehow fallen into their clutches. They reiterated that it wasn't Simon's fault and there was a quote from Ben saying the same thing.

I couldn't believe it. I reminded myself that I was in a dream. Could I wake myself up? Did I want to? After all, it wasn't as if I could do anything about something that occurred in a dream-world almost five decades before.

I got through the evening without collapsing, confessing, or having hysterics. I'm still not sure how. Though it was probably because every few minutes I told myself, *This is the most extraordinary (and really, really long) dream ever.*

In truth, my subconscious mind began to suspect that "dream" might not be an entirely accurate description.

After dinner, Simon wanted to watch more of a documentary series we'd apparently been streaming about the mafia. In between episodes, I made a comment about how the series *The Sopranos* seemed to have gotten a lot of details right. Simon wrinkled his brow and asked, "What show was that?" I decided not to explain. *The Sopranos* had been one of his all-time TV favorites.

At bedtime I was faced with a new question. Could a person go to sleep in a dream? I had no idea. Still, I was elated to be sharing a bed again with my husband and snuggled in close. Simon kissed the top of my head, unaware of how special the moment was—for me anyway. He picked up a book from his bedside table. It felt so normal that I almost burst into tears. But I couldn't cry without arousing suspicion. I made myself sit up and examine the pile of books on my own bed table, which, unfortunately, consisted almost entirely of biographies. (There was a single natural science book about deforestation—too depressing.) I remembered the Russian Empress's biography that appeared mysteriously—how could I not?

I finally grabbed the book that was on top, opened it at the bookmark, and tried to make sense of the mid-life crisis of a painter I'd never heard of. I couldn't concentrate at all. I was too antsy to read.

I pretended for a while anyway, turning pages, and flipping back to reread.

Simon kept looking over at me. When he finally turned out his light and slid under the covers, he asked if I was okay.

"Sure," I answered. (What else could I say?) I added, "I don't know why I'm this wired. It's not like I had any caffeine since that tea you made me."

"It's odd," he said, with a little frown. "You're normally asleep by 10:30, and don't forget, last night you woke up in the middle of the night and couldn't get back to sleep."

For the record, in my real life I stay up past 10:30 all the time. And how did he know I'd been up the night before? When my creepy dream about hiking with Mabel woke me, I'd been in the real world.

I reminded myself once again that I was in a dream, and therefore all my dream-experiences (including Simon's existence) had to come straight from my own unconscious. Therefore, it made sense that dream-Simon knew what I knew.

I said, "It's probably because I took such a long nap."

"I guess." He stifled a yawn and asked, "Anything on your mind in particular?"

Ha!

Only a dream in which dead people are alive and alive people are dead and my brother has a daughter and I didn't seem to be waking up.

"Not really," I said.

That got a sleepy nod from Simon, who patted my hand and was soon softly snoring. I loved that sound.

I studied my husband's face as he slept. I thought about how long it had been since anyone—other than my dog and (occasionally) Bill—noticed my sleeping habits. I got up and went into the bathroom where I closed the door, sat down on the side of the bathtub, and cried as quietly as I could manage before getting back in bed.

Crying must have helped me sleep. I woke briefly some hours later. Simon slept beside me. I spooned against him and allowed myself a moment of contentment. Did it matter if I was stuck in a dream? It was mostly a good dream. My eyes closed.

It turns out you can have dreams within dreams—even if they aren't really dreams.

I was in some kind of park with Gretel. My big dog pulled me steadily as a grassy area gave way to woods. Soon there was barely a path to follow between the encroaching trees. Typical Southern California species—oaks, eucalyptus, and sycamores—transformed into frightening tangles of black and spiny knotted branches like the dark forests of Middle Earth and Hogwarts. I expected monstrous spiders. All I could see were Gretel's white patches as she towed me ahead. It was tough to stay upright over the rough ground and I lamented my bare feet, absolutely inappropriate for the terrain. I kept getting leaves stuck between my toes, but Gretel was going too fast and I was scared to let go because then I would be well and truly lost.

When Gretel finally slowed, we faced a mound of dirt and dead leaves. One little California poppy, bright orange, illuminated a small circle around itself, making its own light to grow here in this shadowy wood.

Gretel woofed her deep melodic hound's bay and began digging at the mound with her front paws. She was spraying dirt all over me and I tried to call her back; I even tugged on the leash, but she ignored me. As Gretel clawed away at the dirt, the poppy plant slid down, but now the light seemed brighter, an intense orange that backlit Gretel's enormous outline.

Dread grew in me. There was something under the pile of dirt, and I knew that whatever emerged would be ghastly. I was right. In a few moments Gretel had unearthed the bluish, mud-smeared young body of my sister Lily, several days dead. I looked at Lily's empty eye sockets, at the worms investigating the ear closest to me. Gretel began to lick my sister's face clean, which was sweet but horrible. I wanted her to stop. When I tried again to pull her away, Gretel turned and growled at me, her huge canines reflecting blood-red in the light. I woke up crying, trying to catch my breath.

CHAPTER TEN

Simon wasn't there.

I looked for my phone on the bedside table. Two-forty-six A.M. I saw
the boring biography, then looked at the place where Simon had been
sleeping. The pillow was indented. It was the middle of the night.

Was I still in the same dream? How could that be?

I wandered into the kitchen and found Simon drinking lemon
balm tea, Gretel at his feet.

"Bad night?" I asked.

He nodded. "You too, it seems."

"Yep," I said and sat down. "Is there more water in the kettle?"

There was. I poured myself a cup of chamomile and we sipped in
silence. I rested my bare feet on Gretel's warm back, trying to forget
her frightening dream growl. I watched Simon as he noodled on his
phone, looked out our kitchen window, then back at his phone. Being
up in the middle of the night is different when you have company,
especially easy company that requires little effort, few words, and no
explanations. I decided that this might be another moment I wanted
to savor—dream or not.

When my eyelids got heavy, I kissed the top of Simon's head. He
smiled at me fondly, then, as I stepped away, asked, "Are you all right,
Lexie?"

My brain switched from sleepy to alert in an instant. "Um, yeah.
Sure."

"Huh," he said. "I don't know, all of a sudden you seem… tentative, I guess."

Tentative didn't begin to cover it, but how could I respond? *This isn't real and I'm dreaming, and in this dream things are the same but different, and in my real life you are dead.*

I sat down again. "I'm not sure what you mean."

"I'm not sure what I mean, either," he said, with a little laugh. "You just seem confused. I don't know when it started but I noticed it when Ben was here yesterday. Do you think you should go to the doctor?"

I swallowed. Was my behavior *that* out of line? I'd better not seem reluctant, though. That might be suspicious. But of what?

"I don't feel any different," I lied. "If I feel the same, is there a reason? I mean, unless you think it's necessary. You could be a better judge."

Simon stared into his tea cup.

I added, "I've been a bit preoccupied." I realized my mistake as soon as the words were out.

"With what?" Simon asked.

Damn. I couldn't let Simon know I was preoccupied with what had happened to Lily. It didn't seem plausible—it was years and years ago—plus Simon had made it clear that subject was closed. And, what if I revealed that I was in a dream and that convinced Simon I was suffering from some type of mental illness? Even worse, what if it woke me up and ended my time in this lovely place where we were together?

"You know," I faltered. "Probably a better phrase would be absent-minded." That was true enough.

"You mean like forgetting things absent-minded?" Three horizontal grooves appeared in Simon's forehead. They'd been in the making when he'd been younger, but now they were deep.

"Oh, no, not like that," I assured him.

Not quite. Not like dementia. But what if this *was* dementia? What if there were people whose dementia took the form of thinking they were dreaming and imagining dead people?

"They have a few new drugs now that can help if you're diagnosed early," he said. "I do think you should make a doctor's appointment. I can do it for you if you want."

I could make the argument that Simon was jumping the gun, but I could also see how stressed out he was. Still, I didn't think a visit to the doctor in this dream world would be helpful for anyone. "Let's see how I feel in the morning," I said, and headed back to bed.

The full force of my circumstances hit when I woke the next morning. It had been about sixteen hours since I'd taken a nap the afternoon before. Yesterday, I'd assumed that instead of waking up, I'd moved from one dream into another. In the morning's light it seemed obvious: *This cannot possibly be a dream.* I sat up and threw the covers off.

How *could* it be a dream? My activities in recent hours now included a night of sleep and a dream within my dream. It made no sense. Logically—and I *was* trying to apply logic—the most likely option was dementia or another serious mental illness. In real life, I might be lying in a coma somewhere with my thoughts working overtime. I was surely hallucinating, going through the motions in my brain as if it were reality. It had to be something like that. Which was terrifying.

My body responded to these thoughts, oh so kindly, with a hot flash, complete with adrenaline, flush, and the always charming release of an unreasonable amount of sweat. It had been years since that happened. I tried to think back to what I used to do when I'd had hot flashes. Mindfulness, that's right. I tried to stop thinking about anything but breathing, and relaxed a little bit. I chalked up yet

51

another physical reaction that shouldn't take place in a dream. I tried pinching myself again. It still felt real.

When I finally made myself get out of bed, I discovered that Simon and Gretel had gone out already. *Okay*, I thought, *I'm on my own—now is the time to figure this out.* I went back to my office and sat myself down at the computer. The irony of using a computer to better grasp reality did strike me, but I had no other ideas.

I found a few answers, some of which I'd gathered from my research the evening before. The date—year and month—seemed right. I was indeed in Santa Monica, California. I recognized some names in my email inbox. Then I looked at newspaper sites.

There were unexplainable anomalies. Our senators, for example, were men. Our governor was a woman. The California I knew had sent at least one woman to the Senate for years, and our governor was a man. I saw references to all kinds of things that were slightly skewed. A famous older singer I'd never heard of. A reference to a blockbuster film from the 90s that I absolutely would have seen if it existed— keeping up with films had been part of Simon's job, after all. There was a huge online retailer that wasn't called Amazon but resembled it right down to union busting and crowding small businesses out of the market. In my real life, I kept up, listened to NPR, and consumed news about world and national events with a dutiful citizen's sense of responsibility. But many of the items reported that morning looked unfamiliar. Some better, some worse (in my opinion), yet significantly different from the world I knew.

That's when I began to get an inkling of another (yes, farfetched) possibility.

On the science page of a newspaper website, I followed a link to an article, then more links, and more articles. I had heard about the concept of the multiverse more and more over the years, especially since that film about it won an Oscar. I did know that the theory was something about different choices leading to different worlds, but past that, I'd never paid too much attention. It was too abstruse for me. Not to mention improbable. Redshift, string theory—I'm all in for fun facts about plant biology and the natural world in general, but those kinds of physics concepts require a much bigger brain than I either have or want.

Scientists disagree bitterly about multiple universes, of course. There were quotations from eminent physicists on both sides of the issue. And the kicker? Nothing can be proven one way or another. Just as we weren't there to document the Big Bang, no one can go to other dimensions—let alone universes—and come back with a report. We can never know if life is sustainable in any of these theoretical elsewheres. Physicists seemed comfortable admitting that, but the crux of the pro-multiverse argument seemed to be that it gets them out of a few difficult mathematical conundrums that are ultra-technical (quantum mechanics, anyone?). I could barely fathom the explanations.

Yet, it did add another possibility. Now my choices were: (1) dream, (2) hallucination, (3) alternate universe. Did it help me feel better? Not really.

I heard the front door and quickly minimized the window on my computer, as if whatever was on the screen would confirm my confusion, the confusion that Simon was worried about. He called hello from the hall and the leash clunked down.

At that moment, more than anything, I wanted to be by myself.

I had to think.

My predicament was absurd, but that didn't stop me from wanting to understand it. My first order of business should be to try to figure out where I was.

I was somewhere I didn't quite recognize. It did feel real, though, that was something. It did not *feel* like a dream.

I emerged from my office and told Simon I had been inspired to "declutter." That would cover me if he came in and saw me going through files. After all, decluttering was all the rage (...where I came from?). More importantly, it seemed to satisfy my potentially alternate husband.

I sat on the floor in front of my file cabinets, a handy trash bag at my side, and looked through family mementos—our marriage license, our children's birth certificates, documents from the sale of our house— which seemed mostly the same as I remembered them. Some of our friends were different—there were birthday and congratulatory cards from names I didn't know. I thought about the mathematical odds of all the details and I thought about causality. I couldn't imagine a way to take it all in, codify it, or even make a chart.

I found my parents' obituaries—nearly verbatim from what Lily and I wrote at the time, though in this version, Lily predeceased them, not Ben. I also found Simon's parents' obituaries, which gave me a bonus tidbit: Simon's father hadn't died of cancer, as "my" Simon's father had, but of Alzheimer's.

Psychologically speaking, for this Simon, my absent-mindedness might be a prelude to a steep mental slide. Going to the doctor at his request would be a kindness. But it might not allay his fears, especially if the doctor decided I *was* suffering from dementia. Didn't they ask all kinds of questions in a dementia test—basic knowledge—like who was president? I would probably need to study. Had World War II happened the same way? What was the deal with global warming? Were there Whole Foods and Starbucks on every corner? Which corners? The list of what I might not know or have wrong could be huge. I knew I'd be able to recall lists of words after five minutes, and draw a clock, but what if I blurted out something about thinking I was in a dream or didn't remember where one of our kids had their third birthday party?

CHAPTER ELEVEN

At dinner, I reiterated to Simon that I was fine. I assured him I wasn't trying to hide anything from him (yeah, right) and that he shouldn't worry. But, I added, if he wanted me to see a doctor, no problem.

It was as if I'd intoned a magical incantation. His face relaxed, and he sat up straighter.

"I'm still not exactly sure what upset you," I said. "What am I doing that seems off to you?"

"You seem, I don't know… more vague," Simon responded. "Usually you have your feet firmly on the ground. I rely on that."

He smiled at me and I beamed.

But I don't think of myself as all that practical. Sure, I can manage my world, (though recently I had to wonder how well I was doing that) but I'm actually more of an idealist. Even though my work centered me in the here-and-now, it also gave me a way to act on my values—try to do the right thing for this California desert in which we've been maintaining golf courses and other too-thirsty plants for way too many years.

Simon held out his hand and I took it. "I'm truly grateful that you're willing to do this for me. Go to the doctor, I mean."

"Of course—I know your dad's issues left their mark."

My newfound awareness of Simon's father's dementia had helped me grasp why Simon was nervous but understanding it didn't mean I necessarily agreed. His worry seemed premature at best. It had only been a day, as far as I could tell, since Simon noticed anything different about me.

Simon looked at his plate. "You seemed so strange when Ben was over. Like you didn't know where you were"—he held his hand up to keep me from interrupting—"and I know you said you were sleeping deeply, but you were more confused than that. And since it was late in the day, there's that sundowner's syndrome? And Ben seemed to think you were acting strangely too." He sighed. "And then you brought up Lily…"

"I know." I hung my head. That mistake had left outsized damage. "I don't know what I was thinking when I said that."

"What in the world made you bring it up?" Simon looked at me, almost pleading for an answer that made sense to him.

I hovered as near truth as I could with my answer. "I think it leaked over from the dream I had." A good call. Which I then negated with a mistake. "You know how those things hang on for me." Simon's forehead wrinkles reappeared instantly.

"What things?"

Oh dear. "Dreams, fiction, movies…" It was a lousy shot in the dark.

"You don't even read fiction."

I threw up my hands, but only inside my head, where Simon couldn't see that I was furious with myself. "That's why. It gets to me."

"See?" said my husband of forty years. "I'm telling you, something is off. You've never said that about fiction before. I thought you just liked reading about reality more. And, in all our years together you have never told me about a bad dream."

I bluffed, such a stereotypical wife bluff, but it was all I had. "I've told you before, but you must not have listened."

As much as I wanted to please Simon, I also felt trapped, so the next morning I made the doctor's appointment. I figured I'd do my best to catch up on world news, family events, personal contacts—whatever I could cram in—all under the guise of continuing to "declutter" my office.

I had an idyllic few days, in spite of my nerves about being discovered as an imposter, I ignored every inkling of dread in my belly and enjoyed having my husband around. Things weren't quite as I remembered—*he* wasn't quite as I remembered—and yet I convinced myself that it was my memories that were off. After all, the last years of our lives together had been shaped by his illness.

I was a bit tentative with Simon about being overly affectionate—after all, if I was a person with two feet firmly on the ground (as he had described me), could I also be a person who sat with my arm around his shoulder when we watched television? Could I make a tiny detour to kiss him on the top of his head while he sat at his desk or the kitchen table? These actions seemed to earn me smiles, and they felt great, but I had no idea if they added to Simon's anxieties about my mental health. Regrettably, I hadn't unearthed a file called *Lexie's Usual Routine* that I could memorize.

I noted a few anomalies on my travels through files and mementos: the California drought wasn't quite as bad—there had been a few more El Niño years that had helped the water table (and made it more difficult for me to convince my clients to use water-wise plants). Taiwan was firmly and irrevocably part of China. Photos of the kids growing up showed the same pets, plus a snake I absolutely would have remembered if we'd had one. Our old house was painted a different shade of blue. Technology was mostly the same but some of the car model names were different. Simon and I had met the same way. That one had been tough to figure out, but it seemed important that I know it, so I searched diligently and found a note he wrote me on our first anniversary—an item that even the "practical" me of this world had been sentimental enough to save.

I was also worried about the physical portion of my doctor's visit. What if I had a different blood type or a drastically different resting heart rate than the previous me? It wouldn't be evidence of dementia, but it still made me nervous. I decided to cross that bridge only if it appeared before me because there wasn't a darned thing I could do about it.

I studied. I had a lot to cover in the three days before I saw the doctor. I made a list on my computer to keep things straight—including political facts and a little recent history—events and people I probably should know as a well-informed citizen. I placed all my research in a new folder on my computer which I named "Yucca Taxonomies" to discourage prying eyes. In its way, it was kind of fun, especially because I found the differences interesting. How does a world end up one way and not another? How does a family?

It turned out to explain a lot, that multiverse idea.
It also made no sense.

How and why would a seventy-plus year-old woman wake up in another universe? I got the "different decisions create different universes" concept, but that didn't come close to resolving how *I* might have ended up in a universe not my own. For one thing, I was still me. And the dream or world I found myself in didn't seem all that different either, at least on the surface. It was the details that differed. To me they were big differences, but on the grand universal scale, who lived, who died, who got elected—that was tiny stuff.

I realized that if I didn't want to panic, to give in to my rising hysteria and freak the heck out, my only option was to keep moving forward—dream, multiverse, hallucination, or whatever. Sure, I could try to find answers, but I shouldn't let that get in the way of enjoying my lost loved ones, whether they were real or not. It seemed my life in SoCal had made me more of a Buddhist than I knew.

One tiny positive thought bubbled into my consciousness: *If this is an alternate universe, then I'm not actually crazy!* I didn't feel crazy—but then again, I didn't know if I even knew what crazy felt like.

My research had made me more confident. The night before my 9:30 a.m. appointment, I was nervous, but not enough to keep me awake. I trusted my short-term memory to come through. I had always been a good student—and it didn't matter if the me in this dream/universe was too, because it was ME who studied in the here and now—and I'd prepared myself well.

I set my alarm for 7:00 a.m., determined to start my morning with a cup of nicely caffeinated black tea and give my brain plenty of time to wake up before I saw the doctor. His office was in Santa Monica, and no version of me had apparently been there before, because there were detailed instructions about how to get to their new location on the office's message. Simon wanted to take me, and though I'd have preferred to go alone, I was doing this for him, so I decided that the less I protested, the more it would appear as if I had complete confidence in my mental state.

I woke up the next morning wondering why I hadn't heard my alarm. And why was Gretel on our bed?

My phone said 6:00 a.m., which meant I hadn't slept through my appointment. I put my phone back on the bedside table and saw, not the dull biography I'd been slogging through in that other place with Simon, but the lovely cozy mystery I'd been reading in my real not-a-dream life where I lived alone.

I was back. In my proper world? In my right mind? I did not know which.

CHAPTER TWELVE

I couldn't help it. I burst into tears. I felt gut-punched, and I cried for Simon, for Ben, and for myself. I didn't want to lose everyone all over again. My sobbing alerted Gretel, who pushed her big head and morning breath in close and slobbered. It finally forced me to get up and wash my face.

It might be time to go back to Dr. Graham, here in my own world. But how was I going to communicate my experiences? No doctor, no man of science would believe my story. Nothing was verifiable, there was no evidence one way or another. And what would I do with evidence, even if I could gather it and transfer it from one existence to another?

I made myself take Gretel out, so absentmindedly that I forgot my key and had to wake up the building manager.

I needed to confide in someone. I needed to understand what was happening to me, to get some control over whatever it was—and none of that seemed remotely within reach. I couldn't answer the simplest of questions when Nora called me. I had to ask if I could call her back later. When the phone rang about twenty minutes later, I decided not to answer it. Bill's voice came through on voicemail.

"Lexie," he said. "What's going on with you? I've left three messages and you haven't called back. Are you okay? I hope so. I was calling to get together. It's been a couple weeks and I miss you. Call me back, please. I'd appreciate it. I hope …" there was a pause and then a dial tone.

The phone rang again. "Lex, sorry. I got cut off. I was going to say I hope you're okay. So, uh… that's it. Please call me back."

Yeah, I'd better call him back. Simple politeness dictated a response. But it would have been helpful to have even a single memory of the last few days in this world.

I wanted to give myself a few minutes before I listened to the rest of my messages—have a cup of tea and let the caffeine do its job—but the phone rang for a fourth time. It was my youngest son, Anton.

"Hey, Mom," he said.

"Hi sweetie, what's going on? How's that adorable baby?"

"She can't wait to see her grandmom," said Anton.

"Are you coming to L.A.? Can you stay here?"

Silence on the other end of the line.

Then, "Mom, you're coming here next week. For Halloween, remember?"

Did I remember? No. Well, sort of.

Yes, I had bought a ticket to Seattle a few months before, when it seemed like my newest grandchild's first Halloween was a not-to-miss event. Back when my life made sense. When I still knew who I was. Where I was.

I blushed with embarrassment, grateful we weren't video chatting. "Of course! That's right," I said, trying to recapture my wits. "I must have lost track of the dates—" I went to peer at the calendar on my refrigerator. "Wow, that's coming up next week."

"Yeah, that's what I said." Anton's voice sounded deliberately deadpan. Then he added that most dreaded of questions. "Are you all right, Mom?"

I forced a laugh, so he wouldn't think it was anything too serious. I thought as quickly as I could but all I came up with was, "I've been having the most intense dreams."

More silence.

Then, "About what?"

How could I tell the story without including too much bothersome detail? "You know when a dream starts out the same as real life, but then goes another way?"

I heard a mumbled grunt in reply.

"Well at first it was little things, but recently they've gotten bigger. Like dreaming about dead people being alive? It's a little overwhelming. And hard to wake up from." I hoped this sounded good enough.

More than good enough, it seemed. Anton's voice sounded brighter, "I love it when I dream about Dad."

"Yeah," I answered. "Exactly. Me too." We were both quiet for a moment, thinking.

"Sorry but I've gotta go," Anton said. "I'm glad I checked in and reminded you about next week. And now I've got some other stuff to do while the baby's napping. Everyone told me they take up all your time, but I didn't get it until Edie came along."

I gave another little laugh. "Every parent on the planet feels that way."

I was tickled to hear that little Eden had a nickname already – Edie. Very sweet.

"Mom, are you sure you're okay?"

"You'll see for yourself," I said.

The conversation had pulled me a little out of my confusion-gloom. I would take a shower. Cleanliness usually helped my frame of mind. Then I'd return the rest of my calls.

Someone had moved the clothes around in my closet.

My sweaters and long-sleeved shirts were now nicely organized on lower shelves; the linen trousers, tank tops, and other summer clothing were folded and moved to the top. It was the time of year I usually rearranged things—hot weather clothes put away, cold weather clothes down, easier to reach. But I hadn't done it yet. I stood dripping, my shocked face partly visible in the mirrored sliding door.

Everything was arranged by color. Everything. I had always arranged my shelves by warmth. Long sleeve cotton in one pile, long sleeve wool and warm sweaters in another pile, used mostly for travel and the occasional cold wind. But whoever had rearranged my clothing had done it as if each pile of shirts, neatly folded, was a display of paint chips—blue: navy to turquoise, red: maroon through pink. Whites all together on top of the grays which were on top of the blacks. Et cetera. I never would do it this way. Never.

I sat down on the floor, head in my hands. When I looked up again I expected to see my shirts and sweaters and pants back the way they were in my head. But no.

Gretel's face peered at me around the doorframe. She generally stayed away while I was in the shower (she's not a fan of running water). But now she lay down, big head on her big paws. She gazed at me stoically as if to say, "This is unusual, but I'll try to be patient."

Even my dog is starting to worry.

Water seeped from my shoulders and hair into the carpet. The mirror reflected wild eyes and sopping hair plastered to my head. I looked like an inpatient at a mental facility. "It's come to this," I thought, and then had to laugh at my overreaction.

A new thought hit me. For the first time, I contemplated another different Lexie—a me who might have been "here" while I'd inhabited her life "there." Was that what had happened? If not, in the days that passed while I'd been gone, dreaming in another universe, who had taken care of Gretel? Someone had to have fed her and walked her, or there would have been ample evidence of neglect. Had I switched places with my counterpart in another world? It certainly would explain Bill's messages. Also, Simon did describe *other*-me as organized. If my closet was evidence of that other Lexie, it was also the work of an orderly mind, one much more so than my own. Other-Lexie might even be OCD.

How could this be the first time I'd thought of her? She probably missed her own real life too.

I got dressed and put all my sweaters back the right way. Well, the right way for me.

I went into my office—which looked as it had before my little foray into alternate reality—and checked my blog. Were there entries I didn't remember? No, I'd been absent from the online world for over a week. At least I hadn't posted anything that might have proclaimed to the entire world that I was losing my mind. For now, at least, it was my secret.

Who could I talk to? Was there anyone who would take my experiences at face value and not assume immediately that I was insane? It was possible that the only other person who could understand what I was going through was me. Another me. It was also possible that I'd simply forgotten most of the last week of my life. Or that I'd developed a split-personality, or what they call a dissociative identity disorder, one that included hallucinations masquerading as dreams. It was time to go back to Dr. Graham. There had to be some less farfetched reason for all the craziness inside my head. I'd call today and make an appointment for when I got back from Seattle.

I called Nora first. She seemed a little too happy that I'd remembered to call her back. She was on the way to pick up the girls from school so she let me off with no recriminations for being out of touch. I reminded her that I was going to Seattle the next week, and we shared a laugh at Anton's remark to me about how babies take up time—a nice mother-daughter bonding moment.

Then I had to call Bill. He'd been right. Along with the solicitations for carpet cleaning, extended auto warranties, and a few check-ins from friends, Bill had left three other messages.

What was I going to say to him? *I've been in an alternate universe so I missed your calls? Oh, and while I was there, I slept with my late husband?* Well, not that. Obviously.

I'd have to wing it. Drat.

Bill picked up right away. "There you are, Lexie. I was beginning to worry."

"I'm sorry," I said. "I listened to your messages as soon as I got home from walking Gretel."

"All of them?"

I did not hesitate. I said, "There were two, right?" It seemed that I was not going to be honest with Bill.

In my defense, I couldn't tell him I hadn't listened to any of my messages until today—it left me open to too many questions. If I said I got his messages last week when he left them, but chose not to call him back, he might be offended. I probably would have been offended too.

"No, I left you three others before today," he said. "Did you not get them?"

I thought quickly, trying to shore up my lie. "Oh dear. I figured it was something like that, but I've listened to all my recent voice mails and there was nothing."

"That's odd," Bill said. "I checked my phone. The calls were there. I thought I might have mis-dialed but when I looked, it was the right number."

"That *is* weird." Various excuses from a power outage to messages erased by my non-existent housekeeper ran through my head. I should simply move the conversation right along. So, I said the best—and the worst—thing I could have. "I missed you."

It worked for Bill. His tone lifted and he asked, "How's tonight? Or tomorrow?"

What the hell. I said, "Sure, I'd like that."

After feeling at home with Simon, how could I pretend with Bill?

I cursed my cowardice as I got dressed. I plastered a smile on my face as I walked to his car. At our very nice dinner I drank enough wine to be pleasantly bleary, and back at my apartment I poured him a brandy. When I got back from my around-the-block walk with Gretel, I poured my own brandy and we moved to my bedroom.

I thought, *this is how women do it. They just do.* It wasn't difficult. It wasn't any different than it had been before, when Bill was technically my one and only. But *I* was different, and I had no idea what to do about that.

I was definitely feeling more anxious than I had in a long time—not being in one's right mind (or world), is unsettling, to say the least. But my apartment and my life had been thoroughly ordinary since I'd been "back." Normal. Still, I hadn't been sleeping well. A change of scene might be just the ticket. I felt excited as I packed my suitcase for Seattle. Yet, the next morning when I took Gretel to "doggie camp," I found myself in tears. It flustered me, and downright alarmed the receptionist. She asked me if something was wrong. I said I was just being a silly old woman. Gretel trundled off happily enough, though she did turn to look back at me as the door closed behind her. I headed to the airport thoroughly annoyed with myself.

I settled into my uncomfortable airplane seat, took out my book and phone, and used my foot to push my purse under the seat in front of me. I was looking forward to seeing Anton—always my baby—and spending some time with his baby too. I liked Anton's wife Irina; she seemed a good match for my sometimes-persnickety youngest son. A few days with my newest grandbaby would be worth the hassle that now seemed an inevitable part of travel.

I extracted half of a tranquilizer from my pocket and dry swallowed it, puckering at its bitter taste. I turned off my phone, watched passengers stream by me, and listened to the flight crew's announcements, my eyelids already drooping. I was sound asleep before the jet took off.

I remember nothing else at all about the flight. I slept through the beverage service, the snacks, and any announcements or turbulence we might have encountered.

Two-and-a-half hours later I woke up to pressure in my ears indicating our imminent arrival in Seattle. The flight attendants were making their rounds gathering trash, advising passengers to raise their seat backs and put away any connected electronics. I yawned, conscious of my terrible sleepy breath. I used my foot to pull my purse out again and rummaged for a mint.

We landed. A flight attendant reminded us to stay in our seats while the plane taxied. Then she said, *Welcome to Spokane.*

What?

CHAPTER THIRTEEN

Spokane? I had boarded a flight to Seattle. I knew I had. A surge of panic cut right through my comfy tranquilizer haze. Had I gotten on the wrong flight? Anton would be so angry with me. He was supposed to pick me up at SeaTac, the Seattle airport.

How could this have happened anyway? They had checked my documents at every step. I tried not to hyperventilate as I searched for my boarding pass. What was going on? When I found it in my bag, the boarding pass read, very plainly, "Los Angeles to Spokane."

I never would have booked a flight to Spokane. Anton lives in Seattle. Not only did I know that, I'd visited him there just nine months before, when Eden was born.

I pulled out my phone and punched in Anton's number with a shaky hand. I needed to let him know I wasn't in Seattle. The call didn't go through. I tried it four times before finally noticing that the phone had an entirely different number for Anton than the one in my head. That number didn't go through either. I dialed the number the phone called "home," and reached my outgoing message which said, "Leave a message for Lexie. Anton, if this is you, please, please call me on my cell. I'm coming to find you." The message sounded desperate, scared and determined. When—and why—would I have recorded such a message?

I looked through the phone. Text messages from Anton had stopped three days before. Text messages from Nora and Tom begged me not to go to Seattle—but why? My regular news sites were blacked out and linked to a government site that wouldn't connect—the server was busy. I was advised to try again later.

My fellow passengers listened attentively to the flight attendant's next announcement, which was all about how we were not going to use the jetway, but would be escorted across the tarmac to the terminal by the soldiers waiting for us on the runway. A smattering of applause arose from the passengers at the mention of the soldiers. No one seemed confused except me. I struggled to open my window shade but it stuck. When I finally got it all the way up, the airfield looked strange. There were troops on the tarmac who seemed to be supervising airport personnel as they guided our plane to a stop near the terminal. The sky was dark with something like smoke. When I looked away, the couple in my row was already in the aisle.

I quickly stood up, grabbed my luggage from the overhead compartment and followed the other passengers down the aisle. I stopped to ask a flight attendant what was going on—Why the troops? Why the smoke? How had I ended up in Spokane?—but she was talking to an elderly man who needed help down the stairs. A man in back of me yelled, "Hey, we're all in a hurry here." Embarrassed, I moved along. On my way off the plane, I saw that the pilot and copilot were dressed in military gear, complete with guns at their sides.

As I entered the terminal, I checked the display screen. Flight 46 from Los Angeles. That was the number on my boarding pass. I saw more troops in the airport. A few looked like they were barely old enough to shave.

I walked by a newspaper display with huge headlines. One screamed, "HOMELAND SECURITY ARRESTS SEVEN IN SPACE NEEDLE NUCLEAR BLAST."

My stomach sank, and I nearly sank with it. I gripped the handle of my wheelie bag and managed not to collapse. What about Anton? Was he okay? This must be why I was in Spokane. I grabbed the newspaper and looked at the stories below the fold: "Seattle Tech Firms Offer Rewards," "Protestors Decry Wildlife Contamination," "FEMA Short Handed and Short Funded." The woman behind the counter barked, "You gonna buy that?" I hastily returned it, but not before I caught the first sentence of the article: *The attacks at Ellis Island, in Chicago and now Seattle have strained FEMA's resources to the breaking point.*

I thought—I hoped—I had hallucinated those disasters.

Clusters of people stood under the ubiquitous news-blaring televisions. I stopped and watched with growing horror as reporters informed their viewers that there was no entry into the Seattle-Tacoma area, that survivors had been quarantined, that the death toll was unimaginable. Several cried as they spoke to the camera.

Was I in another dream? Hallucination? Universe? None of the disasters—Ellis Island, Chicago, now Seattle (and who knew if there were more?)—seemed to have occurred in my world or the world where Simon and Ben were alive. But right then, I didn't have the time or mental energy for speculation. I needed to find Anton.

There was still no text from him on my phone. If I didn't hear from him, I would rent a car and drive to Seattle—this was why I was here, I was sure of it.

I tried to make my way out of the terminal. Crowds buffeted me in all directions. On the off chance that I had an unknown-to-me pre-arranged plan with Anton, I decided to wait for half an hour at the passenger pick-up area. If he didn't show up, I would go west.

Time ticked along slowly. I checked my phone every few minutes. No Anton in his beat-up Subaru rolled in to pick me up and erase my fears. I paced the sidewalk restlessly, earning suspicious looks from everyone who passed me, the traffic cops, and the military personnel who stood guard. The sense of urgency in the atmosphere was palpable. People picking up their friends and family members burst into gushing tears when greeting their loved ones. One couple hugged themselves right onto their knees, blocking traffic, but instead of blowing his whistle furiously, the cop approached them quietly, patted the man's shoulder, and helped them up. No one honked.

After half an hour, I grabbed a shuttle to the car rental area.

Five of us got off the shuttle at the rental car lot and were instantly stopped by a National Guard soldier. He asked for ID, proof of car rental, and our ultimate destination. I looked through my purse and found nothing to help me out, nothing but my driver's license, which showed my address in Santa Monica. When it was my turn, the guard asked, "Business in Spokane?"

"No, um, family," I answered.

"In Spokane?"

"No, in Seattle. I need to get there to see if my son is okay."

He looked at me and sighed, sadness and pity in his voice. "You can't take a car to Seattle. You can't even get close."

I opened my mouth to protest.

A middle-aged man in back of me interrupted. "Hey, can you wait and talk about this after he checks me? I'm gonna be late for my meeting."

I couldn't help it, my mouth dropped farther open. The officer shook his head. "Wait a sec, will you ma'am? I'm going to help this gentleman and then I can talk to you." He examined the man's documents and let him through.

Then he turned to me. He was probably in his early thirties, but the expression on his face was strained, worn out. "Look, ma'am, I'm here to help out the rental company. They won't rent you a car if you say you're going to Seattle. You won't get through. You *know* you won't get through."

"But—" I tried to speak. He put his hand on my shoulder and shook his head again. "You're about the eightieth parent, brother, sister, cousin, friend, or girlfriend who has tried to get a car and go to

Seattle. That's just today. Tomorrow there will be more. Yesterday there were hundreds of you, the folks who got on planes as soon as they saw the news. That's why I'm here. It's easier for me to stop you than it is for the employees. People were threatening them. It's not their fault."

"I know," I said. "I didn't say it was but…." My voice broke. "What can I do? I have to help him. I can't just sit and wait."

The soldier put his arm around my shoulder and I started crying in earnest. He led me to a bench where I squeezed in next to a distraught young mother jiggling a baby on her lap. A baby that was not my granddaughter. My chest tightened thinking about Eden, Anton's baby, and I cried harder.

Eventually I got hold of myself. The officer said, "I'll wait with you until the next shuttle comes. Your best bet is to go back to the airport and fly home. If your son is able, he will get in touch with you there. Otherwise how will he find you?"

I tried to answer him, but I couldn't get words out. I needed to appear respectable, coherent, a woman of action, but I couldn't even speak.

He continued, "You won't be able to drive out of the airport. There are guys stationed at the exits to double check stories and they've got checkpoints on all the highways now."

I tried to take his words in. They meant there was no hope. If Anton hadn't tried to call my cell phone, maybe he would reach out to Nora or Tom and they would call me.

Anton, his sweet and funny wife, and the new baby girl who had scarcely begun her own journey, were they all gone? I jumped up and ran to a trash can that stank of rancid food and cigarettes and threw up. There wasn't much in my stomach but I stood there heaving while the soldier watched from the bench. I dug around in my purse for tissues and mints and approached him once more.

"Thank you, sir," I said. "You've been very kind." I wanted to hug him, but I knew I smelled terrible.

I did what he said. I got back on the shuttle. I stood in line at the airline counter and begged my way into a standby seat on a plane back to Los Angeles that left in five hours, the first available. I returned through the restless crowds, back through security. Back to what would be my gate. I sat as close as I could to a television monitor and tried to listen to the news, which rapidly became repetitive, showing the same footage, the same maps, the same interviews, over and over.

A dirty bomb. Four different organizations claimed responsibility for this and the other bombings.

Underneath my sorrow and terror, I had questions. It had been two days since the attack in Seattle. Yet, when I boarded my airplane in Los Angeles, a scant six hours before, the world (or at least this part of it) had been fine. Wasn't this evidence that I was in either a dream or another of those (impossible to get to) alternate realities? How had I ended up here? Had a different Lexie who lived in this universe made a plan to try to get to her beloved youngest son? That other Lexie—the one who'd had time to let the horror sink in, who got it together to board an airplane to as near to Seattle as she could get—might have been better prepared to fight, to sneak through, to lie about where she was going and get in the rental car and go.

I sat weeping, then hiccuping, wiping my face with my last torn tissue. I wasn't the only one in my row of attached chairs crying. People sat all around me waiting, some frantic, some quiet. Eventually my tears ran out and I dozed.

CHAPTER FOURTEEN

"Alexandra Brooker, please call the operator at Star Five Oh Six." It came to me softly through my dream, my dream of being lost in a crowd. I sat up. My eyelids felt pasted on my eyes. I tried to focus. I heard the P.A. message again: "Alexandra Brooker, please dial the operator at Star Five Oh Six. Your family is looking for you." I took out my phone. Nine texts from Anton, all along the lines of, "I'm here," and "I'm waiting outside for you," and "Where are you?" Thank goodness. He was okay. I exhaled a sigh of relief loud enough that the kid eating a sandwich two seats down turned to stare at me.

The dense crowd watching television had thinned to just a few bored travelers. The monitor ticked stock market information along the bottom, and the newscaster was in the process of reciting sports scores—no mention or footage of a disaster. I sent up a silent prayer of thanks. Whether it had been a terrible dream or reality, my world was back to what it should be. I could relax.

I called Anton.

He picked up, sounding scared and pissed off. "Mom! What the fuck? Where have you been? I've been flipping out."

"Oh, honey, I'm sorry, I must have sat down and fallen asleep." It wasn't going to get me out of the mess I'd made, but I didn't know what else to say.

Anton would not be calmed now that he had begun to scold me. "I brought Edie with me to give Irina a little break, but when you didn't show up, I had to park and get her out of her car seat, and that woke her up… "

I could hear the baby fussing in the background. "I'm sorry," I interrupted, "I'll be right there."

"I'm standing outside the baggage claim. They wouldn't let me through security without a ticket."

"I get it, I'm so sorry sweetheart, I'll be there as soon as I can," I said, and walked rapidly toward Baggage Claim.

Anton was truly angry, as angry as I'd seen him since he was a teenager decrying one moral injustice or another. He was trying not to let his anger show, whether for my sake or the baby's, I wasn't sure. We headed out of the terminal to the parking lot and loaded Edie back into her car seat. She protested her confinement at great volume and continued to scream almost all the way to Anton's, which made conversation impossible. Then, in the time-honored habit of all babies, she fell asleep about five minutes from the house. By that time both Anton and I were too frazzled to even try to talk.

Irina came to the door and gave me a welcome hug. Edie wailed and held out her arms to her mother who took her off to the rocking chair to nurse. I sat down, enjoying the view of my granddaughter, now quiet and held close by her mother. A moment of welcome peace.

Anton was not nearly as easy to appease as his daughter. I could sense the impending tirade. He paced around the living room, and as soon as Irina took the baby away to change, he said, "Mom," in the superior tone of someone about to embark on a serious lecture. "What happened?"

I sat up straighter, trying to recover some motherly authority. I tried to explain. "I must have fallen asleep. You know I sometimes take a tranquilizer when I fly. I sat down when we got off the plane—I thought it was for just a minute—and I must have nodded off. It's embarrassing but it's not the end of the world."

Anton rolled his eyes. "Mom, no one sleeps in those chairs. They're designed so you don't. And how could you not feel your phone vibrating? Or hear the call on the P.A.? It makes no sense." He started pacing again.

"Actually," I said, "it was hearing my name on the P.A. that woke me. I couldn't have been asleep for too long."

"Mom, it was an hour and a half from the time your flight got in…" Anton said.

Oh dear.

"It was?" I blinked, thinking. "It couldn't have been. I only napped for a moment, trying to get some of the tranquilizer out of my system. I even had a cup of coffee," I lied.

"Was the line for coffee long? Did you sit down and finish the cup without looking at your phone? What were you thinking? How could you be that irresponsible?"

I knew my son, and I knew my scolding had just begun. He had to say his piece at least five times to get it out of his system. He had always been this way. "I told you," I sighed, "I was asleep. And I'm really, really sorry."

Anton's phone vibrated and he looked at the caller info. "Yeah, hi," he said, "No, she's here now. She says she fell asleep." He kept up his pacing as he talked.

I realized that it must be either Nora or Tom. My bet was Nora, the go-to person for both her brothers where complaints about me were concerned.

"Yes," Anton continued. "She said she took a tranquilizer for the flight." He listened to the voice on the phone then said, "Sure, here she is." To me he said, "It's Nora."

Yep. I was expecting this. I took the phone and prepared to hear another of my angry children chew me out. "Hi, honey."

Nora went on for a few minutes about how I was going to have to get checked out by a doctor, because napping for over an hour once you got off an airplane was completely outrageous unless I had some kind of brain damage. I didn't agree with her—it seemed the most natural thing in the world for a woman my age with any amount of tranquilizer in her system to fall asleep. The irony of having my mental stability questioned because I said I was asleep, when in reality I had been in an awful-yet-real-seeming version of my world, well, that wasn't lost on me. And I already had an appointment with Dr. Graham. I should probably let Nora think it was her idea.

"Fine," I said, when she had finished. "I'm happy to go to the doctor. You can come with me. I'll tell you when I get an appointment."

The rest of my visit to Seattle went along without any hitches. Irina had borrowed an adorable bunny suit with a hood and pink ears, nice and warm, for Edie's first trick-or-treat experience, and even though we only went to a few houses and acquired candy the baby wasn't allowed to eat, I was glad to be included.

Anton continued to steal anxious and annoyed glances at me, but he gave me a big hug when he dropped me at the airport, and I could feel him watching me as I went into the terminal. I had promised not to take another tranquilizer and I didn't. I had also promised to text when I got home, and I did.

CHAPTER FIFTEEN

Nora drove in from Santa Barbara to take me to see Dr. Graham. She had asked another professor to cover one of her classes, which only added to my guilt because I knew she liked to save those favors for when the girls had to stay home from school. Stupidly, I tried to joke with her about how driving all this way to take me to the doctor made me seem untrustworthy, but she didn't think it was funny. It seemed clear that she'd already decided something was wrong with me and that she was going to end up having to manage my "decline." No amount of levity would change her attitude unless the doctor told her not to worry—which I fervently hoped he would.

While Dr. Graham's longtime nurse took my vitals, she and Nora traded updates on their children, who were about the same age. I tried to stay calm and remind myself—as I had been doing since Spokane/Seattle—that I was here for information; everyone, especially me, wanted to know what was going on. Of course, my blood pressure was sky-high, which the nurse noted with raised brows but no comment.

Dr. Graham came in, greeted both of us, and listened to Nora's well-rehearsed (I could tell) speech. I'd been forgetting to call her back, she said. Days went by before I returned calls. I'd fallen asleep at the Seattle airport. I'd been vague, and then there was that bump on the head I hadn't properly accounted for.

I trusted Dr. Graham to note that I hadn't said a word yet. Nora had all the complaints.

Under her watchful gaze, Dr. Graham gave me a cursory physical exam—listened to my heart and lungs, looked into my ears and mouth, thumped at my reflexes, and shone the light into my eyes so that I could see all my capillaries on the periphery of my vision. Then he asked us to meet him in his office, "where we'll be more comfortable talking."

"That wasn't much of an exam," Nora said as I put my blouse back on. We made our way from the exam room down the short hall to the office. We sat in matching chairs across from the doctor and waited for a pronouncement.

"On the surface, everything looks normal," he said. "And since your last MRI was—when was it...?" He flipped through the papers in my file, "Six weeks ago—"

Nora stared at me. "You had an MRI?" She sounded outraged. "And you didn't tell me?"

"I didn't want to upset you," I said, feeling illogically embarrassed.

"Mom—"

"Hang on Nora, just give me a sec," Dr. Graham interrupted. "Your mom had some concerns. It shows she's taking care of herself, right? And the scan showed no problems. But there are a few more tests I want to do to set both your minds thoroughly at ease."

Nora stopped glaring and favored Dr. Graham with a small smile. "Thank you," she said.

Dr. Graham smiled back. "Would you mind waiting outside? I can't have you coaching your mother."

"As if she'd give me the right answers," I said, unable to resist an attempt at lightening the mood.

Dr. Graham winked at her. "I'll get you back in here when we're through."

Nora patted my hand. "Okay, Mom, I'll be right outside." She sighed and stood up.

Dr. Graham asked me a number of general questions from what looked like a standard form for diagnosing dementia. I had recently prepared for a test like this in that other place, where it was still-alive-Simon who worried about my mental state. Here, there was no need to prepare, but I knew I should be extra cautious.

As expected, Dr. Graham began by asking me the date and who was president. Then he gave me five words to memorize, had me draw a clock face with a specific time on it, and asked me some stock questions about my diet, sleeping habits, and exercise. Then he asked me the five words again. Easy. He also asked if I was having any memory issues—finding words, feeling lost, things like that. I had to say no, not exactly.

The last time I'd seen Dr. Graham, I'd taken his "you're fine," as gospel, even though I hadn't been. So, fearful as I was of the consequences, I did want to tell Dr. Graham what was going on. I just didn't know how.

"I can't see a thing wrong with you," the doctor continued. "I wish all my patients your age were in as good shape."

We both smiled. I looked at my lap. I had no idea how to communicate my problem.

Dr. Graham's brow wrinkled. "Lexie, is there anything you haven't told me?"

Here was my chance—an open-ended question. Either fess up or give up. Someone should be on my side in all this, I thought. Why not a medical professional? I nodded and realized my eyes were wet.

"What is it?" Dr. Graham prodded.

I blinked the tears away. "I was going to come see you anyway, with or without Nora. There is definitely something wrong, and even though I want talk to you about it, I know it's going to make me sound bat-shit crazy."

"Bat-shit crazy, huh? Is that your considered diagnosis, Dr. Brooker?"

Thank goodness he had a sense of humor.

"Yup," I said. "It is."

"Sooooooo…" Dr. Graham drew out the word.

I wanted to spit it out—wasting the doctor's time wasn't going to do either of us any good. I tried to assemble the words—not because I couldn't locate them, mind you, but because I was trying to choose them carefully.

"Remember how at our last appointment I said I've been having these dreams? And they're especially vivid? Like while I'm in them, they seem one hundred percent real. They're not like my normal dreams. They seem to last for days."

"Hmmm," said Dr. Graham.

How else could he—or anyone for that matter—respond?

"So, have you lost time? Days you don't remember?"

"To tell you the truth, doctor. I'm not sure."

Well, that got his attention.

I gave him an abbreviated version of what I had experienced when I flew to Seattle and recounted the trouble it had caused. Dr. Graham wanted to know about the tranquilizer I took (which had been prescribed by my internist for the express purpose of flying) and whether it had ever had any similar side effects. Was it old? Expired? I said no to all the questions.

Then we went over how I slept, whether I snore, and if I felt rested when I woke in the morning. Did I wake up by myself or with an alarm? Did I read from a tablet before bed?—a whole bunch of questions that sounded to me like grasping at straws. I replied that I thought I slept fine, I read the old-fashioned kind of books, and that I didn't used to snore and didn't know if I'd started. Without asking

82

specifically about the content of my dreams, Dr. Graham asked if I thought this might be a matter for therapy. I said I had nothing against therapy. If it helped me stay out of my dream worlds, I was all in.

The doctor buzzed and in a moment, Nora was with us.

"Nora," said Dr. Graham. "I have not found a thing physically wrong with your mother. She passes all the cognitive tests easily. The root of her problem, as she describes it, is that she's having extremely vivid dreams, and as you know, that's not strictly my department." He picked up a pen and scrawled in my file while he talked. "But we're not done, yet. I'm going to order some blood tests, a sleep study, and another brain scan to check against the one we have already." He closed my file. "I know we just did one, but on the off chance that it changed, it won't hurt to do another and compare the two." He added, "And you can decide yourself about the other possibility."

"What's that?" asked Nora.

"Therapy," I said. "The dreams."

"That part is up to her," said Dr. Graham. "We'll draw your blood now, and you can check with the nurses on your way out to set up your other tests." He stood up. "It was a treat to see you both. I'll call when all the test results come back."

We shook hands. On our way out, Nora (rather ostentatiously, if you ask me) took the printouts from the nurse at the front desk. It was more than possible that she didn't trust me to follow up.

CHAPTER SIXTEEN

I took Nora out for sushi—her favorite—to thank her for the trouble she had taken driving down to L.A. and accompanying me to the doctor. We settled in the farthest corner of the restaurant—the bar hadn't felt private enough—and examined our lunch menus. Though I was tempted to have a glass of wine or a nice light Japanese beer, I knew I had to be on my game. Nora wanted to know all about those "vivid dreams" I'd discussed with the doctor. I tried to relax and not feel judged.

Nora's brothers called her bossy because, though she was the middle child, she tried to mother them both. Frankly, she could be a bit strident. I hoped I hadn't (unwittingly) instilled care-taking tendencies because she was The Girl, but I reminded myself of the many times when I'd tried to convince her—gently and also not-so-gently—that she wasn't in charge of everyone's well-being.

How was I going to explain? What happened on the airplane was only the tip of the iceberg. How could Nora understand if I didn't open up completely? I wanted to tell her all about the world where her father was still alive and her uncle had never overdosed.

I jumped in with very little idea where I'd end up. "I'll tell you about the airport dream first, and that should give you an idea what's been going on."

"Mom, you don't need to edit with me. I can take it, whatever it is."

Okay then. "So, I took half of a tranquilizer when I got on the plane because I hadn't been sleeping too well, which was because of the other dreams."

That was confusing. Not the best beginning. But now it was out of my mouth and I was stuck with it.

"Anyway, I fell asleep almost instantly, and when I woke up, I was on the plane, but the announcement said that we had landed in Spokane."

I watched Nora's brow crease. As I told my unlikely tale, I realized that all the peculiar obstacles I had encountered made it sound like it *had* been a dream. Nora listened gamely while I told her about the National Guardsman who had sent me back to the terminal, and how I'd fallen asleep waiting for my return flight to L.A.

The waitress came over with our drinks and took our sushi orders. My tea was too hot to drink, but I cupped my hands around the fine ceramic mug feeling its delicate ridges and its warmth.

"That sounds like such a scary dream," Nora said. She reached across the table and took my hand. "But what made you think it was real? I mean, that's the problem, right? That you thought it was real? You know you aren't normally a suspicious person. You usually believe what you see."

"It felt real, that's all I can say. Like, my muscles felt tired when I pulled my suitcase around the airport. I felt like I had a hangover from the tranquilizer while I was walking around, and when I was crying my nose ran. That doesn't happen in dreams, at least not to me. I mean, sure, I get frustrated in dreams, but there's usually no physical sensation. Also, the half hour I waited for Anton felt like half an hour. I kept looking at my watch to see if I could go get a rental car yet. And though I knew it didn't make sense for me to wait for him to pick me up in Spokane, I decided I didn't know the rules of that reality, so I kept waiting."

"What did you mean by 'that reality?'" Nora asked. "Do you mean because it was a dream, he could be living in a different place?"

"Not quite." I sipped my tea for something to do and burnt my tongue. "Ouch." I took a hasty swig of ice water.

"Oh, Mom."

I felt incompetent, but anyone can burn their tongue, right? I took a deep breath and said, "In these dreams, things are different. It feels like I'm experiencing another timeline, another possibility for my life—but I'm only dipping into it long enough to be confused. I've been reading about something called the multiverse…"

Nora made a face. "Sorry, but Mom… other universes? Really?"

"It's the only thing that makes sense. Even though I know it doesn't make sense," I answered. "Since it started I did some research."

Nora jumped in. "When did it start?"

"Gosh, about three months ago—not the research, that was recent—but the, um, the weird stuff. I kept seeing things that couldn't be there—one was a photo of me with Ben and your dad where we all looked as old as I am now, and I also heard your dad's voice in the apartment. Of course I thought I was hallucinating, which is why I went to Dr. Graham originally and had the scan."

Nora nodded. I went on.

"Then, about a week ago, I woke up from a nap to what I thought was a dream—I was in my same apartment but your dad and Ben were there—and it went on and on for days. I had to wonder if I *was* dreaming. I went to sleep each night and when I woke up I was still there with your dad. I think it was during that time when you said I didn't call you back."

Nora took an ice cube from her water glass and put it in her tea. She swirled it around and then took a sip. She was stalling. I knew that trick myself. She'd probably gotten it from me. It's a good way to seem thoughtful when what you actually want to do is yell *WTF?!* at the top of your lungs. She asked, "Did you tell Dr. Graham this? I mean the specifics?"

"Not entirely." I added, "It does sound awfully far-fetched when I say it aloud."

"Yeah," Nora agreed. "It does." She took another sip of her tea. "What else?"

I told her. Not every detail, but as many as I could manage without going into too much detail. I said how happy I was to be back living with her father. How the apartment had an extra room, and how Gretel was virtually the same, and how I felt I was constantly having to figure things out to avoid screwing up. And how Ben was alive and happy and had a daughter. (Nora didn't ask about Lily so I didn't tell her.) I described my research, and how being in an alternate universe was the only option that made sense—besides being in a coma and imagining the entire scenario, that is. I also told her that in the other life, Simon thought I was acting strangely and wanted me to see a doctor. We had a little laugh about that, and then the sushi came and we ate quietly for a while.

"Mom?"

I looked up from trying to negotiate a particularly slippery piece of fish with my chopsticks. These were the fancy plastic ones, which don't grip.

"What was it like having Dad around again?" Nora's eyes had that shine to them, the way they always did when she talked about her father.

It was my turn to reach out and pat her hand. "It was... it was amazing. I fell into it like it had been that way forever, which, well, it had. He retired and was doing some consulting and some charitable stuff." I tried to blink away tears. "And it all worked, even the sex."

"Ewwww!" Nora laughed as she said it.

I laughed too. "Yeah, even hypothetical sex between your parents is gross, huh?"

"Even when you're grown up," added Nora.

"But seriously, I guess this could also be a brain tumor making me think I'm living in memories or concocting alternate scenarios—I don't know. And if it is, I will accept it. It can't be too bad a way to go out."

"Mom don't say that." Nora shook her head vehemently. "My kids need you to be their grandmom. If it were up to Jack's mom, they'd be dressed in crinolines and bonnets."

I had to smile. "Thanks, I appreciate that," I said. "And how's that garden doing anyway? Are the girls helping you like they promised when we set it up?"

"You're changing the subject, Mom."

"I am. I don't know what else I can add." I took up my chopsticks and ate the last piece of my roll. "What are you going to tell your brothers? You know they'll be calling you soon—if they haven't already."

Nora picked her phone up from the table. "Yep. Text from Anton. Nothing from Tom yet, but you're right. What do you want me to say?"

I shrugged, overwhelmed by the thought of talking about this anymore, at all, ever, especially later that day. "I don't know. Whatever you want? Or—" I couldn't help it, I giggled. "Mom's having a great time flitting between universes and checking out the lives she's lived, plus some she hasn't."

"So, like, you're enjoying travel in your senior years?" Nora actually grinned.

I felt just a little triumphant. "Yes, that's it!"

It took only a moment for Nora's expression to turn pensive. "I wish it were that, Mom, I do." Nora swallowed and added, very softly, so I had to lean forward to catch it. "But I'm scared."

I sat back in my chair. "I'm kinda scared too," I said.

CHAPTER SEVENTEEN

When I got home, I had two voicemails, one from Anton and one from Tom. I assumed Anton had spoken to Nora already—he probably called her while she was driving home. Tom's message said that he hadn't talked to Nora yet because he wanted to hear from me first. I appreciated that, though it meant I'd have to go over what happened at the doctor again, plus what I'd talked about with Nora. My brain was exhausted enough already.

But I had to call. My sons were worried.

Tom has the patience of a saint—he always has. He's also one of those people who was born with a dash of extra empathy. As a child, he would burst into tears over stories he heard on the news and the fate of fictional characters in books and movies. Tom had already heard Anton's complaints about my behavior at the airport, so right away I described what had happened in my dream (or not-a-dream?) in Spokane.

"That would make me a permanent insomniac," Tom said. "How scary to go to sleep when you don't know what it'll be like when you wake up."

"I told Dr. Graham I was having vivid dreams because it seemed like the best explanation," I told him. "But honestly, it all felt completely real. Down to physical sensations. Not like dreams at all. Time passing, the whole deal." I was learning to abbreviate my descriptions.

"Huh," said Tom. "Do you want to tell me about it?"

I tried to include everything I'd said to Nora about spending time in that place where Simon and Ben were both alive. I didn't want one of them to say to the other, "She didn't tell me that!" It was interesting to hear their different questions. Tom asked if I had any feeling of control over the dreams—could I make myself go somewhere by thinking certain thoughts before I went to sleep, or was it random? I had no idea, of course. Like Nora, Tom wanted to know all about his dad, but he also wanted to hear about Ben, who he remembered as an occasional visitor who was happy to play Lego with him for way longer than any other grown-up. He seemed as taken with Ben's new (dream?) life as I was. I told him about the photos I'd seen—Ben's dogs, Ben's house, Ben's daughter.

"So, I have a cousin in another universe?"

I couldn't help smiling. Tom was such an easy sell. Like me, I guess.

"Mom, do you want me to come sleep over at your place for a few nights? Check on you while you're sleeping?"

"That's very sweet," I said, feeling tears threaten for about the fifth time that day. "But let me do these tests the doctor ordered. Then we'll know more about what we're dealing with."

We planned a dinner for the next weekend with Tom's son, Matt. I made myself a cup of tea before calling Anton, realizing—too late—that I should have engaged technology and arranged a Zoom to talk to both of my boys at once.

Anton had already quizzed Nora about my doctor's appointment. He seemed to feel bad that he had been angry at me when I was visiting and spoke as if he was sure one of the tests would return some version of a death sentence for me. I knew this was his way of preparing himself, but when I tried to ask why it wasn't conceivable that I was fine, healthy, sane, and this was some sort of alternate timeline experience, he—my only science-fiction-fan child—was dismissive.

"Look Mom, I know there have been lots of articles and books and movies about multiple universes in the last few years. But that doesn't mean there are holes between worlds you can fall into."

"I know that," I said. "I just don't know another way to explain an experience that feels very real to me."

"Yeah, but it *must* be a medical issue," Anton insisted. "I know it's not pleasant to think about, but I want to make sure you get all the tests—the brain scan, especially."

"And Dr. Graham has lots of years of my old brain scans, which should be useful," I said. "But honestly, hon, from inside this old brain of mine, I feel like the same me."

"Then what else could be going on?" Anton sounded impatient. "Think about when Nora started getting optical illusions from her migraines. Your brain can affect what you see."

"You're right," I said. "It can, but I'm not sure if brain chemistry ever makes different kinds of delusions happen all at once—feeling, hearing, smelling, sensing the passing of time. People who have mental illnesses like schizophrenia hear voices in their heads telling them the world isn't the way it is, but when they look out into it, does it look the same? I have no idea. But let's say it is hallucinations—they aren't just vivid, they have boring moments, too. I've never experienced anything like it."

"Did you ever do hallucinogens?"

"No," I admitted. "Never. All I did was smoke a little grass in high school. Ben was the druggie, not me."

"They call it weed now, Mom," said my son. "And I wasn't ever sure you were telling us the truth—you might have wanted us to believe you were straight because of Ben dying."

"I was always truthful about the important things," I said. "Because I wanted you guys to be truthful back. And again, these do not feel like hallucinations when I'm having them."

"Okay, okay." Anton still sounded like he was humoring me. "But you have to admit that you're not super judgmental—you kinda take things at face value."

"Nora said that too!" I protested. "But why do you both think that? I'm not naive—more like hopeful."

"Remember how we had to tell you that people lie on the internet all the time?"

He had a point there. It took me a while to come to grips with the fact that people put stuff out there that they knew wasn't true. But he was also exaggerating.

"You're logical, Mom," he continued. "But what if you're using incomplete data?

"Look," I told him, "If a doctor tells me there's a physical problem causing my brain to misfire or whatever, I'll believe it. But at the moment, that seems—that *feels*—unlikely."

Anton was quiet for a moment. Then he said, "Let's say you're right and the only workable answer is that you are traveling from our universe—our timeline—to another one. Whether it makes sense or not. And, by the way, it doesn't."

I sighed.

"But answer me this," he went on. "Of all the people this was going to happen to—the Dalai Lama, the president, scientists who study physics and astronomy, science fiction writers, people who drop acid all the time—of all of those people, why is it happening to you?"

"Oh, sweetie," I said. "I don't know."

CHAPTER EIGHTEEN

I had taken the first available time slot for a brain scan and showed up as requested at 8:30 a.m. for a 9 a.m. appointment.

Over the years, I've had a few CAT scans and MRIs, and each and every time I am thankful that small spaces don't bother me. Scans can be a total nightmare for claustrophobes. It's like being stuffed into a cannon headfirst. All you can see is the inside of a metal tube mere inches from your nose. When the test starts, you're bombarded by the deafening sound of metal on metal—cameras like roller coaster cars zipping around you on metal tracks. Sometimes they give you earplugs.

These days, there are improvements. They've made the tubes "open," and there's less noise. Ten minutes after I lay down, I was done. No point in looking to the technicians for clues about my results. I'd have to wait for Dr. Graham to get back to me.

All the happy-go-lucky certainty I assumed for my kids' sakes barely covered my underlying apprehension. I wasn't ready to leave my life yet. I knew everyone facing these kinds of situations feels the same while they wait for test results, but that, of course, didn't help.

I decided to take Gretel for a hike and then go to the cemetery to visit Ben—not the Ben I'd seen in my dream/alternate reality but *my* Ben, my brother who had lived and died in *this* world. It was a chilly day anyway and Gretel could hang out in the car for a few minutes while I chatted with the dead.

Ben was buried in a little cemetery in Westwood where our parents bought plots for themselves after he died. My mother said it was so she could look after him better than she had when he was alive. We all protested—not about the location, which was fine, and not about the sentiment, which was lovely—but that she was planning to take her self-blame to the grave.

I stopped and bought flowers, white tulips for Ben and spray roses for my parents—well, mainly for my mother, who loved roses and had great luck growing them. I thought about the rose bushes she'd planted and tended—were they still in the backyard of the house I grew up in? The house is near the cemetery, but I don't drive by it much because I don't want to see what the people who own it now have done to it.

There were a lot of tourists at the cemetery. Movie stars were buried there, and as much as I liked this small, homey spot, a miniature oasis of green surrounded by tall glass and steel buildings, it was never deserted.

I kissed Gretel's big nose sticking out of the window and made my way across the grass to my family's little plot, careful not to step on the mostly flat headstones. I placed the roses for my parents into the little reservoirs at the base of their markers. They held a few inches of water from the sprinklers, which ran daily in spite of any drought.

I said my hellos, feeling foolish when a tourist's scream (She found her idol's crypt! So happy!) interrupted my little catch-up speech to my mom and dad. I like to talk at graves. But I also like to feel as though it's private, and loud tourists can wreck the mood.

Then, I set out Ben's tulips. The headstone gave his name and the dates of his birth and death, nothing else. That was all my mother wanted. I had lobbied for "beloved son and brother," but she wanted simpler.

Was Ben truly alive in that alternate place I had visited, or had I hallucinated the entire experience? The memory of seeing him after all those years turned quickly into tears. And now, how could I talk to him like I usually did here at his grave, catching him up on my kids and their children, telling him stories that would have made him laugh and about books I read that I knew he would have loved? None of it made sense anymore and I started to feel very sorry for myself. I was certainly in the right place for that. I let myself cry.

Through my tears the world wavered. Suddenly, I was alone with no tourists in earshot. Clouds covered the sun, the wind had picked up, and the grave before me read "Lily Rebecca Brooker," with dates for her birth and death, thirty years earlier. The tulips I brought for Ben had become a lovely branch of fragrant white lilies over her grave. I choked on my tears, began to cough and couldn't stop. I tried to stand up, thinking I'd get my water bottle from the car. I heard Gretel's big bark, but I couldn't move yet. I knelt back down, still coughing.

Then the sun was back, and an official from the cemetery was at my side, brand new water bottle in hand, patting me on the back and asking if I was okay and if Gretel was my dog—and if so, could I get her to quiet down, please? I chugged the water, took deep breaths and looked down to find Ben's headstone again. I had no idea how much time had passed, but I apologized hoarsely and thanked the woman for her concern. I reached down, touched Ben's headstone as a goodbye, and went back to Gretel, who quieted when she saw me coming. She'd attracted a small crowd around my car. One girl wanted to have her photo taken with her, but I couldn't talk to anyone right then.

I very purposefully indulged in three glasses of wine before bed. Between the weirdness at the cemetery and dreading my test results, I was fine with going to bed drunk.

The next day was all about waiting for Dr. Graham to call me back. Bill called on the early side, and I worked hard to keep disappointment and anxiety out of my voice. We made a date for a few days on. If there was something wrong with me, I was going to have to tell Bill, and he would want to know why I hadn't told him about all the tests. Truth be told, I didn't want to. I probably should have examined that thought more carefully, but just thinking about the added complication felt like more than I could handle.

Dr. Graham finally called late in the afternoon. My blood tests were normal, and the MRI showed no significant changes, no tumors, no evidence of a stroke, no lesions.

Phew.

That doesn't begin to cover it. I may have danced around my apartment a little before calling the kids with the good news. I guessed that Anton would be—if not disappointed, then grumbling to himself with some version of "so much for the easy answer." He was right. A tumor would have made my situation clear. And easy answer notwithstanding, I knew he didn't want me to be sick.

Next on my agenda, the sleep study, which was shaping up into kind of a pain. I was going to have to be at their lab for the whole night. I arranged for Gretel to stay at doggie camp.

They told me on the phone to think of the study like a night in a hotel—there would be a TV, a reading light, and a private bathroom. I should bring my normal nighttime meds (but no sleep medicines, either prescribed or over-the-counter, pajamas and slippers (there was no carpet in this "hotel.") They would record my breathing, my brain waves, and my snores (really?).

The very idea that someone was going to watch me sleep seemed ultra-creepy. What would they see anyway, other than me drooling? And what if I went to that "elsewhere" in the middle of the night? Would I simply disappear from the bed?

They neglected to mention the gel—a yucky surprise. They slather it under each electrode and it forms a seal with your scalp. The instant the nurse squeezed it out, I longed for the night to be over so I could shower. Even under my tidy gray bob, having all those wires stuck to my head was quite the indignity. Though I'll admit I was glad the mess would ooze onto their pillowcases, not my own.

They also failed to mention that I had to sleep on my back.

I can*not* sleep on my back. Not well anyway. No matter how I arrange the pillows, my neck hurts and I arch my back and squirm, which means that no actual sleeping occurs. How could this be an accurate study if they tested me doing something I never did at home?

I didn't think I'd ever fall asleep. I watched a little TV, read my book and finally my eyelids fell. But my scalp itched, there weren't enough covers, and it was a skinny hospital bed. When I tilted over slightly to fool myself into almost feeling like I was sleeping on my side, the nurse came in and moved me back. But after a while, I must have slept.

I dreamed that Ben and I were standing at Lily's grave, her headstone identical to the one I'd seen briefly at the cemetery. Old-growth trees surrounded the grave and nearly covered it with fallen leaves. I knelt and swept the leaves off with a whisk broom, collecting them into a bright yellow plastic dustpan that Ben took from me and emptied out a few trees over. There were no other graves, no other people. I had brought California poppy seeds to plant, which are tiny, like specks of dirt, and I tried to funnel them into some holes I'd made, finger sized holes that kept being covered by more leaves. By the time I had scattered the seeds, more dead leaves had fallen, and I began to sweep again. Then more leaves, more sweeping, again and again.

I woke with a frustrated knot in my stomach. Where was I? Hospital curtains surrounded my bed on two sides and from the third, I could see an entirely unfamiliar night cityscape out a window that had not been there before I fell asleep. Helicopters with searchlights flew in the distance. The sky seemed smoky. I heard sirens and the background drone of a newscaster reporting something about an emergency I couldn't quite catch. I had no electrodes on my head. I could feel an IV in the crook of my arm and there was a clip attached to my finger, and something on my legs was compressing my calves with intermittent poofs of air. Rhythmic beeping came from machines behind my head.

I tried to sit up but an alarm clanged. The metal guide in the ceiling rasped as a nurse pulled the curtain back and hurried over to turn off the alarm. I could see a hospital corridor through the now partially open door. It seemed full to capacity—patients in beds, patients in chairs, every space occupied. EMTs, doctors, and nurses negotiated narrow walkways, hurrying in both directions. The nurse helped me lie back down and checked my IV.

"What's happening out there?" I asked, gesturing toward the hall.

"Oh, dear, you shouldn't worry about that," she answered.

"But" I said, "the helicopters, the sirens, what's going on?"

"They're calling it an 'incident,'" she said, and patted my hand. "We're very busy, though. Maybe you should try to go back to sleep." She turned a dial on one of the machines and before I could protest, my incipient panic smoothed over into sleepiness.

When I opened my eyes, the nurse from the sleep lab was reattaching electrodes to my skull—apparently I had pulled them off. I was back where I'd started. No background TV, no sirens, not even the staccato whir of a distant helicopter.

The next morning I asked about pulling off my electrodes, and the nurse said she'd taken care of it—only about ten minutes would be missing from my sleep test. As expected, she said I should call my doctor for results.

Before I left, I did try to wash off my head in the bathroom sink. I couldn't stand it for another minute.

On the way to pick up Gretel and go home, I couldn't stop thinking about my middle-of-the-night experience. After what had clearly been a dream, I'd woken in a room that looked the same but was *absolutely not* the sleep lab. Also, if the sleep study was missing those ten minutes, how would it help me?

CHAPTER NINETEEN

By lunchtime I was sniffling. I hadn't dried my hair before I left the lab, and it had been nippy outside. Add chilly air to a wet head and you have a time-honored recipe for the common cold—either that or my immune system was compromised from all the stress of going back and forth between universes. I had to laugh at my own stupid joke.

I called Bill to warn him and let him off the hook for our date that night. He was over at his daughter's house babysitting his sick grandkids and said he wouldn't mind being exposed to my germs, if I wouldn't mind being exposed to his. We decided to eat spicy food on the off chance it might ward off our incipient viruses.

My favorite Indian restaurant was never very crowded, but especially not as early as Bill and I liked to eat. We had our pick of tables and sat at a window, even though it was already too dark to enjoy a view. We ordered, and chatted about the news, and then, in a mistaken attempt to entertain, I told Bill about my sleep study.

"Why did you have to have a sleep study?" he asked. This, of course, was a reasonable question. He continued, "You don't snore. How could you have sleep apnea? How would I not know that?"

I took a sip of my wine, reached for the naan and tried my best to look nonchalant. "My neurologist thinks—"

"You have a neurologist?" Bill asked.

"Yes, because of the migraines."

"I knew about the migraines, but," Bill shook his head slowly, "I didn't know about the neurologist."

"But this isn't about migraines," I said, digging myself in deeper.

"Then, why the sleep study?"

I thought as quickly as I could with my clogged brain. I hadn't told Bill about my little (possibly illusory) adventure at the airport, obviously. I didn't want to seem like a lunatic.

"So," I said, trying to keep anxiety out of my voice, "when I went up to Seattle to see Anton, I took a tranquilizer for the flight. After we landed I was sleepy and I sat down in a chair at the gate—I thought it would be for only a second—but I fell asleep and didn't make it downstairs to meet Anton until I heard them calling me on the P.A. Anton called Nora and Tom and they all sort of piled on and insisted that I get checked out."

"Why didn't you tell me this before now?" Bill looked genuinely distressed. "I care about you. I want to know about it when you go to the doctor"

"I'm sorry," I said. "I didn't think it was a big deal." I took another sip of wine, adding, "which it isn't," and tried not to sound too defensive.

Bill shook his head. "But the airport, it was a one-time episode, right? Why are your kids so worried?"

"It's an abundance of caution," I reiterated. "I didn't want to bother you."

Bill leaned toward me across the table, a look of pained sincerity on his face. "I want you to keep me informed," he said, patting my hand. "And if I worry, it's my choice."

I smiled at him. I had to. He was sweet. He cared.

If he had medical tests, would I be as insistent about checking up on him? The thought pushed my guilt button. I wondered briefly if he understood the limits I placed on our relationship. He must, right?

Bill left early the next morning to get back to his still-sniffling-grandkids. I pictured them all sitting on a kid-friendly squashy couch watching Sesame Street or the equivalent with a box of tissues at the ready. I called him later in the morning to see how it was going.

He was on his third load of laundry, one of the kids was sleeping, and he thought the little one's cold might have morphed into an ear infection. I told him I hadn't had this kind of high-level conversation since Nora's kids were babies, and we laughed.

Dr. Graham called a few days later to report that my sleep study showed nothing out of the ordinary. He said my apnea qualified as "minimal," which meant I hold my breath no more than a few times an hour—healthy and normal.

Dr. Graham assured me he would continue to think about my "interesting problem" and consult with a few colleagues. All he could suggest at this point, he said, was to pursue the therapy option and see if it helped with my "vivid dreams."

I considered telling Dr. Graham that I had woken up in a different place during the sleep study, but it would have sounded like an ordinary nightmare. I knew there was no proof—no electrodes, no data.

I texted Bill: *Talked to Dr. Tests normal as predicted. All is well!* He texted back with a happy face and a thumbs-up emoji.

Which left me to contemplate therapy.

How could therapy fix universe swapping? Okay, it might actually make me happier *about* universe swapping. Therapy could absolutely do that for all kinds of difficulties. But confessing to a therapist seemed like it might create a whole new set of problems—especially if the therapist decided I really was off my rocker.

I spent a little time in therapy after Ben died. Simon insisted. My therapist helped me climb up slowly from the depths of misery and guilt—though there are only so many times you can hear, "It's not your fault" without screaming at the well-meaning person in the chair across from you. Intellectually, I already knew it wasn't my fault. I didn't tempt Ben into using heroin. I didn't sell it to him or stand by while he was snorting it. Of course I had worried about him and checked in with him and even talked to my parents about some of my concerns, but my children were very young and Ben couldn't be my top priority. If I'd thought he was in as deep as he was, I would have done something—but I'm still not sure what. Woulda coulda shoulda. All too late. I ended the therapy in the lamest way, missing sessions with "emergencies," and eventually not calling for new appointments. I thought I was too busy, and that I had healed as much as I was going to.

After Simon died I thought about going back, but my old therapist had retired. I went to see her designated replacement but we didn't hit it off and I quit after two sessions. Instead, I attended a grief group through a local church on and off for about a year.

None of this experience was useful in my current situation. It's tricky finding the right therapist for the most run-of-the-mill circumstances so how was I going to find someone who would listen to my stories about being whisked off to other worlds and not call the folks with the white coats to take me away?

In an attempt at embracing modernity, I crowdsourced. I sent out a group email to some good friends asking for therapist recommendations, for "a friend who is experiencing some issues adjusting to a new reality." That's how I put it. I had never lied about my own therapy before and I certainly didn't think looking for a therapist was cause for secrecy or shame, but admitting that I was the person looking for a therapist didn't seem like a good idea in the moment. I didn't want to field all the kindly-meant phone calls and emails that would come my way.

I was running through my contacts to see if there was anyone else who might have the perfect therapist for me when I came across the name of a very old friend from elementary school, a guy who had been more Ben's friend than mine. I knew he had gone to MIT and that he now taught physics at UCLA. We were friends on social media but I'd never had a reason to do anything more than "like" his occasional posts. Maybe he was the perfect person to help me understand multiverse theory! I tried to compose a message that sounded breezy and curious instead of desperate.

Hey Paul,

> *Lexie here. Well, you know that.*

> *Listen, I apologize for taking up your time but I'd love to get together and ask you some questions about multiple universes. Yes, it's totally out of the blue, but I have my reasons—and it's not for a blog or for publication of any kind. Personal reasons.*

> *Vague enough to intrigue you?*

> *Let me know.*

> *Thanks,*

> *Lexie.*

I didn't expect to hear from him right away—he didn't seem like the type to check social media frequently—but within an hour, I heard back.

> *Wow, Lexie, great to hear from you. I'm sorry to say that I'm on sabbatical this semester and won't be back in LA until after the new year. I sincerely hope it can wait til then. In the meantime, I've sent some links below that might help.*

> *I think of Ben more often than you'd imagine.*

You're welcome!
Paul

His P.S. included the links and some books about the multiverse he recommended as "good-for-amateurs." I ordered all three.

And I tried to read them.

I have a decent enough brain, but this stuff is truly perplexing. Just getting my head around the idea of a regular universe—infinite, alternate, or otherwise—is tough enough. Trying to expand my understanding by reading book-length explanations barely helped. These are issues I've spent a lifetime trying *not* to think about.

It turns out you can't explain why there might be multiple universes without explaining the main points of relativity, the Big Bang, the Doppler effect, and about thirty other "basic" principles of physics. From there, each book described the different types of multiple universes that may (or may not) exist. Some seem to be versions of each other; some, like the "holographic universe" are more akin to an idea or a philosophy about our (or any) universe's reality.

Also, not one of the books mentioned even a hypothetical way to travel to or from these (potentially fictional) other universes.

My personal upshot was a headache followed by nightmares, the regular kind where (fortunately) I woke up in my own bed in my own universe.

In the meantime, the kids called more regularly than usual. Tom and I talked several times and eventually decided we should take Matt to a currently popular science fiction movie (it seemed appropriate) on Friday night, and then to dinner. Nora asked if I wanted to come up and stay with her for a few weeks, which was probably because she wanted to keep an eye on me. I put her off. Anton still seemed skeptical that my doctors hadn't found anything pertinent, but I thought I should probably give him and his need for answers a break.

CHAPTER TWENTY

Over dinner at one of the trendier new restaurants in my neighborhood, I proudly informed Bill I'd been reading about advanced physics. I tried to pass it off as another amusing aspect of my science nerd personality.

"But *three* books?" he asked. "Couldn't you have read just one?"

Maybe it *had* been a bit excessive. I shrugged, "I was good at science. The only reason I didn't take more in college was because everyone in those classes was pre-med, and I didn't want to be like them. I thought I was too hip."

"I'm sure you were." Bill grinned.

"I totally aced my Bio SAT—or whatever they call that."

"Achievement test," he said. "That's what they call it. What did you get, Miss Un-Competitive?"

I had to laugh. "790."

"Pretty great," he said, laughing too. "But it's not physics."

"I know," I said. "I was showing off for Mr. High-Powered Entertainment Lawyer."

Bill pretended to twirl the Snidely-Whiplash mustache he didn't have and waggled his eyebrows for good measure. "Ex-High Powered. My current title is Diaper Changer Extraordinaire, though I also moonlight as a Nose Wiper."

"A useful calling," I said, smiling back. "Here's to being useful."

We clinked glasses.

Bill took a sip of his wine. "How 'bout we go see that new sci-fi film? The one about all the extra dimensions? Especially since you've been reading all those books."

I made a face. "Tom and I are taking Matt to see it on Friday. I'm sorry. I didn't know you'd be interested."

"Why don't I come along, too?" He said it casually, but I could tell he'd put some thought into asking, that he'd been waiting for an opportunity.

I practically winced. "Not this time," I said. "I'm sorry." It had been stupid of me to bring up the outing at all, what with my suspicion that not having met my family might be a sore point for Bill. I don't like knowingly disappointing people.

Bill shook his head. He put down his fork. He looked worse than disappointed. He looked angry. "Lexie, when *will* it be time?"

I exhaled. I felt shitty, but also, I felt I should explain. "I don't get a lot of time with Matt. I've barely seen him since school started this year. And, we're seeing the movie all the way in Orange County which means I have to leave early or the traffic will be a nightmare." That was an outright lie. Despite the traffic, Tom and Matt were driving up to Santa Monica after Matt got out of school.

I reached for Bill's hand. He didn't reach back. "Next time, I promise," I said.

Bill shook his head again. "You know," he said with an audible sigh. "I'm tired. I think I'm going to drop you off and head home."

Was he trying to punish me? Not very mature, I thought. And the evening had started out so pleasantly. I gave him a chance to change his mind. "We'll set up a get-together the next time I see Tom and Matt. It will be soon, I promise."

"I think we're done." Bill put out his hand to summon the waiter. "Can you bring us the check, please?"

On the way home I made an attempt at small talk, but Bill barely spoke. He dropped me off saying, "Call when you have a plan that includes me."

I went back into my building thinking about whether Bill was right to be annoyed with me. Why was I reluctant to mingle these two parts of my life? I had no doubt that my kids would like Bill. Yes, I had met his daughter and grandkids early on, but that was because I was at his condo doing landscaping work. Should I be worried that he wanted more from our relationship?

I was deep in thought as I walked Gretel. Maybe I should stop seeing Bill altogether. His anger felt out of place, unnecessary. Was it insane to hope I might end up back with Simon in that other place? Who was I being disloyal to—Simon or Bill? From a widow with grown children, a canine companion and a kind-of-boyfriend, I had morphed into an adulterer with two versions of most of the people in my life. My questions and quandaries felt overwhelming. I *did* need someone to talk to, but what on earth would I say?

As luck would have it, I heard back from a few friends with therapist recommendations. I decided to meet the three most convenient—by which I mean all three were short drives away and boasted, crucially, available street parking. This is Los Angeles, after all.

I called the numbers and said (on voicemail, of course) that I planned to treat our initial session like an interview, and that I was going to see a few people before I made a decision. It seemed like a good idea to let them know in advance that I wanted to get a feel for them before I would commit for the longer term.

Within a day, all three therapists called me back. Each remarked on what an excellent idea it is to interview therapists, and wondered aloud why more people don't do it. I didn't think I should explain all the (obvious) reasons on the phone—first there's the financial aspect of paying to talk to someone you might never see again, and then there's the emotional toll it takes to tell a story once, let alone several times, to several different strangers.

How should I approach these initial interviews? I could jump right in to my "vivid dreams" problem, but then would they instantly dismiss me as a lunatic? I could be entirely conventional—talk about my relationship with Bill and how it was making me feel guilty, and see how that went. Afterwards, I would assess how much about my "travels" it felt safe to disclose.

It would be good to talk to someone, I knew, even about decidedly ordinary un-quantum psychological troubles.

Late Friday afternoon, as the hero triumphed over squadrons of extra-dimensional aliens, I snuck a look at Matt, sitting next to me in the movie theatre. His eyes were shining. He gave the film a rave review over dinner. His newest ambition, it turned out, was to be an astronaut.

"Yeah, Grandmom," he said, through a mouthful of burger, "I've been streaming all the *Star Treks*. I know they say the Transporter Machine would never work in real life, but—"

"They do?" I asked. "And who's 'they?'"

"Scientists." Matt said, and nodded emphatically, adding, "But that doesn't mean that we can't still go into space. It just makes getting down to planets hard."

"I guess it would," I said. I returned my attention to my salad, trying to think what might have inspired Matt's latest aspiration.

I was about to tell him how he would probably need excellent grades and to be in top physical shape when he said, "Dad said you've been having all kinds of dreams about being in other worlds."

I looked at Tom, eyebrows raised. He shrugged.

"That's true," I said. I hesitated, then thought, *why not? Who would believe me if not a twelve-year-old?* I said, "I'm not totally sure they're dreams."

Matt stopped chewing. "That's amazing."

"Yeah, it kinda is," I said. "But we shouldn't talk about it outside the family. People will think I'm nuts."

I didn't add, "especially your mother." If Matt's mother Denise heard about this, she'd be sure to call me delusional and use it to keep Matt away from me.

Tom started to speak but Matt talked over him. "I shouldn't say anything to my mom, right?"

Tom laughed, "I was going to suggest that myself." He ruffled Matt's hair.

I put on my most officious grandmotherly tone. "You know it's never a good idea to keep information from your parents. I don't want you to think I'm condoning that. But since your dad knows this is going on, and your mom worries, I think it's perfectly safe to keep it between us."

"I know," Matt said. He looked at the little ceramic dish in which the waiter had served a dollop of ketchup, barely enough for the burger and leaving none for the fries. "Can I get more?" he asked, holding it up.

"Sure," said Tom. "I'll ask the waiter." He slid out of our booth on his way to the restroom.

"What are they like, your dreams?" Matt asked, clearly torn between waiting for ketchup and eating his fries immediately without it.

"My dreams?" I said. "They're kind of like falling into different versions of my life." I didn't want to go into all the dead people I was communing with. That seemed too potentially disturbing.

"So, like, you're you, but your life is different?" Matt asked. He was now holding a couple fries at the ready.

"Yes," I said.

"Multiple universes," Matt said.

"How do you know about multiple universes?" I asked.

"They're on TV shows all the time."

"Huh. Which TV shows?"

A server approached with an additional small bowl of ketchup, and Matt dunked the fries he'd been holding.

"I don't know if you'll like those shows, Grandmom," Matt said, with his mouth full. I decided not to comment. "They're mostly cartoons."

I have no problem with animation. I'll take my potentially fictional information in whatever form it might appear.

Matt went on, "Sometimes they do different timelines. Like, the dice rolls one way and a series of events happen. Then they show you another possibility. You should watch..." and he named several shows that used that particular narrative device, both cartoons and live action. I got out my phone to note them.

Tom slid back in his seat and reminded Matt to use his napkin and not talk with his mouth full.

I thought about how glad I was that Bill hadn't been around to hear this conversation. Then I remembered I was supposed to set something up for Bill to meet my family. It had completely slipped my mind. Maybe I should discuss it with Tom alone before I brought it up in front of Matt.

We stopped back at my apartment after dinner so that Matt could see Gretel. Matt loved dogs and had always had a special relationship with Gretel. It was a pity that his mother Denise said she "didn't believe in sharing a home with an animal that should live outside," and Tom's long hours at work often involved visiting building sites where a dog would not be welcome.

When Matt was a toddler, he spent one (glorious) night a week with me while Denise took a class. His other grandparents didn't volunteer to help, and Denise wasn't about to give an extra night to Tom (the divorce was still new). I was a consistent, eager, and free babysitter who happily made the drive both ways. Denise knew Tom often saw his son on those nights, but she chose to ignore it.

Gretel was a puppy when this started, and growing even faster than Matt. From the very beginning they adored each other. Danes are famously lazy, but as the years went by, Matt's visits always brought out the puppy in her.

Tom and I sat down to chat while Matt threw Gretel her favorite toy, the ball she would never retrieve when I threw it. When Matt asked if he could take her around the block for her evening pee, I was grateful, and handed him the baggies and the leash.

"Matt didn't seem even slightly bothered about my weird experiences," I said.

Tom laughed. "That's 'cause these days it's popular culture. Those ideas are all over now, but I think *The Matrix* movie might have started it."

I shook my head. "I've never seen it."

Tom was still giving me a run-down of the plot—and the plots of the sequels—when Matt came back through the door with Gretel, cheeks rosy from the November weather. "Make sure she has water," I called to him and heard the bowl clanking in the sink as he filled it.

"He is amazingly helpful when he's with you," Tom said.

"It's good to be Grandmom," I said, grinning. "Even without Denise's craziness, you'd be having issues now that he's almost a teenager."

"Ugh," said Tom.

"I know, right?"

Gretel and I both stood slightly downcast at the front door after receiving our good-bye hugs. I leaned down and gave Gretel her own hug. "I am glad you are here," I said. I could see that I was a poor substitute for Matt, but she still licked me.

Once again, I realized I'd totally forgotten to say anything to Tom about meeting Bill.

I woke up in the middle of the night thinking that Gretel had nudged my shoulder and said my name. But it couldn't have been Gretel. She can't speak except in woofs and whines.

I turned onto my back and opened my eyes. A man leaned toward me. I gasped, and my brain sifted through possibilities—*not Gretel, Tom?, Simon, an intruder??*

Who was sitting on my bed?

CHAPTER TWENTY-ONE

It was Ben. The Ben I saw in that other place, Ben who was dead in my universe. How was he here?

Was I somewhere else again?

I sat up. Gretel snored on in some dream of her own, legs twitching.

"Ben? What are you doing here?"

"No idea, sis." He scratched the back of Gretel's ear. She opened her eyes and shook her head, ears flapping in slow motion, as if she too, were disoriented. She stared at Ben, then me, dropped her head, and slept again.

"Some watch dog," I said.

"Well, we're in a dream," said Ben. "You can't expect Gretel to get all frazzled when it's not real."

"But, wait—" This was confusing. "Are you dreaming too?"

"Yeah," said Ben, adding—in a moment of brotherly immaturity—"Duh."

I stuck out my tongue—an automatic response, a holdover from childhood I had not known still existed within me. But there it was. Alongside sorrow, loss, and threatening tears—an irresistible impulse to annoy my brother.

"But..." I peered at Ben in the dim light of my nightlight. "I dreamt about something else, and now I've forgotten what it was."

"My dream must've won out," said Ben.

"You know, you're... You're dead in this world," I hazarded.

"Huh?" Ben sat up straighter.

"Simon died, too." The filter between my thoughts and my mouth seemed to have turned itself off.

"What?" Ben's forehead scrunched in confusion

"Yeah, of cancer. Twelve years ago. But you…" It took me a moment to continue. "You died of an overdose when we were 34."

"What?" Ben repeated. "An overdose?"

"And Lily's alive." Unplanned though it was, this chance to own up to Ben felt like an amazing opportunity and—once the words were out of my mouth—a huge relief. It hadn't been an option when I saw him that first time with Simon. I said, "I've been going back and forth between realities. I don't know what to do."

"Go back to sleep," said Ben. "That's what I'm going to do. I can't be in a world where I've died, right? Unless I'm a ghost."

"I guess not," I said. "But it could be an in-between place, where we are now, right? In our dreams."

"Like *The Wood Between the Worlds*," said Ben.

I blinked tears out of my eyes. Would anyone but Ben have made that reference? We used to play our own twin-game of *Wood Between the Worlds* from the book *The Magician's Nephew*, and make up elaborate tales about the outlandish places we went from there. A purple sky and insect people, a world where we could breathe under water, and always—always—worlds where animals could talk.

I smiled and leaned back against the headboard. "Since I have you here," I said, putting my hand on his. "How are things?"

Ben smiled back. "All I know for sure is that I went to sleep—so, I must be dreaming, right?" He shrugged. "And in this dream you said I died."

"Yeah."

"Of an overdose?"

"Heroin," I said.

Ben exhaled. "Wow."

"You didn't do drugs in your world?" I asked.

"Yeah, but... Not like that. Not Heroin. Mom and Dad must've..." He shook his head.

"It almost destroyed them," I said, feeling a surge of anger and grief. "I would have given anything to have had this conversation—any conversation—with you back then. Or to warn you... We were all..." I stopped, not wanting to pile on blame where it didn't belong.

"I'm sorry," said Ben. "But it wasn't me."

"I know. But it's hard to... to completely *get* that." I shook my head. "I mean, I never knew you, um, my-Ben, when he was as old as you. It's so confusing."

He picked up both my hands in his, leaned in and kissed my cheek. "Go back to sleep, Lex."

It was probably good advice. I took one more long look at my brother and lay back down. I would try to calm my brain, breathe, and go back to sleep, as instructed.

When I opened my eyes, Ben wasn't there. Gretel wasn't spread out next to me, either. Simon curled under the covers facing away from me, snoring softly. It had happened again. I had returned to that other life.

I got out of bed as quietly as I could. My brain raced, but my body was suddenly very, very tired. It protested as I padded down the hall toward the kitchen. I felt sore all over. Was this a side effect of whatever transported me here?

Here were the beautifully labeled tea canisters I had seen (hallucinated?) in my own reality. As I pulled out the chamomile, I realized I was a little bit jealous of "other Lexie's" (as I began to think of her) fancy labels, each printed in an elegant font and featuring a line drawing of the flower or plant from which the tea was made. My own labels were handwritten and sloppy. I should make attractive labels like hers when I got back.

I suppressed a snort. Idiocy.

As the tea steeped, I wondered if sleep would take me back to the place I thought of as my home, my real world. But there were too many unknowns. For one thing, there seemed to be no guarantee that I would go back to the place I came from. I could easily wake up here again, or even in that worse place, the world where all those cities had been terrorized. For all I knew, there were many other universes which were worse, each in its own way.

I took my tea to my office and turned on my computer.

The calendar said it was Saturday morning. It had been just last night—Friday—when I saw the movie with Tom and Matt. Huh. Time seemed to move at about the same pace in both worlds. Good to know.

I thought about my most recent visit here. I'd been about to go to the doctor at Simon's behest. I'd missed that appointment when I'd been taken back to my own world. How had it gone? Had I passed the dementia tests as easily as I had when Nora took me to Dr. Graham? Was Simon still preoccupied with what he called my confusion? Or had the "me" (other Lexie), who was (in theory) not confused about the events of her own reality, managed to placate him?

Also, had Ben and I dreamed the same dream?

Well, *that* I could find out. The clock said 4:00 a.m. I shouldn't call, but that's precisely what email is for.

In my world, Ben had died before internet communication was commonplace. But in this world, I bet I sent him sisterly emails all the time. Yes: When I typed in the first letters of his name in the "To" box, Ben's email address appeared. I typed on.

118

Hey Bro,

I have a weird question for you. Did you dream about visiting me last night, like about half an hour ago?

If not, uh, a big never mind.

If so, I'd love to talk about it. Call me tomorrow if you have a chance.

Love,

L

I sent it. Then I thought I'd get a jump on the news in this world. But before I could click on a story ("Readers Weigh in on Congressional Gridlock"), Ben emailed me back.

I'm up too. Funny, I woke up from a dream where you told me I was dead in your world. As you might imagine, I couldn't go right back to sleep. Yes, we should talk, but I have an overnight guest and I don't want to wake her up. Currently trying to convince the dogs it isn't morning. Sheesh.

I'll call tomorrow.

Love,

B

I felt happy and weepy all at once. Whatever the experience had meant, we had shared it! I swiped at my eyes and wrote back:

Thank you thank you thank you. That's the best news ever. At least for me. All this was making me feel completely alone. Call tomorrow. Any time.

Love,

L

Now I just had to hope that I'd be "here" tomorrow.

CHAPTER TWENTY-TWO

I checked out a few other news stories, and finally let my exhaustion take me back to bed. When I woke up later, at a more civilized hour, I saw that Simon had left a note to say he (and Gretel) were meeting some friends for a hike.

The phone rang as I was rinsing my breakfast dishes.

"Did I dream that you had a dream with me in it?" It was Ben.

I grinned. "That's a catchy way to start a conversation. I think the answer is yes. Either that or you had a dream with me in it. Actually, the freaky part is that it's both."

"Ha!" Ben chuckled. "Listen, I'm coming to Santa Monica for an afternoon meeting. Can I stop by?"

"Sure," I answered, and then thought about it. "But we should meet somewhere else."

Ben understood immediately. "You're worried about Simon," he said.

"Uh huh. Would it be weird to him if I go meet you somewhere? Or should I not tell him at all?" Suddenly I was full of questions. "Do we ever get together without him? Is he still super worried about me?"

There was a brief silence. "It's weird that you don't know any of that," Ben said. "No, we don't usually, but it'll be okay."

"I don't want to make him suspicious," I said.

"He's already called me to talk about it."

Oh. Good news *and* bad news: my instincts on that subject were accurate. "He has?"

Ben said, "Yeah, but don't worry. We'll think of something."

As I remembered, Ben could talk anyone into anything. That is, my Ben could. It's how he managed to be such a successful drug user.

In my world.

He was, after all, a different person here.

I got to the coffee shop early. As I stood in line, I realized I didn't know anything about my brother's current taste in coffee—was he a macchiato guy or did he drink lattes? What about matcha tea? This Ben had lived more than thirty years longer than "my" Ben had. This Ben might have developed an aversion to coffee, or cut out caffeine or dairy, or might drink only green juice—this was Southern California, after all.

Ben strode through the coffee shop door and I felt a rush of joy. I started to tell him why I hadn't ordered for him and he laughed and hugged me. Then he ordered a regular cup of coffee. With cream.

We sat at one of the little tables at the edge of the room. And it was down to me. I had to explain what had been going on. The dream we shared made me realize how much I needed Ben to understand my predicament—that I believed I had come from somewhere else entirely—even if I didn't understand it myself.

"So that first day when I woke up from a nap and you stopped by" I said, "It actually started before then, with these not-quite hallucinations but…"

Ben cut me off. "What started?"

"Uh, I've been going back and forth. Between worlds, or realities, or timelines." I knew I wasn't expressing myself well. I tried again. "At first, I was seeing things and people that don't exist." Not much better. One more time. "That afternoon when I woke up and you and Simon were in the living room? That's when I started to wonder if I was losing my mind."

I ought to be getting better at explaining this.

"That was what? Ten days ago? A few weeks?" Ben asked. "You know, when I was there that day, I thought you were a bit off and …"

I couldn't help it, I began to cry. Ben scooted his chair around to let me weep on his shoulder, which muffled my sobs, but when I raised my head to root around for a tissue, I saw people staring. That was the least of my problems. Ben got up and brought me a few napkins.

"Sorry." I blew my nose. "I don't think I can say how losing you… Lily and I—We never got along or had much in common. I mean, I love her…"

Ben put up his hand. "Whoa. One thing at a time."

I stopped my babbling and drew in a big breath.

Ben said, "Go back to your story."

I finally collected myself enough to give Ben a decent outline of my newly weird life, how and why I'd decided I was in an alternate universe. I detailed some of the differences between our worlds and told him about the other world I'd experienced—the terrorist attacks when I tried to fly to Seattle to see Anton.

I described how I'd seen my-Ben's grave become Lily's, and I told him about the mistake I made mentioning Lily to Simon. I also relayed my theory about Simon's dad's Alzheimer's—that it made Simon oversensitive to any vagueness on my part.

Ben sipped his coffee and asked occasional questions, especially about Lily, my kids, and Simon's cancer. He looked remarkably unperturbed. Sharing our dream the night before might have made me sound slightly less insane, I don't know. There was also every chance he was simply indulging me, his suddenly certifiable sister.

I had to ask. "You seem super open-minded about all this. Why do you believe me? Even a little?"

"Ha!" Ben replied. "Great question!" He shrugged. "I have no idea. Maybe it was the dream that did it, maybe I'm just as nuts as you are. All I can say is that it makes a lot of pieces fall into place. But the jury's not exactly back yet."

I nodded—I was lucky he was even listening to my wild theory.

"I know this is going to seem a bit selfish," he said. "But can you tell me more about what happened to me in your universe?"

"Yes, of course," I said, "but it's bad."

"That's okay."

"No, it isn't really, but..." I took a sip of my now-lukewarm tea and thought back.

When had Ben's drug use gotten out of hand? When had he started dabbling in the more dangerous drugs—the coke, the heroin, the pills?

There was nothing that had seemed serious about Ben's drug use in high school. We all smoked pot, surreptitiously, in outside places we thought were safe, in bathrooms with open windows, giggling and hoping, foolishly, that we weren't too obvious. We avoided our parents and teachers and feared the police. We were paranoid, we laughed uncontrollably, and we trusted each other to check on each other. As far as I'd known then, back then, Ben hadn't done much more than what all my friends did.

After high school and our different colleges—I stayed in Los Angeles and he went to upstate New York—we didn't hang out together much outside of family events. It took me a long time to fully grasp that we'd "gone our separate ways." I didn't even realize that Ben wasn't sober very often until we were in our mid-twenties. He had moved out before I did, and when I visited him, his apartment smelled like weed at first, and then it didn't anymore. One time he offered me cocaine and I said no. He never asked again.

Ben had a job writing reviews for a film magazine, which meant he was out most nights watching new releases and going to revival houses. His schedule was the perfect excuse, if that's what it was, to not see people with more "normal" work hours. As time went on, and

Simon and I got married (Ben gave a fabulous toast at our wedding), we saw him less and less. He didn't see our parents much either. One Thanksgiving, I could tell Ben was coked out of his mind, but that year Tom was a toddler and required constant supervision at my parents' un-childproofed home, so I couldn't pay attention to anything else. It was Ben's last family Thanksgiving. After that year, and on through the last years of his life, he'd say there was a film festival he needed to go to during the holidays, or he'd be out of town with a girlfriend.

In the end, my brother's downward slide escaped me.

"People who do drugs are good at keeping it secret," this Ben said, rather kindly.

"Yeah, I know." I looked at him. "I went to therapy."

It was such a relief to tell my story. It was even more of a relief to ask this grown-up, responsible version of my brother all my questions about how his own life (this version) had turned out. I'd always known he'd be a great parent. Lousy husband, but a devoted father. My Ben had been great with my kids, at least the few times he'd come over apparently sober.

This Ben seemed to revel in both his fatherhood and uncle-hood. He caught me up on his daughter and my own kids' lives in this universe, which was very helpful, and as a bonus he told me about "his" Lexie, the person whose body and life I seemed to be inhabiting. Apparently, the dementia tests Simon had requested had all turned out fine, but she had complained to Ben privately that she was having on-and-off memory issues.

"It's upsetting for her," Ben said. "And for Simon, too, though she hasn't talked to him about it much because it's such a trigger for him. I've felt a bit in the middle, if you know what I mean, with them both confiding in me."

"I'm sorry," I said. What else could I say?

"Lexie doesn't want Simon to worry, but she's been forgetting whole days," Ben said. "She doesn't seem to have any memories from when she's, um… in your world."

"I think she re-arranged my sweaters," I said, "the last time we switched."

"What?" Ben sat back in his chair, looking even more astonished about that than the whole universe-hopping thing.

"Yeah, I looked in my closet, and she'd put my summer clothes away and moved my winter clothes down. She arranged them by color, which is totally different from how I do it."

"Wait, what? People switch their clothes around for different seasons? You do that?" Ben seemed mystified.

"Yeah, I do it every year. Mom used to do it too."

"It's a thing?"

"Yeah, though it might be a girl thing."

"Riiight," Ben stretched the word out to show me how ludicrous he thought it was. "Well, uh, leaving that aside, Lexie was freaking out—she said her whole last week had been a blur, she said it felt like she'd been unconscious—but she didn't want Simon to know."

"That's worse," I said, thinking about how it would feel to lose whole days.

"Worse than what?"

"Worse for her than for me. Not being aware while you're somewhere vaguely familiar, then waking up and having only blurry memories—that seems a lot scarier than what's happening to me. I know I'm in the wrong place, and that's scary enough, thank you very much. Though maybe…"

I'd have to think about that. What if people experienced alternate universes all the time, but didn't remember them? What person would think, *You know those days I don't remember? I bet I was in another universe!*

Ben looked at his watch. "Shit," he said. He dialed his phone and told the person on the other end that he'd be there shortly.

It was only after we hugged goodbye—me holding on a little too tightly—and Ben ran off (literally) to his meeting, that I wondered how he'd ever communicate with me if I went back to my world. It wasn't like we could count on meeting in our dreams—say, once a month—to exchange important information.

I drove the short distance home thinking about staying here in this alternate life—growing old peacefully with my husband, minding the kids and grandkids, walking the giant dog, and hanging out with Ben. Would it all be at Lily's expense? Was it an either/or situation, or was there another place—another world entirely—like this one, but one where *all* my loved ones survived to live long healthy lives? That's the world I wanted. That's the world we all want. No trade-offs, no tragedies.

CHAPTER TWENTY-THREE

Ben,

When I got home Simon was suspicious. Also mad that I didn't stop by the market which I guess I was supposed to do.

I want you to know—and yes I know I'm being sentimental—that I have missed you for over thirty years.

Telling you about my "situation" helped, but how do I keep in touch with you if I go back to that other universe? Going back and forth seems entirely random. And how will I communicate my alternate universe theory with the "other" Lexie? She certainly deserves to know. I'm darned sure emails and phone calls from one reality to another are not gonna happen. (Is there an area code for Alternate Universe? A domain name?)

Having lost you once, I really don't want to lose you again. Though strangely, when I was back there, simply knowing you exist here—confusing as it was—it made me feel better.

Big sigh.

I should also add that I have started to feel like I don't belong here. And especially if the other Lexie is stuck in my world—I feel shitty about that. Plus Lily died in this world and didn't in mine. How do I reconcile that? And while I'm at it, how the hell did a normal grandmotherly-type landscaper end up with all these bizarre dilemmas?

Yours, with too much philosophizing,

L

He wrote me back right away.

Lexie,

I've been thinking about why I believe you when you say you're a different person than my sister. All I can say is that I do. Maybe it's some kind of twin intuition? Maybe you just seem different. I'm not sure it matters. Even if you are the same sister I've had my whole life and this alternate universe idea is your insane fantasy, and that dream we "shared" was a hallucination or a coincidence, I still want to help. So, let's take it as a given that I'm on your side.

The Lexie I know, my twin in this world, well, she doesn't ask many questions. She's a "take it as it comes" person. But in order to deal with whatever the hell is going on, some context might help, so here goes:

After Lily died, Lexie told me she wasn't even going to try to make sense of it. She threw herself into her kids and her work, and on the surface everything turned out great. Well, her kids definitely turned out great, and her landscaping business was successful. Simon was dealing with guilt on top of his anger and I think Lexie became the "get-it-done" person in the family. She was a rock for our parents, and for me, too.

It sounds simplistic, but I'm not sure Lexie ever fully grieved for Lily because she was focused on trying to alleviate Simon's sense of guilt. As I think you've noticed, he's never gotten over Lily's murder, and in his heart he blames himself. I think that's why he's become so much more controlling over the years. You might also want to know that Lexie wanted to name Nora "Lily," but Simon wouldn't have it, even as a middle name. It upset him too much.

My two-bit psychologizing. Benjamin Freud Brooker, at your service.

As for communication, maybe we should try 1-800-WTF? Or send emails to @alt-uni.infinitecosmos?

Yeah, I tried.

But here's an actual idea: what if you left Lexie a note for if/when you trade places again? You could even explain your multiverse theory. I'm not sure there's a downside. But telling Simon is a different matter entirely.

More soon,
Love B

I thought about Ben's suggestion. I liked the idea of writing other-Lexie a note. My first concern—and it was a big one—was what if Simon saw it? That might cause all kinds of trouble. Also, if I was going to do it, I should do it ASAP because who knew when I was going to be whisked back to my own universe with no warning?

Where could I leave a note that only other-Lexie would see?

Then I had an inspiration (one I might patent for future tech-savvy universe travelers?)

What if I emailed her? I could send the email to my/her/our address and while I was here, I would leave it unopened in the inbox. Then (potentially) when/if we switched back, other-Lexie would open her email, see the one from me and read it. It might help her cope.

I tried to think through any drawbacks.

For one, other-Lexie might (or would, probably) think she was truly losing it if she got an email from herself that she didn't recall writing. It sounded like she was already having serious doubts about her memory and sanity. But she'd probably be curious enough to open the email, and if she went on to read it—voilà, communication!

Another (less likely) snag would be if other-Lexie thought she'd been hacked or that the email from herself was some new sort of spam. But she'd also have to question why anyone might want to pull off such a stunt—there was no money request, after all—and she might read it anyway, phishing warnings notwithstanding.

My last concern was that if Simon had her password, he might check her email occasionally himself. He was a suspicious guy, it seemed, at least a lot more so than my Simon. If he saw an email from Lexie to herself, it could convince him she *was* losing her mind. No good would come of that.

I tried to think it all through. I could run my plan by Ben. That was when the next cartoon light bulb went off in my head: I could and should (and would!) cc Ben on the email I sent to other-Lexie. If she had questions or problems, Ben would be there for her. Corroborate. Help her understand. Whatever she needed.

So I wrote her, and cc'd Ben.

Dear Other Me,

You probably think you're crazy—seeing an email from yourself that you have no memory of writing.

YOU ARE NOT CRAZY.

If you hold on for a minute and take the time to read this, it might help you figure out, at least up to a point, why you think you've been forgetting things. It also might make you feel better. So give it a whirl.

You are getting this email from a different Lexie Brooker. I'm another you. I live in another universe.

Now take some deep breaths.

After a fair amount of research I think I know what is happening, but I have no clue why or how. In the last few months I've been falling out of my world and into other "alternate universes." My own world is similar, but not the same as yours. Weird as it sounds, I think we're traveling between universes, exchanging places with each other. Or, our consciousness is. Yes, it sounds one-hundred-percent loopy but it also will help you see why you're losing hours, days, even.

As for me, I've been to other universes too, but mostly I seem to come here. I think it's because Simon and Ben are alive here, and somehow their presence pulls me in. In my world they both died. My Ben died of an overdose when we were 34, and Simon died of cancer 12 years ago.

And then there's Lily. In my world, nothing bad ever happened to her. She's alive there and happily divorced from a good guy that she still talks to, and she remains the country club gal she was always meant to be. We've never been too alike but I love her, and I can't tell you how guilty it all makes me feel, though (obviously) her death here in this reality wasn't my fault.

I haven't talked to Simon about this theory of mine, but you'll notice I cc'd Ben on this email. That's because I told Ben about it. After you read this, you can call Ben and he might be able to explain better than I can in this email.

I don't want you to think that you're losing your mind. I thought I was, too. I realize that getting this email and my whole multiverse supposition might feel like another straw on the camel's back, but I'm hoping it makes you less freaked out.

I feel like all this is my fault even though I have no idea what I might have done to make it happen. I also don't know if I can fix it (or how), but you have my promise that I'm going to try.

Write me back! Send an email to your own email address and leave it in your inbox for me to open if I get here/there/wherever.

Love,

Me

I worked hard on that letter. I didn't want it to be too long, but there was a lot of information to get across. It was like writing a letter for a time capsule, except that I wasn't talking to myself from the past. I was talking to myself from some elsewhere. Location to be determined. Or possibly not ever to be determined.

Ben approved the letter—if somewhat briefly:

L,

Got the cc. Fine job. Not sure if I would have said the stuff about Lily but that's okay. Warn me if you decide to tell Simon.

CHAPTER TWENTY-FOUR

I emerged from my office a few days later to find Simon in the living room on the phone with Nora.

"Oh shit," I said. Simon had told me she'd called earlier, but I hadn't called her back yet.

Simon proffered the phone to me with an irritated look, and I talked to Nora, assuring her that I was fine, just "busy" (doing what, I didn't say).

Simon's reproach landed the minute I hung up and handed him back his phone. "What the hell is going on with you?"

I had known it was coming from the look on his face, but I didn't expect the vehemence.

"Oh God, sweetie, I got distracted by bright and shiny objects on the internet and forgot to call her back."

"Our daughter called and you forgot?"

"Yeah, it happens. She's a grown up—she'll survive." Now my back was up—I had to justify myself. "I'm sure I would have done it soon enough."

"How would I know that?" he asked. Anxiety seeped out with each word. "You know, Lexie, I don't know how you got the doctor to think you're fine. I still believe something is wrong with you."

"I'm so glad you're on my side," I said. As soon as I said it, I realized my sarcasm was probably counterproductive.

"How am I not on your side? I want you to be fine, but you won't tell me what's going on, and you keep making excuses." Now his voice was loud. I'd forgotten how good he was at being intimidating. My Simon could do it too, but he only used that voice at work. The kids and I used to say it was his superpower. We were glad he only used it for good.

Disturbed by our raised voices, Gretel got up and left the living room. Duly noted.

I gestured at her and asked, "Do you think shouting is going to make me do better?"

He stared at me. I stared back. I started to walk back toward my office.

Simon stopped me with, "Where do you think you're going?"

"I don't have anything else to say. I already apologized to Nora, who after all was the 'injured party,'" (I used air quotes) "and you've made your own disappointment obvious. I'm tired of apologizing for not being perfect." I kept walking.

"Lexie, get back here. We don't do this."

"We don't?" I turned around. "How would I know that? For the last, uh, couple months you've been angry with me for what I think are perfectly normal failings. Nothing earth-shattering. A little forgetfulness."

His expression looked cold. "You're different," he said.

You're dead, I thought, and my insides protested. At least I hadn't said it out loud.

If Simon hadn't been so hostile I probably would have admitted right then and there that I *was* different. That I wasn't his Lexie, and all the rest of my strange, sad tale. I briefly reflected that the other me must be more of an apologizer and a soother, but this me? I get angry right back. I said, "And you're perfect? The same guy you were 30 years ago? Sharp as a tack? On top of every little thing? I would never claim that, and frankly I think your anger is totally out of proportion, not to mention inappropriate."

133

"Inappropriate? Whole days disappear from your mind and you've gone from apologetic—at least that helped—to nonchalant about it. I live here too, and take care of everything, and the least you could do would be to thank me."

I snorted. "Do you actually think, one, that you take care of everything? Or two, that this is a good way to get me to apologize?"

Simon gave a theatrically big sigh. "Lexie, it feels like you're a different person. I don't know how to deal with it, and with the kids calling to complain to me—and no, it's not only Nora—it's too much. And add in that *you* don't think you're doing anything different or wrong..." He picked up his wallet from the table and stuck it in his back pocket. "I need to calm down. I'm going for a walk." He took Gretel's leash from the hook next to the door, called her, and out they went. She didn't even look back at me. Here, she was definitely Simon's dog.

Just when I was feeling better, too. I'd been so happy to find an ally in Ben, to finally not feel alone. And instead of being able to enjoy my beloved husband—though this wasn't my beloved husband, at least not as I remembered—we were fighting.

I went back into my office, but I was too worked up to be productive. I wished I'd been the one to leave with the dog. I sat down on my office floor to try some relaxation exercises. Instead of calming, my mind galloped through the whole spectrum of words and phrases I should have said—from contrite to self-righteous.

After a few more inhalations and exhalations, I considered expressing a little remorse by cooking dinner for my angry husband, but I couldn't remember for the life of me if we had plans. Were we going out? Were we having friends over? Somewhat creakily, I got up off the floor.

There was nothing helpful on my calendar, so I checked in Simon's office. Nothing there either, but there was a long list of sites about dementia on his browser history. He had googled "forgetfulness" and "passes doctor's tests." It looked like his next move would be to crowdsource with a post on some medical forum along the lines of, "My wife isn't normal, but the doctor thinks she's fine."

When Simon and Gretel came home, I offered to help with dinner, and Simon grudgingly told me I could make a salad. We ate almost in silence and then I took Gretel around the block. She didn't seem particularly keen. My Gretel was always eager to get to the outside world; this Gretel was hung up on Simon. Maybe it was because she somehow knew I wasn't her Lexie.

When we came back, Simon was watching television. I sat next to him, waiting for him to look at me, to apologize, to try and talk about it. No dice. After about half an hour, I went to bed.

My Simon hadn't been the pouty type. This Simon was. Ben said Lily's murder had caused Simon long-term issues. Maybe over time, it had changed his personality.

So, there we were: two people who were different than either of us expected.

I woke up in my own reality. I could tell by the empty bed. I felt terrible for the other Lexie who was going to have to contend with Angry Simon without a clue about what had occurred. At least I'd written her that email. If all went as planned, she could read about her/our situation. It might help.

I lay in bed for a good while, thinking about all the ironies laid bare by my visit to that other reality. For years now I had lived by myself and missed my family. Missed Simon and Ben and my parents—all the people who had passed from this life.

Yet, here I had my children. Children I had birthed. Children I trusted. I couldn't say that about my children "there"—who I hadn't yet seen in person—though genetics and circumstance probably made them quite similar.

I thought back to their childhoods. It had been noisy, and annoying, and I never seemed to get anything done—but feeling overwhelmed had also been part and parcel of a full life, a busy life, a life where, at the very least, I hadn't had the time or energy to feel sorry for myself.

When the kids were little, plunking myself down on the couch meant that in all likelihood, I'd be asleep in ten minutes. I used to make myself a cup of tea after dinner just to stay awake and read them their stories. Now if I had caffeine late in the afternoon, I'd be up all night cursing my stupidity.

And Simon, well, he was not living up to the vision I had about how it would have been to grow old with the man I married. As it turned out, I was relieved to be living by myself again.

But there I had Ben.

Gretel seemed especially glad I was back. I still couldn't find any physical differences between her and her counterpart. All the black and white patches seemed to be in the same places. I wondered if she— possibly like other-Gretel—could tell the difference between me and other-Lexie. When I finally stopped ruminating and got out of bed and dressed and got the keys and the leash and the bags, she backed me against the front door and put her two front feet up right near my shoulders and licked my face. *I am glad you are home*—that's what I think she meant.

We walked and came home and she spent the rest of the morning by my side—no normal laissez-faire dog stuff like going off to lie on the couch if I was in my office, or staying in the office if I went briefly to the bathroom. If I moved, she went with me. She even stopped and looked back at me on her way to drink from her water bowl in the kitchen. Whatever was happening to me was getting to her, too.

CHAPTER TWENTY-FIVE

The next afternoon I had my first therapy appointment. It was a mere ten minutes away, but I left early to try to find a spot on the street—my friend had warned me that parking in the building was expensive.

Dr. Mallik was in an office with four other therapists. The waiting room was homey, with lush plants and a trove of back issues of a favorite magazine of mine, one that had devoted attention to water-wise gardening early on.

The friend who recommended Dr. Mallik had said I'd like her because she had a green thumb. And she did. When she showed me into her office, with its upscale floor-to-ceiling windows looking out on the Santa Monica Mountains, I saw a row of low open bookshelves adorned with healthy plants in attractive ceramic containers. I gave Dr. Mallik immediate points for compatibility, at least in this area.

It also got our conversation off to a comfortable start. Dr. Mallik had heard of my blog and my old business. Talking about drainage problems turned out to be a decent icebreaker. Then she asked me why I had come to talk to her.

I didn't want her doubting my sanity right off. Though I'd rehearsed a much more detailed version of my story, my nerves in the moment made me compromise. I told her I'd been seeing my late husband and brother in "vivid dreams."

Dr. Mallik racked up a few points for diligence as she made sure I'd seen a physician and noted the tests I'd had. She also questioned me about my history of headaches.

"I think you've got two intertwined circumstances, Ms. Brooker," she said. "One: your dreams are affecting your waking life. Two: the content of those dreams brings up old sorrows and losses. Is it possible that you haven't worked through those losses to your satisfaction?"

Of course, I thought, nodding agreement. *It might even hit the nail on the head.*

I gave her my best condensed version of how my life had changed in the twelve years since Simon died, emphasizing as I often do that I have a good life, with many comforts and joys, foremost among them my excellent children. I mentioned my ambivalence about Bill. I also may have blathered on a bit about what a good companion Gretel is.

When I finally meandered to a halt, feeling somewhat sheepish, Dr. Mallik folded her hands in her lap and asked: "So, why do you think this is happening now?"

It was, indeed, the question. "That's why I'm here," I answered.

I left the office with a good sense of who Dr. Mallik was. She would be empathetic and kind, and we had a certain amount in common. And yet, Dr. Mallik didn't seem like a person who might ever consider the possibility that I was visiting other universes.

I knew that last item on my therapist wish list might not be reasonable, I really did.

My second appointment was two days later. This time, the therapist was a man, and my friend had described him as a Buddhist who specialized (naturally) in acceptance and living in the moment. I considered myself pretty good at living in the moment, but acceptance also sounded like a worthy goal. Would I feel comfortable enough to admit that what I was trying to accept was travel between universes?

Dr. Bissing was a small man with a white beard several shades lighter than his silver hair. His office was appointed in dark wood furniture, a wine-red Persian rug, book-lined shelves and dim lighting.

Very traditional, and not at all what I expected. He dressed conservatively and precisely in a perfectly tailored classic suit with an unremarkable tie, and he wore undoubtedly expensive shoes. This was a Buddhist? I couldn't picture him folding himself onto a yoga mat for the life of me.

We sat down across from each other. Dr. Bissing fixed me with an intense gaze, his light blue eyes behind old-fashioned wire rim spectacles. I waited for him to say something. But he didn't. As minutes ticked by, I became more and more annoyed.

This guy clearly practiced a "wait it out" strategy. I couldn't decide if my choice to not speak until spoken to was childish. What if his approach had some concept behind it that I didn't know about or understand? But I was irritated. I felt manipulated. I'd talk when he talked. So, after about five minutes of waiting—staring at him, then down at the carpet, then up again—I stood and headed to the door.

"I'm sorry this isn't working for you," said Dr. Bissing (finally) from his chair.

"I've done all the helping myself that I can do," I said, instantly glad I'd stuck by my guns. "I need someone who doesn't play therapy games."

"I see that now. I am probably not the right therapist for you."

Damn straight, I thought, and walked out.

I drove home thinking about Lily. How she was the assertive one. Walking out of Dr. Bissing's office—that was absolutely something Lily might do. Throughout my childhood and on through adulthood, I'd been both envious and exasperated by Lily's ability to get what she wanted and leave behind what she didn't.

I thought about how strange it was that Lily's strength and force of will might not exist in some other world. I'd never thought of her as a person who could be pushed into anything and I wondered if the other Lily, the Lily who had been a victim in that other world, had been less of a force of nature than my own. I certainly didn't want to call up a "blame the victim" scenario, but I imagined that if my Lily had been confronted by a man with a gun she would have knocked it out of his hand, picked it up, and shot him. Undoubtedly unrealistic, but running the scene through my head made me smile.

When I got home, I called Lily. It would be silly to tell her that I wanted to hear the sound of her voice. She didn't have even one sentimental bone.

"What's going on?" I asked.

"Not much." Lily proceeded to tell me how the event she'd arranged for that night had been canceled because the honoree had been admitted to the hospital with heart issues. "A lot of time and planning down the drain, but what are you going to do? I guess we're all getting up there."

"Yes we are," I said.

"This man?" she continued, "he was a heart attack waiting to happen. Eats too much red meat, and he has a mean serve which means he can plow through games without a lot of actual exercise. It came back and bit him."

Lily's assumptions about people sometimes threw me. "You're saying he was in bad shape to begin with?"

"I hear you making that face," said my sister. "You're a softie. But sometimes, you know, people get what they deserve."

"Was he a bad person?" Three minutes in and I already wanted to argue about her worldview. How did I always end up here when I started out with such good intentions?

"Of course not. Would I be arranging a gala in his honor if he was a bad guy? But if you don't take care of yourself, it catches up with you. That's all I'm saying."

"I know, babe," I said. "I know. But it can all come across as a little… harsh."

"No doubt," said Lily. She laughed. It was a very good sound.

"What are the chances of us seeing each other at some point in the not-too-far future?" It just came out of my mouth. I hadn't planned it.

"Really?" Lily laughed again. "I mean, I'd love to see you Lexie, but... "

I could practically hear the cogs in her mind turning. *Why did Lexie call me? What's wrong? What doesn't she want to tell me over the phone? How will I fit her into my busy schedule?* Lily excels at moving people around like pieces on a game board. Her world is set up meticulously. Unexpected events, like a visit from her sister, didn't take place without a lot of shuffling.

"I know, you're asking yourself how we'll get through a meal without throwing food at each other," I said. "But I have been overcome by a powerful urge to see you. I'll drive down, spend some time with Tom and Matt, and afterwards, you and I can have a drink. If we're still speaking after one drink, we can have dinner."

"Huh," said Lily. "That has potential. But I know it can't be that simple. There must be something you're holding back. Did you break up with that guy you were seeing? Are you sick? Are the kids okay?"

"Everything's great," I said. "Bill and I haven't broken up, at least not that I know of; I'm not sick, the kids are fine. Gretel is a little needy but it's all good." I could be convincing when I needed to. And it wasn't like I was going to tell Lily about my otherworldly adventures over the phone. It would be way too weird for her. Hell, it was too weird for me.

I called Tom and arranged to have lunch with him and Matt on Sunday. I'd meet Lily afterward at her club in the late afternoon and we'd go from there.

CHAPTER TWENTY-SIX

Matt sprinted up to the table, followed by his father. I hugged each of them and held Matt at arm's length.

"You have grown. What's it been? Two weeks?"

"I know, right?" said Tom.

Matt beamed. "Mom says she's going to have to cut off all my pants into shorts so we don't waste 'em."

"We used to call those high-water pants, but," I looked down to see that Matt's ankles were covered by his jeans. "Those are still fine."

Matt giggled. "High water, like for when the ocean rises, right?"

Was environmental disaster a default prediction for Matt's whole generation?

"Well," I said, "that's not why they got the name. I think it had something to do with making fun of kids whose parents couldn't afford to buy them new clothes."

Tom snorted. "I don't think kids these days—or at least here—" he waved his hands around at the November SoCal sunshine, "are allowed to make fun of other kids."

"We're not," said Matt, adopting a serious expression. "No bullying."

"Does that work?" I asked, then shook my head. "Never mind, forget it. It can't hurt. Let's look at our menus. I'm hungry."

By the time we got to dessert I had gotten the play-by-play for the last two soccer games, including how his team's goalie had been hit in the face so hard by the ball that the only reason he didn't lose any teeth was because his braces held them in place. I also heard about how such-and-such a friend had lice and how he'd put his shaved-off hair in a baggie and took it to school to look at under a microscope, but got in huu-uuu-uuge (a full three syllables' worth of) trouble.

"They sort of overreacted," said Tom. And shook his head with mock sadness.

"Mom was totally grossed out," added Matt. "She thinks they were right to suspend him."

"But there was a protest and they let him back in the next day anyway," added Tom. "Miraculously, scientific curiosity won out!"

When Matt's chosen dessert arrived—an ice cream sundae, what else?—he dug right in. It was a pleasure to watch any creature enjoy ice cream this much. When he finally slowed down, it was all I could do to stop myself from wiping the spot of whipped cream from his chin.

"Grandmom," he said, taking a moment to savor whatever last morsel he'd put in his mouth. "Are you still going to other worlds?"

I could see Tom struggle to not interrupt—he was probably going to tell Matt that it was kind of a rude question. But I loved that Matt had asked straight out.

"Funny you should ask," I said. "Yeah, I've been gone once, for a couple of days. And it was kinda great, considering."

What a relief to discuss universe-wandering as if it were a normal activity in the average grandmother's day.

After lunch, I whiled away a pleasant hour in a bookstore until it was time to meet Lily. When I walked through her country club's front door, she was in the lobby, prompting me to wonder (as I did every time) if she was on the valet's speed dial. She stood arms akimbo, smiling at me, somehow projecting welcome and skepticism in equal measure.

Lily was the athlete in our family, lithe and strong. Unlike me, she continued to dye her hair, which was pulled back into the type of short blond ponytail that looked perfect sticking out from a tennis visor. It had been a good six months since I'd seen her. In April she had come up to donate platelets for a childhood friend. No fuss. That was totally Lily. She showed up, did what she was supposed to, and spent the night with me before driving home in the morning. We had caught up and even had some laughs about a mutual friend who posted very inappropriately on social media.

Another Lily phenomenon: As we walked to the dining room, nearly every person we passed said hello and sang my sister's praises unsolicited. Being with her here was like dancing attendance on a queen. Maybe we should all be allowed a little world like this one, I thought, where the like-minded gathered to appreciate each other and their mutual love—of, in this case, golf and tennis.

The waiter seated us at the best table, overlooking the tennis courts and the path to the golf course between them. The sun was setting and the view—while entirely man-made and definitely not water-wise—was lovely.

"Okay, Lex, what is it?" Lily asked, once the waiter left with our drink order. "Why are you here?"

I looked away from the view into my sister's canny stare. "There's no reason," I said. "I just missed you." When I saw her shaking her head, I added, "That may not sound likely to you, but it's true. We don't see enough of each other. I decided to be proactive."

Lily shook her head some more. "There must be something. You might as well tell me now and get it over with."

I laughed. Lily laughed too. There was no point in holding out.

"Okay," I said. "This is the deal. There's some weird shit going on—some weird dreams, mainly—and I'd love it if I could explain but I can't. The bottom line is that I'm fine. I've been to the doctor and there is nothing wrong with me."

"What doctors have you seen?"

I knew this was just the beginning of Lily trying to wheedle more information out of me. She added, "You know I can always call Nora."

Yes, Nora would tell her. Anton probably would too, but she was closer to Nora. With no kids of her own, Lily had been Nora's favorite aunt, babysitter, cheerleader, and partner in crime (picture blue eye shadow and red lipstick on a six-year-old).

I recited my list of doctors and their tests: internist, neurologist, sleep test, MRI, now back to therapy.

Lily scoffed. "Therapy?! For bad dreams?"

Lily didn't believe in therapy. When Ben died she flat out refused to go, and she wasn't particularly supportive when our parents joined a grief group.

"Why not?" I countered. "If it helps?"

"But aren't there simpler ways to cope with bad dreams?" Lily was heading right toward ridicule mode. I could see it coming. "Cheaper, too? Like trying to think pleasant thoughts before you go to sleep?"

The waiter brought our drinks—iced tea for me and Lily's favorite, a martini.

"I'm sure there are," I answered, "But my dreams aren't like that. And they're not necessarily bad."

Lily took a sip of her martini and gave me her practiced litigator stare. "Then what are they like?"

I should have known complete honesty was inevitable when dealing with my sister. I made my narrative as matter-of-fact as I could. Living in other worlds, Ben and Simon alive, other details different. (I didn't mention that there, she hadn't survived her twenties.)

I watched her as I spoke. She chewed on the inside of her left cheek—an old habit our mom had tried and failed to cure her of. She finished her martini and signaled the waiter for another. She didn't look horrified or even concerned.

"That's quite a story," she said. "But I still don't understand—why therapy?"

"What should I be doing instead?" This was not the conversation I expected. "I mean I've thought of letting it go," I said, "trying to be okay with not knowing where I'll wake up in the morning, hoping it goes away by itself so—"

"Nope." Lily broke in, shaking her head.

I stared at her. "Then what?"

"You need a shaman."

Yes, my beloved down-to-earth legal-eagle sister had just advised me to engage a shaman.

I was so astounded by every aspect of this suggestion that I couldn't speak. Lily wasn't questioning my experiences at all, and she didn't think I was crazy. I suppressed an incipient sob of gratitude and said, "I can't believe I didn't tell you about this a lot sooner."

Lily took me over to another table to talk to a friend, a Mrs. Thompson, whose husband had passed away very suddenly in a car accident about five years before. On the surface, Mrs. Thompson seemed conservative. Tennis whites, cardigan, understated but expensive jewelry and hair. She introduced me to her daughter, who wore the definition of a power suit and seemed the opposite of New Agey. I thought Mrs. Thompson was going to give me a song and dance about a séance, but instead, she told me about how the shaman's ritual had sent her to another place, a sacred space where she could talk to her late husband. She used words like "energy" and "portals"—and "multiverse." She was not embarrassed and had certainly not kept the story from her daughter, who nodded along.

"I don't have his card with me," she said. "But I'll give his number to Lily and she can give it to you. And, if he doesn't think he can help you, he'll say so on the phone and you won't have to waste a drive. Or he'll recommend someone else."

I thanked her profusely, and thanked Lily, too. By the time I got home to Gretel, I was feeling better. I felt like a whole new world of possibilities had opened up.

Also, Lily had already emailed me a note:

There are more things in heaven and earth, sis. Let me know what happens.

She included the name and number of the shaman, Mr. Angelus.

CHAPTER TWENTY-SEVEN

Excited as I was about Lily's surprising suggestion, it was too late to back out of my third and final interview appointment. This therapist practiced out of her upscale Brentwood home in an office that had once been a pool house. The waiting room was decorated simply, and it seemed that Therapist Three also saw children. There were neatly shelved baskets of brightly colored toys, and a low table with two manual typewriters, a rotary dial phone, and an old-fashioned manual calculator. It looked a lot like the pediatrician's office where I'd taken my kids.

Dr. Stewart opened the door at precisely the time of our appointment and introduced herself. We made our way through a short hall to her office, and she motioned for me to sit wherever I'd like.

"So," Dr. Stewart said, "Let's talk about why you're here. What can I help you with?"

I gave her my now-practiced song and dance about "vivid dreams" as well as my pertinent medical history. When I was done, she read over her notes. Silence hung in the room for a few moments before she spoke. "Sorry. This is a new one for me. Most people who come to me at your age are adjusting to a new circumstance—an illness, a loss, more rarely, the break-up of a long-term marriage or relationship."

My surprise must have been visible because she said, "It does happen. Occasionally. It's very difficult when you've been with someone for so long, even if you haven't been happy."

"I can imagine," I said.

"I think my first question for you is," Dr. Stewart continued, "do you want the dreams to go away, or do you think you'll miss them? I'm not saying I can make them go away, but sometimes talking about certain kinds of dreams does dispel them. I gather they are upsetting, but maybe you are looking for help coping with them, not trying to get rid of them."

What a good question.

"I don't know," I began. "I mean, the dreams are incredibly inconvenient. I'm losing days of my life—or that's what it feels like—and my kids are worrying about my sanity. And I am too! I haven't said a thing about them to this man I'm seeing and that has caused some problems." I gave a small chuckle. "But the dreams are super compelling. There are people there who I miss…" I tried to speak more slowly, but I felt suddenly overwhelmed. "And I get a chance to be with those people and enjoy them in a way that feels normal—" By the end of my sentence I was sobbing.

Dr. Stewart leaned over to hand me the box of tissues. She let me cry for a long while, waiting patiently for me to be able to continue. Occasionally she soothed, "It's all right," which made me feel more at ease than embarrassed. I did feel comfortable with her, I realized. Even more than with Therapist One, she of the healthy plants.

When I collected myself and blew my nose, I said, "Sorry, I didn't expect that."

"In the first place, you shouldn't be sorry," she answered. "Also, I could tell that it took you by surprise."

I gave her a wan smile and more tears leaked out of my eyes.

Dr. Stewart said, "Why don't you give me some more details about the people in your dreams."

In between snuffles, I told her about how opening my mother's perfume had unexpectedly brought my childhood back. I told her about Ben, my dearest Ben. I told her about my love for Simon and how much I missed growing old with him. But when I talked about Lily dying, I began to tread on more dubious territory.

"But your sister, she's alive, right?" asked Dr. Stewart.

I nodded, pondering how I'd handle divulging my inner certainty that Lily's horrendous fate in that universe was as real and true as her happy normal life in this world. "Yes, she's great," I ventured. "I drove down to see her yesterday."

"Because of the dreams?"

"Yes."

"And when you say the dreams are vivid, you mean they feel *too* real to you. Is that right?"

I said, "Yes. I know it's strange, but yes."

"It's not that unusual to be affected strongly by a dream, to feel like those events you've experienced have a kind of reality that carries over into your waking life. In and of itself it's not a reason to question your sanity."

We both smiled.

"And I'm sorry," she said, "but our time is up. I'd be more than happy to see if I can help you. If you decide to continue with me, I think it might be useful if you try to think about that question I asked you earlier—Do you want the dreams to go away? Do you think that's a good place to start?"

"Yes, I do."

"Do you want to make another appointment or do you want to go home, think about it and call me in a few days?"

I didn't need to think about it. I said, "I'd like to make another appointment. Please."

Conventional therapist or shaman? Emotional health provider or spiritual health provider? I thought about it on the drive home and

151

decided to try both—why not?—as long as my conversation with the shaman went well.

I dialed the number for Mr. Angelus (if that was his real name). Many hyperactive butterflies had taken up residence in my stomach. As we all do when making awkward calls, I hoped it would go directly to voicemail. Then I could put off what would undoubtedly be a difficult conversation with a stranger.

But the man himself answered. He had a friendly voice and an unplaceable accent. After I identified myself he said, "Yes, Mrs. Thompson told me to expect your call."

"Oh good," I said. "I've been having a few problems, and she thought you might be able to help. I'd like to make an appointment."

"Can you tell me the general nature of your problems?" asked Mr. Angelus. "I want to make sure I'm the right person to help you."

"Sorry?" I asked, confused by the question.

"Issues usually fall into loose categories," he said. "For example, some people need help with physical pain. Some are looking for peace with a departed loved one, and some want my help with energy troubles. I can help with many things, but occasionally, I recommend another practitioner."

"I'm sorry," I said, annoying myself for apologizing again, "but my situation doesn't fit in any of those categories."

"Then why don't you try to explain it now, in whatever words you can?" said Mr. Angelus. "There's no charge. If you're comfortable with it, and it seems like I can help you, we'll make an appointment. If I'm not the right person for the job, I'll recommend someone else."

I was relieved. As advertised, he didn't want to charge me for a service he couldn't provide. "That's great," I said. "I'm in."

There was a pause. I waited for his response.

"Now it's your turn. Describe your problem to me," he said.

I paused. By this time, I had the "vivid dreams" story down pat, but it wasn't fundamentally true. And this was a shaman, right? He had to hear out-there stuff all the time. I took the plunge.

"I believe I'm exchanging places with another version of me—someone in another universe. I decided that was what's happening because I ruled out everything else I could think of."

Silence. I've never been good with silence. I kept talking. "At first I only told my kids my insane alternate universe theory. I didn't want to tell anyone else because they would think I *am* actually insane. What I've said to other people is that I'm experiencing vivid dreams. But I go to sleep in my own bed and wake up in this other place and it's a lot like this universe but—"

Mr. Angelus interrupted. "Let me ask you a question."

"Uh huh?"

"Are you under medical care?"

"Well, yes," I said. "I'm, um, in my early seventies."

"I mean, have you had the requisite medical tests to rule out physical problems—like conditions that might cause hallucinations?"

"Oh yes," I said. "I saw my neurologist and I've had an MRI and a sleep study."

"Okay then," he said. "We can check that off the list. Shamans can help with physical healing, but I always make sure to ask about any physiological causes." He paused, then went on. "I have to say that your problem is fascinating. Only rarely are people so loosely tied to this world that they unwittingly fall across boundaries. There's a good chance I can help. I'll know better when we meet in person. Let's make an appointment."

Mr. Angelus' fee sounded quite reasonable, not that I knew what was reasonable for a shaman. My health insurance was good but not out-of-this-world good, and would surely *not* cover a shaman visit, but my sessions with Dr. Stewart could be partly reimbursed. I resolved to pursue both angles: The traditional and the not. Though, I supposed, shamans had been around a lot longer than therapists, which meant they were actually the traditionalists.

I called Lily and left her a message saying I had made the appointment. I didn't know if I should tell the kids. I'd think about it.

I took Gretel on a lazy walk around the neighborhood, made myself a lovely salad for dinner and settled down on the couch to read my mystery. I thought about calling Bill—it had been a while since we'd talked. For all I knew he was still mad at me.

When I woke up I had the other Lexie's boring biography open across my chest, and Simon was standing over me suggesting gently that I ought to move into our bed for the rest of my night's sleep.

CHAPTER TWENTY-EIGHT

What could I do? I took myself to bed, but I couldn't sleep for worrying. I worried that other-Lexie, now in my world, didn't know about either my new therapist or the shaman and would miss both appointments. I worried that other-Lexie would get a call from Lily, which would flip her out completely. I worried that Simon might notice (again) that I was not acting like his usual wife.

I pretended to be peacefully asleep when Simon came to bed later. As I lay there, trying not to fidget or change positions, I reminded myself that my situation in this world had improved. I had Ben on my side here now. I did my breathing and managed to lay reasonably still until Simon began gently snoring. I gave it another full ten minutes before I got up and went into my office. I wanted to check my email ASAP—and thank goodness, waiting for me were emails from both Ben and other-Lexie.

Ben wrote that, as outlandish as it sounded, he believed what I had told him about my/our predicament. He had told other-Lexie to call him and he'd further explain, and he offered his help with whatever she needed.

Lexie's email was longer.

Dear Lexie,

I wrote this with a few possibilities in mind:

1. As you said in your email, you and I are (implausibly) switching places between our respective universes;

2. I am losing my short-term memory and that's why I don't remember sending myself an email;

3. My time in your life might be some version of a recurring nightmare;

4. Losing my mind is so traumatic for me that I've made up this elaborate meta email story in order to make myself feel better.

While you are experiencing and remembering an existence in both worlds, my days and nights seem to go by in a haze. It feels like cotton balls where my brain should be.

Frankly, I'm scared. I keep trying to assure myself that people don't usually get dementia one week and lose it the next, but Simon's anxiety rubs off on me. I read your(??) email right through to the end, all the while telling myself not to hope too much that it is true (what a thing to hope for! Universe slippage??) Then I called Ben, and now I'm not quite as worried about my sanity, though I am absolutely still scared.

I haven't said a word to Simon. I'm not sure he believes anything I say about my own state of mind, especially since there is a lot I genuinely don't remember. Simon's father had Alzheimer's and was extremely difficult in the early years before they got him diagnosed. He bullied, denied, and lied constantly and his whole personality seemed to change. Simon had to intervene between his parents many times before his father finally allowed himself to be tested for dementia. Then they gave him some helpful medications to calm him down and it got better, but Simon's memories of those experiences are powerful.

Ben has been such a good brother, supportive through all of this. The idea that in your world he died so young, and that Simon died too, is really hard for me to grasp. I've been thinking back a lot about Ben's life and why he might have gone in such a different direction. And Lily? The thought that she might be alive somewhere, anywhere, is too fantastic to fathom.

If I'm losing my memory, I have to deal with it. (Yes, it's terrifying, but I'm not sure I can do anything to stop it.) If you're right, and we're

exchanging places, I guess communication is as good a start as any. So,
thank you.
    Lexie.

It was like reading an email from a long-lost friend. I wrote back.

Dear other-Lexie,
    *It's definitely strange to get an email from someone who is me, but not
me. (But of course you know that already.)*
    *This morning I woke up here—no warning, as usual—and your
email made me feel not as alone. Even if we will never meet or share a
universe, we have a bizarre and unique (no kidding) connection. I wish I
had a clue why you feel like you're in a haze when you're in my world. I
seem to be fully present here, in your place.*
    *First, I have to apologize for the fight I had with Simon right before
I woke up back here in my own world. Your Simon seems more high-strung
than mine was. Ben thinks it's about him having taken on guilt over Lily.
Even so, I don't want my expectation that your Simon is the same person I
knew to screw up your relationship with your husband. That won't help
either of us.*
    *Btw, it's confusing—all these "mine's" and "yourses" and "this" and
the "other"—I have no idea how to express myself most of the time.*
    *I was thinking there might be some practical measures that could
make this craziness easier for both of us. For one, I should try to get along
better with Simon, no matter the differences. Mainly, though, I think
sharing information will help us most. So here goes:*
    *The last time I was in my own universe (long story shorter) I ended
up at the doctor. Since all the tests I took had normal results, I found myself
telling my (our?) kids my alternate universe theory. Strange but true, like
Ben in your world, they seem to have taken my universe-hopping theory
pretty much at face-value—either that, or they're doing a great job of
pretending I'm not nuts when they talk to me.*

I haven't been completely honest with anyone besides the kids, plus Lily and the shaman (more about him in a sec). I'm not even sure yet if I should be fully honest with my new therapist. (Her name is Dr. Stewart, and her phone number and address are on the calendar I keep on my computer if you end up having to go in my stead.)

I didn't intend to tell Lily about any of this, but in her typical fashion, she got it out of me. And also, because my (our?) little sister always does the unexpected, she's the one who suggested I see a shaman. Apparently shamans have some comfort with travel between universes. Makes sense, right? Anyway, the guy's name is Mr. Angelus, and I talked to him on the phone and made an appointment (you can check it on my calendar too) and he seemed excited by the prospect of seeing someone who was experiencing what I am. What we are, I mean. In other words, don't panic if Mr. Angelus calls, or if Lily calls to check up on my appointment.

Then there's Bill. A couple years ago, I got set up with him (to do landscaping, initially) and we've been seeing each other. He lives in the valley and has a daughter there and grandkids, and yes, we do sleep together. More specifics available if you want them but at the moment the important info is that he's mad at me because I've never been inclined to introduce him to the kids. And he doesn't know anything about the alternate reality issue, and I do not feel like telling him.

I think that's it for now. I hope these updates help you. At this point I seem to be putting a stupid amount of hope in the shaman. Also, what do you think about letting Simon in on all of this? Everything might be easier if he knew.

Sorry to go on for so long.

(Other-)Lexie.

CHAPTER TWENTY-NINE

I got myself back into bed as quietly as I could. Simon was asleep facing my side, the now-deeper lines in his forehead drawn together as if engaged in complicated calculations. My Simon used to look like that too when he was dreaming. Sometimes I'd ask about his dreams but he rarely remembered. I snuggled up to this Simon, the comfort and familiarity of his body erasing our recent arguments from my awareness. He mumbled and pulled closer to me before resuming unconsciousness. Within a few minutes, I too was asleep.

My internet project for the day was to try to determine if Mr. Angelus existed in this alternate world, too. While I was searching, Simon came into my office to remind me we were having dinner with friends. I had checked my calendar, and I already knew about the dinner (woohoo!) but as we were talking, Simon saw the search results on my computer monitor and leaned in.

"You're looking for a shaman?"

I forced out a chuckle. "Yeah, shaman sites are a good source for info about healing plants."

I didn't think that up on the spot. I had it prepared it in case Simon asked, along with an entire extra scenario to cover me going to an appointment with Mr. Angelus' counterpart (if I could find him in this world). It was entirely plausible, as lies go.

"What plants?" Simon asked.

This I knew too. "Feverfew, chamomile, elderberry; Shamans have used them to treat pain over centuries," I said.

"Huh," he said, seeming satisfied. "All right. I'm going to take Gretel out and then go to the gym."

I looked up at him and mouthed a kiss. "Have fun," I said.

Alone at last!

Who'd a thunk I would want to be alone, instead of glued to the side of my not-dead-here husband?

The first thing I did was buy another book about multiverse theory—a selection not available in my universe!—in the hope that Simon would pick it up from the coffee table and gently ask (either me or other-Lexie), "Hey, are you having problems staying in your correct universe?"

Okay, I knew that wasn't going to happen. But any little thing that might make it easier to be honest with Simon would be a step in the right direction.

How could I be feeling so lukewarm about Simon? Was it because I had research to conduct, Ben to call, and my own life in this universe to review, in case there was a test? Or was it because I didn't like this Simon as much as my own? Or was it, more simply, that I had gotten used to being by myself and had learned to relish it?

I thought about what might have been different if my Simon had retired in good health, rather than having been forced to step down by the mounting number of doctor's appointments, procedures, physical misery, and fatigue. When my Simon retired, there were no mid-morning trips to the gym or dog walks, no coffees with friends or going to see movies on weekday afternoons, things we'd assumed would be staples of our post-work lives. Instead, there were naps.

Even my Simon's love of reading fell victim to his exhaustion. He'd throw the book down with an angry thump and say, "I've read the same page six times now." Often he'd just fall asleep. Finally, most books became too heavy for him to hold. I bought him an e-reader (a concept which he claimed to deplore) but by that time, it was too late for him to tackle all the books he'd planned to read "someday." There wasn't going to be a "someday."

Ben called as I sat down to drink a cup of tea. "I'm very happy to hear your voice," I said.

"Me too," Ben said. "Though I did just talk to the other you yesterday."

"God, this is confusing," I said.

Ben laughed. "Yeah, very weird. I mean, it's weird for me, but…"

"Yeah, I know. I'm currently winning the weirdness competition."

"You are a little funnier than my real sister," Ben said.

"I guess I should take that as a compliment. Funny is good, right?" I asked, adding, "I've been thinking that I should come see your house, meet your dogs, you know, hang out. It might help me, um, sound better with Simon."

"Of course," said Ben, "Good idea. But you need to catch me up too."

So I did—events of the past weeks, therapists, shamans, my kids, Lily. We talked about Lily for a while. How pushy she was, how we'd grown closer. How much she'd floored me with the shaman suggestion. I mentioned Bill too, then realized my error instantly.

"Boyfriend Bill? Ooooh, bad Lexie," Ben said. And then, in a sing-song, "Two-timing Lexie!" as if we were kids on a schoolyard.

"I can't say I've missed being teased like that." I grinned, "That's a lie. I totally have."

Ben laughed, and then, as was getting to be a habit, I began to cry.

Fortunately, by the time Simon got back my eyes were no longer red and puffy. I had already applied a cold washcloth, composed myself and made a plan with Ben to see his house the next day.

Our dinner with friends went fine. These weren't people I knew in my other life, but they seemed nice enough. It turned out that we had known them since we were all parents at our neighborhood school. I had to vamp a bit, but no one questioned my identity, my sanity, or my memory.

We got home around ten and Simon, mildly drunk, suggested we both take Gretel around the block. We ended up kissing on the corner like teenagers. He was easier when he'd had a couple glasses of wine. I was very much on board when we got home and moved it into the bedroom.

And then I thought about her. About other-Lexie. Whose husband I was enjoying. Was this technically adultery?

The kids call it a buzzkill, and I think that's an excellent turn of phrase.

I could have turned him down, and I know he would have respected any "not feeling up to it" excuse I might express. But that would be lying too. My body had been all in before my brain jumped in yelling "not your husband!" It's difficult to think straight when your body is distracting your brain, and the best thing I could think of in the moment was to go along as if I *was* his Lexie. It was also easiest.

Anyone who's been married for a long time and grown through life's changes with their partner knows that sometimes you go along for the other person's sake. I think the politics have gotten muddy about not enjoying 100% of a sexual encounter. It is more than possible to enjoy someone else's enjoyment even when you're not quite as enthusiastic yourself. In my most feminist moments I can't see anything wrong with that.

So I pretended. I pretended I didn't know he wasn't my Simon. I pretended to myself and I pretended to him. No one would be the wiser but me.

Afterwards, Simon (still a bit tipsy) fell asleep. I was left to think about why the passion had drained out of me so suddenly and completely.

That first time I'd woken up here to find Simon and Ben chatting in my living room, my confusion had been tempered by the feeling that I had wandered into an unexpected utopia, somehow created to fulfill my deepest longings. Seeing Simon, making love with Simon, it had been a surprise, a gift.

No longer.

Now I knew I was in fact, replacing other-Lexie. This was *her* husband and I was an imposter. Clothes, money, the car, even the dog—none of them were quite my own. And I was keeping my imposter-hood from my husband, who was in fact someone else's husband. I was enjoying someone else's stuff. It made me feel like a bad guy.

I lay in my bed listening to Simon's quiet breathing. Logic proclaimed I had no control. It wasn't my fault. Further, it might all be a hallucination and I might be the only person affected.

And yet.

CHAPTER THIRTY

The next morning I told Simon I was taking Gretel to Ben's house for a doggie playdate. The eye-roll I got was inevitable, and probably justified.

As I drove up into the canyon following Ben's directions, I thought about my Ben, how he had always been aesthetically inclined. When we were growing up, he curated the posters on his walls, his clothes, and his furniture. Even when he was fighting addiction, Ben's clothes—often unwashed and wrinkled—were carefully chosen. I hoped being in this Ben's home would give me some of the information I craved about his life.

Canyon homes are often built right up to the road, but Ben's house was about eight feet back. In the smallish front yard, a raised bed held large succulents separated by short gravel paths. Gretel and I got out of the car and were met by Ben and his dogs, Ursula and Wallace. Wallace and Gretel greeted each other with woofs and a happy dance. Ben and I tried to stay out of their way as they bounded around each other. Ursula attempted to bark everyone back into proper order.

"That's how it goes," said Ben. "Ursula is very controlling." He was perfectly turned out in black jeans and a vintage t-shirt that looked almost familiar. As I got closer, I read the text—*Talking Heads '77*—but the album cover I remembered had green writing on a red background. The colors were flipped on Ben's t-shirt—it was green with red lettering. Huh. Someday maybe I'd get my brain around the differences between worlds, but until then, I could only marvel at the cosmological roll of the dice that made t-shirt colors different.

We moved inside, where an over-excited Wallace instantly slid across the hardwood floor and bumped into one of the many floor-to-ceiling windows. Ursula jumped straight in the air repeatedly, barking at Ben as if to say, "Hey! I can't stop this nonsense! Can you?!" Ben picked up Ursula and let the other two dogs out to play in the back yard.

The house had been built in the 1930s, and Ben told me that when he bought it, he stripped the house to its walls and put in wood floors which, in the living room, were whitewashed. He used the simplicity of the architecture to showcase his several collections—constructivist posters, an assortment of brightly colored period chairs and couches, and mobiles, lots of mobiles. It must have been tricky to have dogs with all these pristine pieces, I thought, but dog beds artfully covered to match the people furniture sat in the corners of every room.

I gazed out a window overlooking the backyard, the canyon and city beyond. To one side, there was a wooden deck with green slatted metal furniture, some covered against the elements.

Everything planted was drought tolerant. Different colors of rocky paths meandered around nicely grouped plantings and led down to a lower level where the back fence was shielded by Palo Verde trees.

"You did the landscaping, you know," Ben said, handing me a cup of tea.

"It looks terrific," I said. I wanted to go outside and inspect my counterpart's work, see how all the various plants had established themselves. But being with Ben was more important.

"When I moved in it was all raggedy lawn to there." He pointed. "With the oldest swing set in captivity. Where the yard sloped down there were layers of ancient ivy. My dogs then—Ernest and Edith—loved finding the rats and lizards in there. They'd come back disgusting—covered with dirt and sometimes bloody."

165

I wrinkled my nose. "How long before I made you change it?"

"About two years after I finished the house remodel. But with me, nothing is ever finished."

I nodded. My Ben had been the same.

He took me on a tour. In his office, a display of movie one-sheets that he designed coexisted with photos of Tasha at every age. Ben pointed out items in the photos – a favorite toy I had bought her, a hand-me-down sweater from my kids. He said he had moved to the tech side of publicity early on, and now worked freelance. He had clearly done well for himself. My Ben had trouble holding a job, though the people who hired him loved him and apologized sincerely when they fired him.

Tasha's room was the only contrast to the minimalist aesthetic of the house. A giant bulletin board covered the wall above her desk with a jumble of photos, cards, and mementos. About two dozen sports trophies cluttered the top of her bureau, some with medals hung by ribbons.

"You let her go wild, I see," I said as I examined the items on the bulletin board. "You must have kept the door closed when Architectural Digest came around."

Ben looked puzzled. "What's that?"

Huh.

"It's a magazine. You must not have it here. I was trying to say that this room is very different from the rest of the house."

"I got that," Ben said. "It turns out that children are mess-making machines."

"And all those trophies!" I inspected the metallic labels. Most were for soccer, a few for cross-country. "You went to soccer games and cheered from the sidelines like regular parents?" I couldn't picture it. My Ben had been completely un-sporty.

"Yeah," he said. "I kind of got into it. It wasn't my idea though, the sports. Tasha's mom is into sports. She coached a few of Tasha's teams."

Tasha's mother was named Claire. She and Ben had never married, and when she got pregnant from what Ben characterized as a "friendly one-night stand" they each decided that it was their last chance to have a child.

Ben said, "It was the best decision either of us ever made."

"I hope I get to see her," I said.

"She'll be back for Christmas break." Ben led me out of Tasha's room and we sat down in the living room. The peculiarly shaped red couch was unexpectedly comfortable. "I guess you don't know if you'll be here."

"Nope." I sighed. "I don't."

Ben brought the dogs back inside where they lay panting at our feet. I had a short agenda, one item to discuss with Ben in person. I told him wanted to be honest with Simon, tell him I wasn't his Lexie, that I was from a different world altogether. I knew Simon wouldn't believe me, at least not at first, but I hoped he would come around and that it might alleviate his fears in the long run. I laid it all out for Ben.

"Honestly, I don't know," he said. "I mean, Simon isn't open to woo-woo New Age concepts—these days it seems he's against all unfamiliar ideas on principle."

"Huh." That was different. My Simon was open enough to try all kinds of treatments for his cancer, treatments that some people might call New Age. We had long discussions about the power of positive thinking and whether it might help, or if it was only a media-hyped version of wishful thinking, and/or a way to blame the victim. To be honest, of all of the not-strictly medical treatments we tried (so-called healers recommended by friends, magnets, guided imagery) there were only two that made a difference: acupuncture and a macrobiotic diet.

I ate the bland but healthy vegan food alongside Simon until the day he said, "It's just not worth it." We went out for steaks.

Ben said, "My opinion? Simon will instantly question your grasp on reality. Now that he's gotten the idea in his head that you're having memory lapses, he can't stop speculating that you're covering up some form of dementia."

"It's not like I colluded with the doctor when he said I was fine," I said. "Simon's got to know that nothing is medically wrong with me."

"There's knowing, and then there's knowing," Ben said. "The suspicion is there. It's like he has some version of PTSD from his dad's Alzheimer's, and the smallest seemingly unrelated, not-even-slightly-verifiable indication that you might be forgetting something—I'm guessing it makes Simon anxious and he overreacts.

"You think it's that bad?" I asked.

Ben nodded thoughtfully. "Yeah, I do. Between Simon's father and his guilt about Lily, he lost a sense of control over his life."

"What you're saying is that I shouldn't tell him."

Ben nodded again.

Damn. Not what I was hoping to hear. "Okay then," I said. "Worst-case scenario—what do you think will happen if I do?"

"I think he might do something drastic."

"You mean he might try to have me institutionalized?"

Ben held my gaze. "I don't think it would work, but is that a fight you want to have?"

"No." I shook my head. "Still, how can I have a decent relationship with someone I'm lying to?"

Ben grimaced. "Alright, then let me play devil's advocate here. That's a terrific principle. But haven't you ever lied to make a relationship easier or better? Even with "your" Simon? I know I'm not the best judge, having never sustained a relationship myself," he shrugged. "But you love Simon, right?"

"Oh God, that's a big question," I answered. "I absolutely loved *my* Simon. I'm not sure they're the same person now. And anyway, this is about who *I* am," I said. "I'm a different person than his Lexie. At some point I'm going to have to—"

Ben interrupted me, "Look, I understand, but it's dangerous. And it's not fair to my actual sister if you put her in that position. She'd have to go along with your scenario whether she wants to or not."

I considered, somewhat abashed. As much as I felt bonded to this version of my brother, other-Lexie was his real sister. He might like me, but he had to be loyal to her. He loved her.

"Good point," I said.

I hadn't thought about it like that before. Was I jealous of their relationship? I certainly was jealous of anyone whose beloved sibling hadn't died, but my relationship with this Ben felt all good, a complete gift, and I didn't want to mess with it.

"But wouldn't it help in the long run?" I asked. "Isn't explaining to Simon going to help her eventually?"

"Yeah, I get that," said Ben. "And I would back you up. But please, please, be careful."

Ben had wanted to FaceTime with Tasha while I was there, so I could see the niece I'd never known, but she didn't answer. I couldn't blame her. She didn't know that I wasn't her regular Aunt Lexie. She didn't know it would be my first—my only?—chance to meet her.

I roused Gretel, we said our goodbyes to Wallace and Ursula, and walked to the car. I got all 120 pounds of Gretel into the back seat and then I had to kick Wallace out. He loved cars and thought he could come along too.

I hugged Ben goodbye, trying not to get teary. As I drove home, I tried very hard to be happy for the life this Ben had been given. It was exactly what I would have wanted for him. It felt good to have seen it, to have spent a morning with my brother, to have been able to catch up as if we had only been apart for a few weeks, instead of for a lifetime and a universe.

CHAPTER THIRTY-ONE

By the time I got home, I felt even more muddled than usual. If I was going to spend more time in this world, and not wreck other-Lexie's marriage, I'd have to come clean. But confessing my imposter-hood to Simon (against Ben's probably-better judgment) would be risky. If sex with her Simon made me feel guilty, how would I feel if I got her locked into a facility for people with dementia?

Back and forth my brain went as I lay on the couch trying to concentrate on the Russian biography. Simon was heading out and I asked him if we still had the Talking Heads' first LP. I wanted to see the cover for myself.

"I think it's in with all the vinyl in my office," Simon answered. "Take a look." And then he did the brow-furrow-worry face that I'd come to associate with an upcoming test of my sanity. "Why? What made you think of that?"

Easy. "Ben was wearing the t-shirt."

"Oh," Simon nodded and his face relaxed. "Great album." He smiled and leaned down to pat Gretel and kiss my cheek.

I leaned back. I wondered why I kept reading this book of other-Lexie's. She would surely come back to find the bookmark moved along but have no idea what had happened to the Russian empress in the pages I'd pretended to read. Maybe my next email to her should include an update, like those study guides kids use when they don't want to read the actual book.

In the meantime, I was very sleepy.

I dreamt I was back in Ben's house, but it was empty. No furniture, posters, photos, residents. Gretel's toenails clicked on the bare floor as we walked toward the window that looked out over the overgrown back yard. Tendrils of ivy crept up toward the deck and weeds poked through crumbling cement. Gretel was on high alert, her ears pricked, her chest rumbling with a low growl. She was entirely focused on something outside I couldn't see. I put my hand on her back—there would be no hunting in the underbrush for my dog—and soothed, "It's okay, girl, we're fine." She didn't seem to hear me. I felt her growl grow and her muscles tighten. Before I could hook my hand under her harness, she sprang. Where her front paw hit, the window shattered in an outward spiral of cracks and splinters, screeching nails-on-chalkboard as shards hit the floor inside and the deck outside. Gretel bounded through toward something emerging from the ivy. I tried to follow but my foot slipped backwards on broken glass. My knee landed on a large fragment, which further fractured, cutting through fabric and flesh. I looked up from the blood seeping from my knee to see Gretel fighting with a creature, the monster that came out of the ivy. It was horned, fanged, and angry. I tried to push myself up to go to her aid, but wherever I put my hand, glass shredded my skin. The floor was slick with my blood.

The landline rang. I sat up frightened, panting. I looked for the handset. It was there, on the coffee table, and I grabbed for it.

"Hello?" I said, trying to make my voice sound calm.

"Lexie? Are you alright?"

It was Bill. I was back in my own world.

CHAPTER THIRTY-TWO

"Yeah, I'm okay," I said, trying to catch up with my surroundings. Gretel, snoozing on her dog bed, raised her head to look at me. She stood up and headed over. "I had a bad dream, that's all."

"I'm sorry I woke you," Bill replied. "Do you want me to call you back?"

"No, it's fine. Just give me a sec." I put my hand over the receiver. Gretel stood over me sniffing. She licked my face and tried to get on the couch with me. I hugged her and made her get back down, then spoke into the phone. "Bill, I'm glad to hear from you. I thought…"

What had I thought?

"You thought I wasn't going to call again."

"Um," I said. "I guess so. I mean, I guess not. Well, you know what I mean." I felt like an idiot, taken off guard this way.

"Thanksgiving is coming," said Bill. "My kids are going to Arizona to spend it with the in-laws. I hate Arizona. And I thought to myself, who would I feel comfortable asking for an invitation?"

"Me?" I asked, trying to not betray my incredulity. But, why not? It wasn't like I was agreeing to a lifelong commitment. So, I said, "No, you're right, it would be a perfect opportunity to meet my family. This year we're doing Thanksgiving at Nora's in Santa Barbara." As I said it, it felt good to offer an invitation in return for his forgiveness.

"Sounds great," Bill said.

"Can I ask you a question?" I added.

"Sure."

"What day is it today?"

I heard Bill's laugh come down the phone line, hearty and unforced. "I thought you were going to ask me a completely different question," he said. "But it's Thursday today. Thanksgiving is in two weeks."

"Oh good, that's what I thought," I said. I hadn't missed either my appointment at the shrink or the shaman. "I lose track sometimes now without work."

"Makes sense. Taking care of my grandkids is the only reason I know—school days vs. not school days, at a minimum," Bill answered, then added, "I have a question for you too."

Uh oh.

"You *are* being honest with me, aren't you? About your health? You're okay, right?"

Phew. "Yes, clean bill of health all around." No lie, that—I *was* absolutely physically fine. I asked, "What did you think? Wait, don't tell me, I know! You thought I was going to ask you why you'd forgiven me."

"On the money," said Bill.

"So?" I asked.

"Life is too short," he said. "You've been a good friend, to say the least. And as I said, I hate Arizona."

I laughed. "All's fair. You are welcome to share Nora's guest room with me, but the bed isn't huge. Or get a hotel room if you'd be more comfortable. Though if you want to do that, you'd better make those calls today," I added.

"I'll probably take you up on the guest room," he said, sounding cheerful. I felt cheered up too.

Gretel looked at me expectantly. She seemed perky, even energetic, and it took me another moment to realize she wanted a walk. This wasn't the same Gretel who'd exhausted herself running around Ben's backyard with Wallace. I had to remember that. This was my Gretel, and she definitely needed a walk. And here there was no Simon to share my dog-walking duties.

Dr. Stewart handed me the tissue box. I was crying already, only ten minutes into our session.

"I'm curious," she said. "Why do you feel such ambivalence about inviting your friend-slash-boyfriend to Thanksgiving?"

I had begun by telling her I wanted to figure out what I was doing with Bill. It had seemed like a safe topic. But within a few minutes of describing our argument about meeting my family, followed by Bill's phone call and my invitation to Thanksgiving, I was blubbering away.

"You've been widowed for more than ten years," she added.

I nodded through my tears and blew my nose, trying to get control. Crying was probably a useful catharsis, but I should use my time with Dr. Stewart better. I took a deep breath. "I don't know. It's not about the principle. I mean, I never swore to my Simon I'd be faithful to him forever, and I know he would never have wanted that."

"*My* Simon?" asked Dr. Stewart

Oh shit.

But then she continued, "Did you ever talk about it, about what might happen after he died? Whether you would date?"

"No. I think we both sort of treated it like it was too sad to talk about, but I also think we both expected me to go ahead and date when I was ready. That I would find companionship." I laughed, surprising myself, "Other than Alfred, I mean." I had to smile.

"Who's Alfred?" Dr. Stewart asked.

"Alfred was our dog back then. A Great Dane. I have another one now. Her name is Gretel. I wish Bill liked her more."

Dr. Stewart raised her eyebrows. "Bill doesn't like Gretel? Or at least you think he doesn't?"

"Right," I agreed.

Dr. Stewart held my gaze and waited.

"I just think he's not a dog person, and since Gretel is a Dane, that's kind of as much dog as you can get," I said.

Dr. Stewart smiled. "Yes, I suppose so. But what makes you think Bill doesn't like her?"

"She's a little possessive, and the whole sleeping in my room issue—" I stopped, contemplating the situation I was trying to describe. "Um, she growled a bit at first."

"I wouldn't like her either, if she growled at me," Dr. Stewart said. "It's hard to like someone who doesn't like you."

"I know, I know," I said, shifting my legs to a more comfortable position. "I need to deal with it. Give him treats to give her, stuff like that."

"Would she hurt him?" Dr. Stewart asked.

I sat up straighter. "Absolutely not. She's incredibly obedient. She's the best dog I've ever had. She's the best companion ever."

"Better than Bill?"

"Touché," I said, laughing. "Good point. Dog or human. Which do I want more? The one who doesn't speak English or the one who does? The one who needs me and has been there for me, or the one who… Oh, I don't know. I guess I've never taken my relationship with Bill seriously enough to find out."

"That's important to realize. Also, I'm not sure it's either/or," said Dr. Stewart. "While not liking your dog isn't the worst reason I've ever heard for sabotaging a relationship, it doesn't sound like that's written in stone. They might get along better if you took some steps."

I knew that.

Dr. Stewart continued, "It might also help to discuss some other aspects of your relationship with Bill. What else isn't working?"

It came out before I could stop myself. "He's not Simon."

Dr. Stewart let that sit in the air for a beat before she said, "No. He isn't."

We looked at each other. I blinked away some more inconvenient tears. My mind ran through all the complications and finally I said, "I guess there's no statute of limitations on missing someone."

"No, there isn't." Dr. Stewart shook her head ruefully. "I do have another question, though. I can't help wondering—with all this loss in your life, why do you have dogs with such short lifespans? They only live, what, at most ten years?"

No worries about straying into multiverse territory here.

Why a Great Dane? Easy answer. "Having Gretel in my life is a joy. One hundred percent."

"If a shorter life comes with the package, you can handle it?" asked Dr. Stewart.

"Yes, absolutely." I went on for a while, waxing rhapsodic about Great Danes and explaining in possibly too much detail why I'd rather have a Dane for fewer years than any Methuselah-aged Chihuahua or Yorkie.

"And Simon," I continued, seeing that she was losing interest, "well, he might not have wanted his lifespan compared to a dog's, but he had what a hundred years ago they would've called a long life—"

A thought came to me unbidden. *But Ben didn't.*

Dr. Stewart must have seen my train of thought stop short. "But?"

"Well, I was thinking about my brother, Ben," I said, reminding myself to be cautious.

"That he didn't get a long life like Simon?" asked Dr. Stewart.

I nodded. "I just wish things had been better for him," I said, trying to keep my voice steady.

Dr. Stewart sat forward in her chair. "That's probably a good place to start next session. Our time is up."

It was still weird, scheduling fifty minutes of emoting per week, but it was good, too. I gathered my purse and crumpled tissues and thanked Dr. Stewart.

Next stop: shaman.

CHAPTER THIRTY-THREE

Or not.

When I drove away after my appointment with Dr. Stewart I was so lost in thought that I found myself heading east—the wrong way. I caught it before I got too far, but on what I can only call a whim, I decided to keep going and headed up the canyon toward the spot where Ben lived in that other world. I knew the address. I had driven myself and other-Gretel there the day before, though it had been a universe away. Was there even a house there in this world? What might be there, where my brother was not?

It was barely lunchtime and the canyon roads were free of their regular rush-hour traffic. I turned right off the main road and followed a smaller street toward the top of the hill. There it was. The house where Ben didn't live. It existed in this universe, too.

I pulled over across from the high-end SUV parked in the driveway. The front yard of the house had been leveled for a basketball court of sorts, the kind where any out-of-bounds shot bounces down, down the hill. I bet there was a veritable basketball cemetery in the scrub below. The mom probably had to buy basketballs in sets of six.

But maybe it wasn't a mom, I chided myself. Maybe it was a single millennial who played with his friends before or after they watched games on the big screen TV and drank artisanal beer. It was hard to tell from the outside. Heavy curtains blocked the windows. Ben had not had curtains. He had modern streamlined shades.

I got out of the car. I felt like I was being drawn toward the house, even as another part of my brain insisted I was on a fool's errand. I could ring the bell and make up a charity or a lost pet. Or a brother in another universe.

Okay, that last idea wasn't going anywhere. Nonetheless, I wanted to see inside of the house.

I gathered my courage, walked to the front door and rang the doorbell. After a short time, I heard footsteps.

"Who's there?" came a woman's voice in heavily accented English.

I said my name.

Perhaps it was that I gave my name, or because I was female, but the door opened revealing an older Hispanic woman in an apron. I said hello and in a moment of inspiration, pulled out one of my old cards which read, *Alexandra Brooker Landscape Design*. "I was hoping to see the back yard," I said.

The woman looked ready to let me walk through, but then I heard another voice, and the clip of sharp heels on the floor.

"Who's there, Estella?" asked the woman. She was dressed for the office and spoke quickly.

"I'm sorry," I said, heart sinking, "there's my card." Estella was still holding it and the woman put out her hand. She was in her late twenties, I gathered, and she didn't need glasses to read the small print.

She looked at me. "Are you looking for landscaping work?" I started to answer but she talked over me. "We don't need anything done, and I'm about to leave," she said. "I had to stop back and pick something up."

I tried to continue. "No, no, I was just curious," I said, instantly deciding that this woman would be unsympathetic, no matter what I said. "I'm retired, but I used to know the person who lived here and they—"

"You knew the Kellys?" she said.

"No," I said, thinking quickly. "Before them."

"But they owned the house for thirty-five years, before we bought it." Now she looked suspicious.

I held out my hand anyway. "Lexie Brooker," I said. "I used to play here when I was a child."

The woman's expression changed, more sympathetic, but still unsure. "Oh," she said. "You shouldn't ring doorbells like that."

"I know," I said, "I'm sorry, but I drove up to see and…"

Now the woman had the look people get when they're assuming you're a lunatic.

"I'm sorry," I said again. "I just wanted to see the back yard."

The woman shook her head, but said, "Alright. Just for a second. I have to leave—as I said—and I don't think I should leave you alone in the house."

I guess the maid doesn't count, I thought.

"Thank you so much," I said.

I walked toward the window that looked out over the yard. I could see a lap pool built into the hill below. Yesterday I had stood here and it had been Ben's house.

I blinked to clear the tears from my eyes. And there, instead of this back yard in this world, I saw the view as it had been in my dream. The giant window began to break again, and the shadowy figure emerged from the ivy. I gasped and blinked again, reaching my hand out to steady myself on the window.

"Are you alright?" The woman's concern sounded genuine, though I'm sure I also detected a tinge of annoyance.

I nodded, trying to breathe normally.

She watched me intently. "Do you want to sit down?"

I shook my head. "No, no, I'm all right. It was déjà vu, I think."

"Oh," she said, now brisk. "I've had that too."

I could see she thought I might find another way to delay her departure—faint? die?

181

"I should leave now," I said. "I appreciate your kindness."

She gave me a taut smile.

"You've made a beautiful home," I added, wanting to acknowledge her in some way. After all, she had let me in. I was grateful for that.

"Thank you," she said. She handed me my card back. Uneasiness still showed in her face.

"Thank you," I repeated.

As she closed the door after me, I heard her begin to speak angrily in Spanish. I walked slower so I could eavesdrop. My Spanish is pretty good. She scolded Estella for letting me in, telling her that now she was late, but their guests were due at seven and... Then I couldn't hear any more.

I got in my car feeling sad and embarrassed. What had I hoped for? For the world to bifurcate then and there and give me Ben in this world too? He still called to me, and I had no idea if that would ever stop.

CHAPTER THIRTY-FOUR

Dr. Angelus' office was on the second floor of a quiet mini-mall in Garden Grove. The ground level had a dry cleaner, a few take-out restaurants, a postal store, and (naturally) a Starbucks. I walked up the stairs and along a narrow balcony that connected the offices. I passed an accounting firm and two dentists on my way to the correct door, glad Mr. Angelus' neighbors looked legit.

It could have been any office. The posters on the walls were abstract, with what you might call a primitive flair, but there were no diagrams of chakras or Egyptian hieroglyphs or charts of edible plants. It smelled more institutional than it did New Age.

As I checked out the magazines, (Real Simple, Forbes and Sports Illustrated), Mr. Angelus opened the door of the waiting room. "Alexandra Brooker?" he asked.

"Yes," I said. "Call me Lexie."

Just as no one would be able to pick out this office as a portal to the otherworldly, no one would ever single out Mr. Angelus as a shaman. Like his faintly accented English, his skin and features might have placed his ancestry anywhere from Southeast Asia to the ancient Americas. His head was close-shaven and he wore gray slacks with a light blue button-down shirt. His face was lined—deep crinkles, especially around his eyes and mouth—yet he moved like a man in his thirties.

In the inner office, the desk faced a window that looked out on the surrounding suburban neighborhood. I obeyed Mr. Angelus' proffered hand as it motioned me to sit on the couch. I put my bag down and nervously scratched at an old mosquito bite on my hand. I took in the posters—exhibits of Native American textiles, African masks, Thai calligraphy and a Man Ray retrospective—and tried to breathe some calm into my brain. Mr. Angelus leaned back in his chair and folded his hands in his lap.

"I've been looking for help in all kinds of ways," I said. "I've seen my doctor, I've had tests—I know I told you that already and I'm sorry I'm repeating myself. I'm back in therapy. Well, not literally back, more like it's new since I haven't seen a therapist since my brother died, if you don't count the grief group I was in when my husband died, but they were quite far apart in time and..." Words tumbled out of me. Mr. Angelus held eye contact. His attention felt patient, sympathetic.

I gathered my thoughts. "So," I continued, "I need all the help I can get."

"But something changed since we spoke on the phone," said Mr. Angelus. "Then you were sure you wanted to stop going to that other place, or at least that's what you said. But now... Have you become uncertain?"

What had given me away? Was it my tone of voice? My obvious jitters? Or was Mr. Angelus truly and deeply perceptive? He was a shaman, after all.

"It's true," I said. "I've been vacillating—There are people there I love... But it's not actually my life, and the more I think about it, the more I realize I'm stealing someone else's."

I had to hand it to Mr. Angelus. His expression didn't change. "Maybe you should go back to the beginning, again," he said.

I laid it out as simply and quickly as I could, describing my experiences in each world, hoping to leave enough time in our session

184

for Mr. Angelus to fix it. (Presuming, of course, that I wanted it to be fixed.)

When I arrived at the present moment, I paused, and asked, "What should I do?"

He smiled at me kindly, deepening the wrinkles around his eyes. "Breathing is a good start. At least in this world."

It made me smile back.

"I'm not here to say what you *should* do," he continued. "First, what do you know about what we—shamans—do?"

"Not much," I said, hoping I didn't seem like too much of a dunce, adding, "I did a little research online, but you are the only shaman I've ever met—knowingly, I mean. And your office, well, it doesn't have any of the things I was expecting."

"Like what?" he asked.

"Um," I tried to recall the webpages I'd perused. "Like drums, or herbs and incense, maybe spirit animals…" I trailed off.

"Yes," he said, "those can all be tools of the trade. But in a case like yours, I don't use them right away. If I am going to heal a spirit, or find a soul that has gone missing, it helps to know what happened in that person's life. How it has affected them. But now that you've said you have mixed feelings about closing the door to that other world, I think it's prudent for you to think about what it is you want, at least for a little while longer."

I felt my guts twist inside me. Was he going to tell me he wouldn't do what I came for? I was surprised by a surge of impatience—I suddenly felt that whatever was necessary, I wanted it done as soon as possible. I guess now I knew what I should say when Dr. Stewart asked me again if I wanted the dreams to stop.

"But my sister's friend," I said, "She didn't mention that it took more than one session."

"Her case was straightforward," said Mr. Angelus. "Without divulging anything too personal, I can say that it was the kind of healing I do most frequently, cases in which I can 'cut to the chase,' if you will, with very little preamble." He didn't seem boastful about it. He was stating a fact. Grief isn't easy for anyone. It made sense that Mr. Angelus dealt with it frequently in his practice.

But how many people missed their loved ones so much that even after decades they accidentally found a way to visit them in other universes? Probably not a lot.

"How did this happen at all?" It burst out of me, this question I'd been trying to find an answer to for weeks and weeks now. "I read a lot of physics books and they all said it can't happen." I tried not to sound too pitiful, but without much success. "I've been telling doctors I'm having vivid dreams because I don't want them to commit me. Even my kids thought I was losing it."

"It's very rare," said Mr. Angelus. "I'd venture a guess that your sadnesses over the years have made you susceptible to that other place because there, those losses never happened."

"But people lose their loved ones all the time," I cried. "They lose their whole families and nothing like this happens. What's so special about me?"

Mr. Angelus remained calm in spite of my (probably) unanswerable question. "It is unusual, but not unheard of. Some people are not quite tethered to this world. In truth, I think it happens more than we know, possibly because most people can't remember it clearly. They don't—or can't—talk about it."

I nodded, remembering how other-Lexie questioned her memory and her sanity.

"There's not a lot of available information. But yes, there have been cases like yours. Society often puts them down to madness or the use of hallucinatory drugs. As a matter of fact, one interpretation of what occurs when people take 'trips,'" Mr. Angelus used air quotes, "is that people see glimpses of those other places, like other dimensions or planes of being."

"Wow," I said. That had never occurred to me.

"Just out of curiosity," Mr. Angelus asked, "did you ever use psychoactive drugs—LSD, psilocybin mushrooms, ayahuasca?"

"No," I said. "A little marijuana when I was in high school and college, but I sort of lost interest."

"Okay," Mr. Angelus nodded. "People often think those kinds of drugs are necessary to shamanistic rituals. But they're not. For one thing, they can be very hard to control. When shamans access the unseen—a broad category, I know—the most important thing is to be open, to believe in the otherworldly. But you *know* it's possible. You have experienced it. I've been thinking about it since you called, and wondering about your abilities. I even googled you." His smile seemed sheepish.

He continued, "I saw your website, and I can tell how important it is to you that our earth is healthy. You may have an affinity for all this." He gestured around the room, as if it encompassed eons of human supernatural beliefs.

It wasn't often that anyone saw my life's work of water-wise landscaping as worthwhile. I thanked him.

"You must also keep in mind that if we succeed, and we anchor you back to this world," Mr. Angelus went on, "you will never again be able to visit the people you love in the other world. It has to be a factor in your decision."

Tears smarted in my eyes. "So..." I faltered. "What now?"

"Let's talk a little while longer."

I sighed. "I'm back in therapy already, did I say that?"

Mr. Angelus nodded. "That's great. It will help you figure out what you're feeling and what you want. Therapy, in my opinion, is a good process when the therapist is good. But your therapist alone cannot help you shut the doors to other worlds."

"But you'll do it? If I want you to? You'll help me try to stay here?"

"Yes," Mr. Angelus' voice reassured me. "If and when you decide you want to go through with this, we'll meet again and I'll do my best. Alas, there are no guarantees."

I sniffled, "When can we do it?"

"When you're ready." Mr. Angelus stood, "Meet with your therapist a few more times and then call me. Though, I have to warn you that I'll be on retreat and out of touch for the next few weeks."

It began to sink in. My fantasy of shaman-as-instant-fix would not be fulfilled today. I practically wailed, "But what if in the meantime I go there and don't come back?"

"I think if you do go back there, just existing in that life for a time will help you decide," Mr. Angelus said. "Try your best not to worry. And call me when you've made up your mind."

CHAPTER THIRTY-FIVE

Crying the whole way home sounds a lot more romantic than it was. Driving with tears blurring my vision should have scared me into pulling over, but I wanted to be home where I could think, without my attention split by traffic and lane changes and thoughtless drivers.

Should I really try to shut the door to the other world, to Simon, to Ben, to this bizarre magical do-over, or could I keep going with the flow, back and forth with no obvious rhyme or reason? Knowing they were there, in that other reality, would I be able to stay here and lead my solitary life? Would it make missing them better or worse? It was all too complicated. A simple "pros and cons" list couldn't contain the nuances of this decision.

Having the power to choose also felt terrifying.

When I finally got home and pulled the car into the underground lot for my building I practically had to pry my tense fingers off the steering wheel. I got myself up to my apartment in a bit of a daze, happy to see Gretel. If anyone was my anchor, I realized, it was Gretel. Sure, she existed in the other universe too, but in this universe, I was her one and only.

We took a stroll around the block. Gretel, in her intuitive way, walked as close as she could to me, never taking her sad hound's eyes off me when she stopped to pee and bumping her head against me softly as we turned corners, as if to say, "I'm with you." She was a good girl.

And she would die too, like everyone else.

I did not want to go there. I reminded myself that I should concentrate on my breathing and be in the moment.

Was all this simply about my inability to accept death? Was I in some way flawed—or were all human beings as furious and sad and despairing about the inevitability of life's endings as I was? How did people cope with their so-much-more-tragic-than-mine lives? People killed each other for reasons I'd never understood; children died of diseases both curable and not; natural disasters occurred all the time. I could see that life and death would be a lot less miserable if you believed in a heaven wherein we'd all be reunited, but I'd always had a lot of trouble taking that literally. I was much more of a "my atoms will rejoin the universe however they manage" type of person. I was fine with that—even good. But this wasn't about *me* dying, it was about others. How do you love people and live on without them in your world?

Gretel and I came in the door to a ringing landline. I heard Lily's voice on the machine, and ran for it. "Hey," I said, a gasping a bit.

"Hey back," said my sister. "I guess I made you hurry."

"Yep, Gretel and I just got in from a walk."

"How is that sweet monster dog?"

"Better than sweet," I answered. "She's all there for me. I might even be more important to her than her dinner."

Lily laughed. "I'm not sure that's true for any dog."

"You know I'm going to disagree." I looked over at the big girl. She turned her usual three circles, plunked down, put her head on her paws and looked at me.

"I saw the shaman," I said.

"I remembered it was today," said Lily. "How'd it go?"

"Confusing, mostly. He says he can help but he wants me to be sure I don't want to be able to go back to that other world… or else I'll have regrets? Or it won't work? I'm not sure. In any case, he said I should think about it."

"Huh," said Lily.

"Yeah," I said. "It turns out that I'm not a simple case. Not many people can do the whole universe hopping thing."

"Big shock there." Lily matched my sarcastic tone with her own. I could tell she felt more on top of the shaman idea than I ever would. She didn't seem at all put off by the idea that science and logic might not agree.

"So, do you believe this stuff?" I asked. "It seems so… unlikely."

"Does it even matter if it fixes the problem?" Just like my sister to steer me back to the straight and narrow. She added, "The ball's in your court,"—another typically Lily answer, complete with a tennis metaphor.

I promised to keep Lily posted. We'd see each other at Thanksgiving—if I spent it in this world, which I fervently hoped I would.

I used to think of myself as the human embodiment of what you see is what you get. I got off the phone questioning whether I truly was all that straightforward and uncomplicated. Had I let the necessities of daily life distract me from introspection, from my grief, from missing Ben? All the emotions I had bottled up over the years seemed to be suddenly seeping through.

Or, more accurately, *I* was seeping through—to somewhere else. Ridiculous, right?

CHAPTER THIRTY-SIX

The Wednesday before Thanksgiving, I dropped Gretel off at doggy camp, then picked up Bill in the valley. We drove west toward Santa Barbara with the rest of the holiday traffic. We chatted, covering the morning's headlines, and then, as we passed the Ventura County line, Bill said, "I'm not used to you doing the driving."

"Well, feel free to take over!" I said, motioning at the many, many other cars slowing our progress.

"No, I think you've got it," he said, leaning back and tipping his hat over his eyes.

I laughed. "You're awfully trusting."

"Hey, I'm hoping this is one of many family outings to come," he answered.

Drat.

What I wanted to say was, *Please don't get used to it!* But of course, saying that aloud was a very bad idea and would not make for a pleasant holiday. What I said instead was, "I'm a good driver, if I do say so myself." This led to the California vs. New York drivers discussion, after which I ruminated on what should have been obvious: inviting Bill to Thanksgiving had probably been a very bad idea.

When we arrived at Nora's, she had run out to the market. Nora's husband Jack was busy in the kitchen, with Audrey perched on a stool watching her father's turkey preparations and Ruby drawing a picture to honor the holiday. Bill and Jack shook hands and Audrey asked Bill, "So, are you our Grandmom's boyfriend?"

Bill glanced at me as if to ask, *Am I?*

Ruby looked up from her little work table. This boyfriend question piqued her interest.

"Yes, sweetie," I said, and left it at that. Communicating the ins and outs of my relationship with Bill was TMI for nine- and seven-year-olds.

Jack to the rescue. "Audrey, we talked about this. It's not polite to quiz people about their relationships."

Audrey looked at me to verify her dad's words. "Your dad's right," I said. "Sometimes it's better to wait for people to tell you themselves."

Ruby giggled and climbed up on the stool next to her sister. "Audrey talks about boyfriends a lot. I think it's stupid."

Jack said, "Ruby, we don't call each other stupid in this house."

"And yes," said Bill, "I am your grandmother's boyfriend. But that probably means something different to us than it does to you."

"Do you go on dates?" Audrey was persistent.

"Yes," we both answered.

"Are you going to get maaaarrrried?" Audrey asked, in the singsong of countless elementary school girls.

We both laughed, "No."

"Why not?" asked Ruby, visibly puzzled.

"You take this one, Lexie," said Bill, amused, but not wanting to go out on a limb.

"Because neither of us wants to," I answered.

"But why not?" persisted Ruby.

"It's not very important to us," I said. And then, unable to resist a teachable moment, I added, "Being married is very special for some people but it's not for everyone. I think Bill and I are just happy to spend time together. He has his own family, too, you know."

We heard the front door, and Nora's harried voice call, "Hi Mom!" She came in the kitchen, dropped her shopping bags on the counter and gave me a hug. "Never," she said, "go to the market the day before Thanksgiving."

She shook Bill's hand and gave him a warm smile. "So nice to finally meet you," she said. "I've been pestering Mom to introduce me for a long time."

Well, that'll win his heart, I thought.

Bill offered to help Jack, and they conferred about all matters turkey while Nora and I re-organized the overflowing fridge to make room. I was on for the salad, my favorite task. We were expecting Lily, Tom, and Matt in the morning.

Nora had planned a low-maintenance pizza dinner for that evening and everyone seemed to be getting along well. The girls were on their best behavior, and I was glad to see that Bill was happy to roll up his sleeves and lend a hand, fitting in easily without drawing too much attention to himself. What had I been worried about?

After dinner Bill and I retired to our cozy guest room, which doubled as Nora and Jack's office. The bed was full size, a lot smaller than my bed at home. It also shared a wall with the girls' bedroom, and was across the hall from Nora and Jack. I had known this, but not thought it through. Hell, I hadn't thought, period.

"I feel a little foolish," Bill said, kissing me goodnight. "Like we should, um, just go to sleep."

"Yeah," I said, relieved. "I don't know about sex in my daughter's house. I should have warned you about the proximity issues."

"It's no big deal," he said. "It's not a problem for me if it isn't one for you."

"I'm glad you're here," I said, "and, um, I think taking it farther is going to make me too self-conscious."

"Okay then," he said. "I'm happy too, being here and spending time with you and your family."

"Okay then," I said and gave him a grateful kiss.

I woke up once in the middle of the night not knowing where I was. My first instinct was to question which universe I was in. A glance reassured me—Bill was asleep next to me. I was still where I belonged. Bill mumbled in his sleep and I thought about how, a few days ago, I'd slept with Simon in one world, and here I was now sleeping with Bill in the other. Bill wouldn't approve of my new/old relationship with my not-exactly (dead) husband, and other-Simon might full-on freak out. Hopefully, soon Mr. Angelus would anchor me to this, my proper universe, and neither of them would ever have to find out about any of it.

Early the next morning Tom called to report that he and Matt and were heading north. There was a final count of eleven for dinner. We moved tables together and assembled plates, napkins and utensils. Audrey, Ruby and I picked flowers and lettuce from the garden. We all set the table and the girls helped me decorate with flowers and herbs in small vases.

Lily arrived from her fancy hotel with her usual contribution, three beautiful pies ordered from the best bakery in her neighborhood. In spite of Lily's lack of domesticity, Audrey and Ruby adored their great aunt. Her secret weapon? Games. It was a mystery to me that my sister had never developed a gambling addiction. Another mystery: other than tennis and very occasionally golf, Lily never watched any televised sport. But whatever it might reveal about her psyche, Lily's competitive spirit made her very popular with the kids. She always played her hardest, whether it was Uno, Monopoly, or a tennis match with her peers. Kids respect that.

Today's game was badminton. Lily had not only brought pies; she'd also brought six rackets, an entire box of birdies and a net. Jack and Bill took time away from watching football and attending the turkey to put up the net.

Soon Audrey was more or less successfully bouncing a birdie up and down on her racket while Ruby practiced her swings. Lily took one side, the girls took the other. Bill offered to referee. After an hour or so of backyard badminton, the girls were exhausted and Lily victorious (as always).

Jack had just challenged Lily to a game when Tom and Matt arrived. Before I could introduce them to Bill, Audrey and Ruby began pulling Matt outside.

"Wait a sec," I said. "Tom and Matt need to be properly introduced."

"Aww," said Ruby, jumping in place impatiently.

"I thought you guys were tired," said Nora.

"Tom this is—" I began.

Ruby interrupted, "Grandmom's boyfriend Bill." She pointed to each person. "And that's Tom, our uncle, and that's our cousin Matt. He's twelve." She turned to look at the rest of the adults gathered around to greet the newcomers. "Can we go play now?"

"Whew," said Tom. "Down girl. Give Matt a second."

Ruby could not be contained. "But it's BADMINTON!" she whined. "Aunt Lily brought us a whole game!"

Lily was laughing and I was trying not to. Bill put his hands up and said, "Far be it from me—" and Nora, shaking her head, said, "Ruby—" but gave up as soon as the word came out.

Ruby led Matt out the French doors to the newly created badminton court, Audrey in their wake. Lily followed the kids out to supervise. I knew she also wanted to play more herself. Adding Matt

196

to the opposition would give her a bigger challenge. Lily loved a challenge. She'd probably been on the treadmill at her hotel gym for an hour before she came over.

Jack's parents arrived—they lived up the coast in Monterey—and more introductions were made. By early evening, the food was ready and we all sat down to dinner.

It started out beautifully. My salad was a hit, the turkey was tender, the gravy and stuffing delicious. Even the green bean casserole was almost finished in the first round. There was less enthusiasm for the sweet potatoes, and Nora threatened—as she did every year—to stop making them if no one ever ate them. Looking around the table at my family comfortably chatting and eating, I felt genuinely happy, sated in the best sense of the word.

Before dessert, we took a break to clear the table, watched a bit of football, and loaded the dishwasher. We put out the pies and plates for dessert. When everyone gathered back at the table, it was time for our family's yearly tradition—expressing thanks.

Nora led off, saying how glad she was to have her family around her.

Audrey, sitting next to her, said, "I'm happy to have a whole four days off school."

Ruby squirmed next to me, and pouted.

"What's wrong, sweetie?" I asked.

"Audrey stole my thanks!" she said.

"That's okay," I said. "It's okay if more than one person is grateful for the same thing."

Jack's parents, veterans of this ritual for years now, said they were thankful for time with their son and granddaughters. Bill said how happy he was to meet my family and spend Thanksgiving with us.

Sitting next to Bill, Lily smiled and said, "I want to thank my sister for having fabulous kids and grandkids. I'm grateful when I get to spend time with them, and I'm grateful when I go home to my own quiet house!" Everyone laughed.

Jack thanked Nora for "absolutely everything," and Tom said, simply, "I'm glad for every moment I spend with Matt—and the rest of you are fine too."

It was Matt's turn right before mine. He said, "I'm grateful that my Grandmom is here in this universe for Thanksgiving and not in that other place."

CHAPTER THIRTY-SEVEN

"Huh?" asked Jack.

I heard Tom whisper to his son, "Matt, I don't know that everyone is up on your grandmother's situation."

Matt blushed. "Um…"

I saw the rest of the family exchange furtive glances. Bill, Jack, and Jack's parents seemed to think it was a joke, but soon their confused smiles turned into confused frowns. I knew it was going to have to be me who cleared this up.

"Don't worry, Matt," I said. "It's just that some people don't know."

Matt looked like he wanted to melt into his chair. "I'm sorry Grandmom," he said.

I shook my head. "Nothing to be sorry for."

I could have kicked myself. How *would* Matt have known I was strategically keeping this information from Bill? Whatever Jack or his parents thought of me didn't feel like a big deal, but Bill? I knew he was going to feel betrayed no matter what I said.

In as light and breezy a tone as I could manage I said, "I've been having a supernatural adventure! Nora and Tom have been following my 'travels,'" (I used finger quotes to play down the word) "and Lily found me a shaman."

My attempts to explain myself were destined to fail, I could sense it. Jack (to whom, it seemed, Nora had not said a word) didn't even bother to hide his expression of astonishment, Jack's parents gazed down at their plates, and I could see Audrey and Ruby were as puzzled by everyone's reactions as anything else. Matt squirmed miserably.

I got up and kissed Matt on the top of his head. "It's okay, sweetie."

Standing with one hand on Matt's shoulder and the other on Tom's for strength and comfort, I tried to continue. "I've had scans and sleep studies and I'm seeing a therapist, in case there's some psychological reason this is happening. After all of it, the only answer that makes any sense is that I've been, um…" I took a big breath, "experiencing an alternate universe."

Bill pushed back his chair and stood up. "Can I talk to you for a sec?"

My stomach sank, but I said, "Sure." I kissed the top of Matt's head again, and whispered, "Not your fault."

I followed Bill out the French doors to the corner of the garden that couldn't be seen from the living room. It was getting dark, but the street lights hadn't turned on yet. I trusted Tom and Nora to talk the rest of the family down, but Bill was my responsibility. I knew he'd think that keeping a secret like this was wrong—probably unforgivable.

"Just tell me," he said. "Is this some kind of joke?" His tone was icy.

I shook my head no. "I didn't know how to explain."

"Explain?" Bill began pacing in a small circle. "I asked about your health so many times—straight out. You said you were fine. Now you've totally blindsided me in front of your family!"

I tried to respond but he cut me off.

"I don't know if you're flat out crazy and your family is enabling you, or if this is some elaborate prank." He stared at me with open hostility. "*Now* I know why you never wanted me to meet your family!"

"That wasn't it!" I protested, knowing I was trying to soften the tiny piece of truth he had hit upon.

Bill glared, turned on his heel and walked away, toward the garden wall. "I'm furious. Furious!" (As if I couldn't tell.)

"You won't let me at least try to explain?" I tried to inject a note of martyrdom in my voice, but Bill was having none of it.

"You could have told me! Damn it Lexie, you *should* have told me." He had begun pacing again. "I asked you specifically about going to doctors."

"I know, I know," I said, now outright crying.

"I can't believe this, Lexie. A shaman? What on earth is the matter with you?" He pulled out his phone. "I'm going to see if I can get a ride home."

"No, don't do that, stay." I heard myself begging and cringed. "Never mind then, be mad at me. But you have to listen."

"I have to do no such thing," he said, "and don't you think it's a bit too late for you to read me in on this insanity?" He took off toward the house.

I followed more slowly. I could hear Bill apologize as he walked through the living room. I heard Jack make a joke about family quarrels and the holidays. Then I walked through the living room myself, past the beautiful Thanksgiving table where everyone was still uncannily quiet. I tried to angle my face away so no one would see my tears.

CHAPTER THIRTY-EIGHT

In the guest room, Bill was pulling his small suitcase from under the bed. He grabbed a few items from the nightstand, and walked by me into the bathroom where I heard the clack of his toiletries as he swept them into his bag.

"Don't," he said, putting up a hand to silence me when he came back into the room. "Don't bother. I'm sorry to embarrass you in front of your family," he gestured in the direction of the living room, "but this is too much. You didn't trust me enough to include me, and what I heard just now—It's fucking insanity!"

I sat down on the bed. I wanted to ask how he would get home, but when he looked at his phone I realized he'd called a car. I blinked hard to re-focus and push back the tears. "Bill," I said, "I want you to know—"

"You want me to know nothing," he said. He left the room holding his suitcase and jacket.

I heard the front door open and close, and within a few moments Nora appeared at the guest room door. "Tom's gone out to try to talk to him," she said. "Are you alright?"

"No." I shook my head. I began to cry again, feeling helpless and angry with myself. And sorry for poor Matt, too.

Nora sat down next to me and I held on to her, crying on her shoulder until I heard someone at the door. Nora motioned to whoever it was. I sat up and saw Tom come in. Matt crept up behind him.

"I'm sorry Mom," Tom said.

"Me too, Grandmom," said Matt.

"Aw honey," I said. "It's no one's fault but mine." I wiped my nose. "Bill left?" This question was to Tom.

"He didn't want to talk to me. Lily went out there too but he wouldn't talk to her, either. A car came and picked him up." Tom sat down on the other side of me on the bed.

"I hope Lily's serving the pies, at least."

"No, we're waiting for you."

I nodded. "I'm going to splash my face with cold water," I said. "And Matt, get yourself a huge slice of each kind of pie. You are my best grandson, and you didn't do anything wrong."

"I don't like pecan," said Matt. "And, you do know that I'm your only grandson, right?"

"Don't be a smartass," I said. I ruffled his hair and headed for the bathroom sink and delicious cold water.

I returned to the table and accepted a hug from my normally undemonstrative sister. She had already prepared a plate of my favorite pie for me—pumpkin with a dollop of whipped cream. Jack's parents were busy trying to cover their secondhand embarrassment with oohs and aahs about the pies, and I caught Jack making one of those eyes-wide faces at Nora that signals, "What just happened here?"

"Are you okay, Grandmom?" asked Ruby. "Where did Bill go?"

No time like the present; I may have gotten that message a bit too late for my relationship with Bill, but now I should answer questions as simply and honestly as I could. "I think he's gone back to his own home, honey. He's angry at me."

"Oh," said Ruby.

"Are you breaking up?" asked Audrey.

Jack and Nora both started to admonish her, but I waved them off. "No worries." I tried to look unconcerned. "I think so." I felt my

203

smile falter, but I went on. "It's no big deal, sweetie. I have all of you, and there's no one—along with your Uncle Anton and his family—who I'd rather be with."

"Even more than Bill?" asked Ruby.

"Yep," I said. "Even more than Bill. Plus, we get to eat pie and he doesn't." I fastened a grin to my face, and the girls and Matt giggled, happy to feel relief from some of the tension at the table. I put a forkful of pie in my mouth. "Yum," I said, but I could barely taste it.

Tom and Matt left for the long drive back to Orange County. Jack's parents went back to their hotel. After giving me another big hug and reminding me to call her, Lily went back to her hotel, too. She was meeting some friends the next day in Ojai.

Clean-up was subdued. I took on scouring the roasting pan with a sense of mission—it was cathartic to attack the dried juices with steel wool. At one point Nora glanced over from loading the final items into the dishwasher and told me to stop. In my attempt to work off my sadness and frustration I had scrubbed the pan shiny again.

Nora and Jack headed off for bed, where I was sure Jack would press Nora for details about my revelation. He hadn't questioned me after Bill left, but I guessed he was waiting for a private moment with Nora.

Though I was exhausted, I was too frazzled to go to my (now lonely) guest room. There was no way I'd fall asleep for a long while yet.

Nora's family computer sat on the kitchen counter and I thought I'd email Bill an apology. But what would I tell him? *Sorry, but I didn't trust you enough?* That was the issue, wasn't it? Along with, *You're not my (dead) husband.* Any of the several ways I might try to justify myself would be reduced to some version of explaining those not particularly flattering statements.

I *didn't* trust Bill to understand. The fact that my kids accepted my story still amazed me.

I should leave it alone. Let him feel righteous and angry. Was he ever going to be the guy who took my hand in *The Wood Between the Worlds* and said, "Let's go!"? No, he would not. I should let him go. Let him find someone more normal.

With the laptop open in front of me, I realized that I should also send other-Lexie a quick heads-up so if we did change places, she'd know about my disastrous Thanksgiving. I opened my email and began:

Dear other-Lexie,

You should know that after half of a wonderful Thanksgiving dinner—Bill's first time meeting my (our?) family—he found out about my world switching. Of course, it confused and angered him—especially because every time he's asked me if there was something going on, I flat-out lied. I'm sure the relationship is over. And you know what? I'm okay with that.

Matt thinks it's his fault because he's the one who revealed my/our secret—by mistake of course. I tried to convince him that it was my responsibility, but if you talk to him, please assure him again that it wasn't his fault. FYI, Tom and Nora and Lily were incredibly supportive. Jack's parents think I'm nuts. Not much I can do about that.

I'm going to try my best to make this nonsense stop—I'll say goodbye to Simon and Ben, and maybe even explain myself to Simon. I'm starting to feel like your dream-come-true world was only supposed to be my dream, not my reality.

Yours,

Lexie.

I thought again about Bill. Part of me wanted to give him the full explanation I hadn't been able to earlier. To confess that I had never been serious about our relationship, and that I absolutely should have said it directly. To tell him that I had impossible standards because I still loved a dead guy. I even wanted to tell him about that alternate universe, in case he might understand, but I knew he wouldn't, especially not now.

What would be the point?

Yet, sending him a short, simple apology would be the right thing to do. I *was* sorry—why not plainly say that? And it would get it all over with, so I could put the relationship behind me.

I typed:

Bill,

I am truly sorry that I wasn't honest with you. I realize there is no point to explaining. Thanks for some good times.

Lexie.

I logged out of my email and surfed around for about twenty minutes, trying to find a decent distraction for my unhappy brain. Eventually, the pixels blurred together. Maybe, I thought, now I could sleep.

I moved as quietly as I could back into the guest room, not wanting to wake Nora, Jack, or the kids. I wondered what would happen if I woke up in the other world and other-Lexie woke up here. At least my email had warned her. That was something.

I couldn't sleep. The bed had felt perfectly pleasant with Bill and me in it, but as weary as I was, I couldn't get comfortable. I usually slept on my right side, but my shoulder hurt—probably from all that pot scrubbing. Each time I felt my eyes close, I startled awake. Was I reluctant to stay in this world and face the end of my relationship with Bill? No, that wasn't it. My insomnia was entirely about my lack of control.

When I finally dozed off, I drifted into a frightening dream. I was outside somewhere, possibly a park. Gretel was ahead and running, pursuing someone or something I couldn't see. She growled and snarled and I couldn't catch up. I shouted at her, but she wouldn't stop. She ran through a stand of oak trees, and then onto what might have been a sports field. I followed, iridescent purple-green AstroTurf crunching under my feet. Finally, she skidded to a halt at a high chain link fence, growling and jumping at it ferociously. With each strike of her big paws, the fence clanged and clattered. When I caught up with her, I saw Simon in a lawn chair only a few yards away. He sat on the other side of the barrier, reading something on his phone, unperturbed by all the noise from Gretel and the fence. I called but he didn't hear me. I tried to climb over, one foot and hand at a time, but when I was almost at the top, Gretel's assault pushed the fence over, flinging me forward on hands and knees. I tried to stand but my shoes were stuck in the fence links. By the time I extracted myself there was no one there at all. Even Gretel had disappeared. I called for Simon, for Gretel, and woke up.

I could feel something had changed. My room felt deserted, dusty, and cold. I got out of bed, put on my slippers and robe, and padded out to the hall. The doors to Nora's and the kids' rooms were open. I peaked in each door. Every bed was neatly made. There were no toys or crumpled clothes on the floor of Audrey and Ruby's room, and no art supplies out on the desk they shared. I wandered down toward the kitchen where there should have been the lingering smells of Thanksgiving dinner. Nothing. The house was empty. No food had been cooked here, no dinner enjoyed.

What world had I landed in now?

It was still dark, but I opened the front door and walked out to the street. The quiet felt eerie, and I could see very few lights from the neighboring houses. I shivered and went back inside. I turned on the living room television. The news channels confirmed my suspicion. They were full of the fallout—literal and figurative—of terrorist attacks.

Nora and Jack must have taken the girls somewhere safe, I thought. Even though this version of my universe gave me little hope, I did hope—fervently—that my children and grandchildren had found shelter from the miseries on the news. In my best fantasy of this horrible version of my life, my children and their children were all together, riding out the storm.

I sat in front of the television news for about an hour wondering what I could do to get myself back where I belonged again. I was tired. My sadness and fear made sleep seem unlikely, but I had to try. Sorrow and worry followed me back down the hall to the guest room, where I put myself back into the cold bed and stared at the ceiling trying to relax, to let sleep take me.

I don't remember falling asleep. At most, I dozed. Early in the morning, though, as a faint light began to show behind the curtains, I heard Audrey and Ruby in the next room. They were arguing about whether it was too early to wake up their parents.

Thank goodness. I was back where I belonged. Bill's rage, how he left the night before—those memories didn't penetrate the comfort I felt to be back with Nora's family, in my very own universe.

The girls' voices lulled me and I finally slept soundly. By the time I woke again, a few hours later, I felt at least rested enough to drive myself home. I threw on some clothes and headed out to see who else might be around.

Nora sat at their kitchen counter on her laptop, checking her email. Audrey and Ruby were in the back yard attempting to bat the birdie between their rackets.

Nora said, "Hot water's on. Jack's gone for a run."

"Thanks, hon," I said. I got a tea bag from the cabinet and poured myself a cup.

Nora closed the laptop. "Are you okay, Mom?" she asked.

I shook my head. "Not really." She was asking about Bill, of course. After the night I had, Bill felt like a fairly minor problem. There was no point in telling Nora about my lousy nightmare and worse visit to that other world. I shrugged. "But I will be fine."

"He did seem nice," Nora said.

"He was." I had to agree. "Mostly. But if you don't mind too much, I don't feel like talking about it—at least not quite yet. I stayed up thinking last night and there's not much more for me to say. I did screw up. But maybe there was a reason I never told him—or maybe I'm only trying to justify my behavior to myself." I sighed. "In the end, it doesn't matter."

"Okay," said Nora. She took a sip from her coffee mug. "If it really doesn't matter to you, then…" She let the words trail off. Then she gave a short laugh. "But I do have to warn you. Jack is fascinated by your experience. He wants to know everything."

"Oh dear," I said. "I wish I knew more myself."

CHAPTER THIRTY-NINE

I hit the road in early afternoon to pick up Gretel before the kennel closed. When I got home—pleased to be back in my own space—I puttered, checked my blog, sorted through the mail and curled up on the couch with my book.

And was immediately hit by loneliness. My dear Gretel was lovely, but without words she couldn't get me out of my own head.

Sometimes I wished I'd been born long ago, when people lived in villages and spent their whole lives together. I reminded myself that their "whole lives" were shorter, often brutal, messy and hard, but if you're going to fantasize about the past, why not cherry-pick? There had to be a few good things about every era, and having your kids live next door, or even in the same house, might be a thing to envy.

My kids called to check on me. Tom gave me a list of distracting comedies to watch and even offered to come up and watch them with me. I almost took him up on it but I knew he had a big project going at work. Nora was dealing with her own issues with the end of the quarter approaching. Anton called on Saturday, most likely at the behest of his brother, sister, or both.

"Hi Mom," he said.

"Oh, sweetie," I said. "Hi. It's great to hear your voice. How's the baby? How's Irina?"

"We're good," he answered. "We went to Irina's brother's for Thanksgiving."

"Right," I said. I knew that. "How was it?"

"Chaotic. Every square foot of their house was decorated and their kids are older, so it worked for them, but the baby wanted to touch it all. Irina was seriously frustrated."

We chatted about the baby, and he asked about the Bill situation—either Tom or Nora had told him their version of our breakup fight. I said I was going to be fine, absolutely fine. He didn't pursue it, and I have to say I was grateful.

Anton told me he and Irina were thinking of coming for the holidays. That bolstered my mood for about five minutes—until I got to questioning whether I'd be in this universe. All the more reason to set something up with Mr. Angelus as soon as possible. When was he back in town?

In the meantime, I had Dr. Stewart.

As soon as I sat down she asked, "What's the matter? You look..."

I supplied, "Terrible?"

"No, not terrible, more like upset," she said. "Tough week?"

I nodded.

"Do you want to tell me about it?"

Was I ready to rehash what had happened with Bill? Already? Ever? And how would I manage it without mentioning the alternate universe situation? I tried to place all my mental ducks in a neat little row. Yes, I could get Bill's anger across without getting into abstract physics. The important information for Dr. Stewart was that Bill and I had broken up.

"So, remember that I invited Bill to Thanksgiving?" I said.

"Yes."

"And everything was great until... until it wasn't," I said. "We broke up."

"Wow," said Dr. Stewart, "what happened?"

211

"It felt kind of sudden," I said. "Though… I guess not. It had been coming for a while."

"Where do you want to start?" she asked. "With the inviting? Or the break-up?"

"The inviting was easy," I said. "And I thought you'd be proud of me for going ahead with it."

Dr. Stewart looked dubious. "Did you think I encouraged you to invite Bill? Because I wasn't aware that I had."

"Oh," I said, "It was probably a combination of circumstances—the idea that I needed to define my relationship with Bill more clearly, which we definitely discussed here—but also I got the sense that you felt it was good for me to commit to having a relationship."

"I didn't think I had expressed that," said Dr. Stewart. "I want to be clear—having a relationship with Bill or with anyone for that matter, is up to you, not me, and whatever went in to your decision to invite him to Thanksgiving should not have been about pleasing me."

"It wasn't."

"Good," said Dr. Stewart. "I just wanted to make sure."

"You did make me think about why I had never included him before, which was actually quite useful. And," I continued, "for what it's worth, Bill was terrific with my family, and the grandkids. But then, when we were finishing our Thanksgiving dinner, my grandson said something about how he was happy I was doing better," (that seemed like a suitably innocuous way of describing it) "and one thing led to another and Bill found out about my weird dreams and my doctor's visits, and he was pissed that I hadn't told him."

Dr. Stewart nodded. "The way you've explained it, he's been more invested in the relationship than you have from the beginning. And it sounds like…" She hesitated over choosing her words, "he didn't like it when there was evidence to that effect."

"I still feel guilty," I said. That was true enough.

"But you aren't devastated?" she asked.

I gave a rueful chuckle. "No, I'm not."

I thought about my session with Dr. Stewart as I drove home. What bothered me most was that I had handled the relationship so badly. I had ignored the most crucial tenets of Relationships 101—communication and honesty. I was not proud of myself.

But I wasn't upset about Bill. From the beginning, I hadn't been straight with him. I knew he wanted more, and I never addressed it. As our relationship continued, I'd used my "secret" to keep him at arm's length. The revelation at Thanksgiving had simply exposed my lack of trust to him.

It should follow, then, that I was happy with Simon in that other world, right? No, that wasn't quite working out either.

I felt like the weight of the world—worlds!—was on my shoulders and I was doing a bad job in both.

CHAPTER FORTY

On impulse, I called Lily when I got home.

"Hey," she said as she picked up. "I meant to call you this weekend but I was dealing with a crisis."

"What crisis?" I wondered how any crisis of hers could compare with the scene Bill and I made at Thanksgiving—and yeah, my whole alternate universe problem.

"Tennis crisis," she said. "Trying to keep the peace while they resurface two of the courts. It's the perfect time for them to do it, because of holiday travels and the weather…"

Lily kept talking on about the politics at her club, and I tried to make interested noises during the pauses. But I felt let down. She'd been there when Bill left. She knew how mortified I'd been. What did she care if a few biddies couldn't get tennis courts when they wanted them? I was not feeling remotely like my best self.

Lily finished her story and (finally) asked, "How are you doing? Did you try to talk to Bill?"

"No," I said, relieved that her recitation was over. "It seemed pointless. He'd already made up his mind. So, Thursday night, after everyone went to sleep, I sent him an email that said sorry and thanks for the good times. Of course he hasn't responded."

"No," said Lily, "he wouldn't, would he? I think you injured his male pride or his ego, or whatever you want to call it when a man thinks you feel the same way about him that he feels about you—and he's wrong."

214

"Yeah. But it was extremely embarrassing."

"Lex, the fact that you're talking about being embarrassed instead of missing him kinda says it all, right?"

Also what Dr. Stewart had said, I noted, picturing Lily's precise expression—eyebrows raised, chin lowered. "Yeah, you're right," I admitted.

"Then what's the matter?" she asked, "Besides the embarrassment, I mean. Jack's parents will dine out on it for a few weeks, but everyone else loves you and understands."

"I know," I said. I did know. "I'm just mad at myself, that's all."

"That's appropriate," said my helpful sister.

I laughed. "Thanks a lot!"

She laughed too. "What do you want me to say? You handled it perfectly? Bottom line, babe, it's not the end of the world. I think there's a very good reason you didn't trust him with what was going on."

"What reason?" I asked.

"How should I know? I only met him the once," said Lily. "Look, it doesn't matter. Lesson learned. Companionship is all very well as long as both parties know what they're in it for, and you two were in it for different things. But you know that. You knew it when it was happening."

"I have a very smart little sister," I said, grinning.

"Yes, you do."

Lily always did surprise me. Pleasantly. How could I ever choose a world without her in it? I couldn't, at least not intentionally. Choosing between worlds where either Ben or Lily was alive was worse than a daunting prospect. It didn't feel possible.

When I woke up the next morning I could already sense I was elsewhere. Something about the quality of the light alerted me. I felt unaccountably weary, as if I'd walked miles the day before.

Simon was not in our bed. His spot looked slept in, but to make sure, I looked on my table to see what I—I mean other-Lexie—was reading. It was a book about World War II with a long and complicated subtitle about the Allies' covert operations. I had never been interested in spy stories—even fictional ones—which meant it was going to take all my stamina to pretend to read it.

I sighed. No point staying in bed. I should do a little investigating so I wouldn't be caught off guard when I saw Simon. I threw back the covers and went to my office to check the calendar and my email.

My calendar looked nearly the same as it had at home. In this world, as in mine, invitations for holiday parties had started to trickle in and, good citizen that I appeared to be in both worlds, I had dutifully sent RSVPs. There was little on my agenda to worry or confuse me—all good. Even better, other-Lexie had sent me an email. I smiled, thinking that maybe we were finally getting the hang of this communication-between-parallel-lives thing.

Lexie,

Just got back from Thanksgiving at Nora's where Tom and Simon got into an ugly fight. Denise decided at the last minute to take Matt to her family's in San Diego for an "unmissable" behind-the-scenes tour they'd arranged at the Wild Animal Park. Simon was furious that Tom let her change the plan. He couldn't stop arguing about it and finally, after dinner, Tom just left. It was very uncomfortable for everyone.

My two cents? I thought Tom was being reasonable. Matt loves animals and was completely on board with skipping our Thanksgiving.

I think Simon should trust Tom to pick his own battles.

We fought about it the whole way home. I hope you're reading this before you see Simon because he's still angry. Frankly, I am too.

Lexie.

What had made this particular Thanksgiving a flash point in both worlds? I had no idea. At least now I was prepared. And I was doubly glad that I'd sent an email to other-Lexie about my own Thanksgiving crisis.

I headed for the kitchen where I assumed I'd find Simon sitting at the table reading the paper, Gretel at his feet. But neither Simon nor Gretel was there. I looked back in the front hall and saw that the leash was gone—they were out for a walk.

That made it a good time to call Ben. He answered on the first ring. "Hey Lexie."

"It's other-Lexie," I responded.

"Oh," he said.

"We switched sometime last night."

"So you missed our fun Thanksgiving?" Ben asked.

"Your Lexie wrote me an email about it. For what it's worth, I had a fun Thanksgiving too. I broke up with my boyfriend—or whatever he was."

"Wow," said Ben.

"I know," I said. "Curiouser and curiouser. But I wanted to call and see if you were a witness."

"I was there," Ben said, "but I stayed out of it. I took the kids outside to play with the croquet set I brought them."

I thought of Lily's gift to Nora's kids, the badminton set. Another near-parallel moment. It wasn't something I could ponder in the moment. Simon had just arrived home, Gretel leading the way.

CHAPTER FORTY-ONE

I looked over the newspaper, while Simon bustled around the kitchen making a smoothie. He asked if I wanted anything, and I realized he was trying to be solicitous.

"I'm sorry about last night," he said, as he sat down across from me. "I shouldn't have lost my temper."

"There's been a lot of that, lately," I said, and silently thanked other-Lexie for preparing me.

"Yes," he said, "I know."

"Some situations are out of our control." I thought it might be a safe statement.

Simon stood up and walked to the sink. "I can't tell you how much it infuriates me, Tom letting her do that."

"You've given me—and everyone else—a good idea of how much it infuriates you," I said, "but that's a separate problem from the anger itself."

"But how can he let her—?"

I cut him off. "We're not going over it again," I said, just as if I had been there for all the arguments. "You need to have a strategy that isn't yelling. Try just breathing instead. Letting it get to you isn't good for your health, mental or otherwise. You need to think about how bad all this anger is for you."

Simon exhaled audibly. "Thanks for looking after me."

I felt myself tearing up. I had tried to look after my Simon with diligence and love, but it hadn't saved him from cancer. Simon saw my face change. "Oh honey," he said. "Don't be upset."

"If you get to be angry, then I have a right to get upset," I said, and tried to laugh to show him I wasn't criticizing.

What I wanted to do was tell him he needed counseling. What I wanted to say was, "You could be a different, happier person."

What I wanted even more was for him to be my Simon.

About an hour later the landline rang.

"Hello?" I said, answering in my office.

"Hello?" Simon had picked up the extension.

"It's Tom," said our son.

Simon's reaction was immediate. "Talk to your mom—I'm not ready." The phone clicked as he hung up.

I heard Tom sigh.

"It's okay, sweetie," I said, hoping that in this universe, as in mine, that's what mothers say to their children.

"Why is he so mad at me?" Tom asked.

"Oh, honey," I said. "I think he's mad at himself and taking it out on you." That seemed safe, plus it was in line with what other-Lexie had said in her email.

"I know, but it doesn't help," said Tom.

"I know," I said. "And you're right, it doesn't."

"When did Dad start being angry at everything?"

Well, that was the question I couldn't answer. Had this Simon been as angry when the kids were growing up? I only had conjecture. I tried to come up with words that would be true no matter what the circumstances.

"I think having more time on his hands has made him more anxious," I said.

"Can't you find him something to do?"

I laughed. "I'd be happy to take suggestions. But try not to hold it against him."

"That's what you said when I left Nora's."

At least I was consistent. "It's good advice, if I do say so myself."

"So, I'm getting Matt this weekend," said Tom. "The whole weekend. I have no idea why, but I'll take it. I thought I'd bring him up for a visit, if that works for you."

"Hmm," I said, looking at the calendar. "I should consult with your father. I'll call you right back."

I found Simon in his office noodling on his computer. He was defensive about hanging up on Tom. I did my best to be patient and understanding. I told him we were getting together with Tom and Matt on either Saturday or Sunday—pick one. We agreed on dinner Saturday night at a local Mexican restaurant. I called Tom back to confirm while I was standing in Simon's office.

"It's going to be really tough for me, you know," Simon mused after I hung up. He shook his head. "I would never talk about Denise in front of Matt, but there's going to be tension." He said "tension" in the same tone a TV reporter would use for a horrific calamity.

I was rapidly approaching fed up. *How did other-Lexie live with this man?*

I needed to speak my mind, but not get caught in a cycle of recriminations. "Tension, huh," I said to Simon, while trying my hardest to sound neither sarcastic nor flippant, "We're going to have to live through that." I gave him my best serious look. "I'm not going to mess up my relationships with Tom and Matt to spare you a bit of discomfort." My no-nonsense tone, I hoped, helped me sound sincere, not critical.

Simon stared at me as if I had grown an extra head. Of course, I sort of had. I wasn't his standard Lexie—I was a feistier version.

"We will get through it," I went on, as breezily as I could. "Tom knows what you think, you know what he thinks—and you disagree. It's not the end of the world." Once I got going it was hard to stop. "I'm so very tired of this argument. For once can we try to make the best of the situation?"

Simon blinked. "Oh." He seemed floored by my suggestion. "Okay, I guess. When you put it that way…"

"I should have put it that way on Thanksgiving," I said. I leaned down and kissed him on the cheek. "I'll be back in my office if you need me."

This was uncharted territory for me. My Simon and I had mostly agreed on matters of child rearing. This Simon was not that man. He picked fights with our son, he questioned my mental faculties, and his generosity of spirit felt, well, ungenerous to me. He was different—not just as a husband, but also as a parent. Of all my family, he seemed the most off-kilter.

My alternate life offered me an entire family I could not quite claim as my own. Even Ben, dear Ben—Ben whose absence in my own world had made a hole in my heart and in my sense of myself—this Ben wasn't my Ben. He was great, he was excellent, even. Other-Lexie should be proud and happy to claim him as her twin. But he wasn't *mine.*

Nurture? Circumstance? Something had changed. In my world, it had to have been before my Ben fell into the drug dependence that eventually took his life. Here, in this world, it must have happened before other-Lily was murdered, when we were in our teens or early twenties. Maybe Lily getting killed scared this Ben straight, or maybe my Ben had a friend with easy access to drugs. Maybe something in this world triggered the man who went on to murder Lily. And then—whenever or whatever it was—my own family's circumstances in this world changed forever.

I reminded myself that when or why this universe veered off from my own was immaterial, all this rumination pointless. It didn't matter. It was all speculation, guesses fueled by fiction and a smattering of pop psychology.

I ought to be dealing with the realities as presented to me, not thinking about why.

I had to face how deeply ambivalent I'd become about being in this universe, in spite of the extraordinary gift of time with Ben and Simon. It wasn't only about how hard it was to keep up with all the changes and act like I belonged. Policing my own behavior was only a part of it. In truth, I couldn't be myself here.

The wishful thought that Mr. Angelus also existed in this world ran through my brain, as did the even more wishful hope that, if he did exist here, he was a shaman like his counterpart in my world. It was time to go back to my proper universe and stay there.

CHAPTER FORTY-TWO

Even though my online search for Mr. Angelus had come up empty once before, I tried it again. After typing his name in every combination of spellings I could think of—nothing. The shaman who might help me return to my own world did not exist in this one.

Were there even shamans in this universe? Yes, there were. When I was here last and told Simon I was researching the history of healing plants, I had found a number of shaman websites. Finding a shaman online didn't quite measure up to getting a recommendation from Lily, but it seemed worth a try. I made a list of potential shamans to call, and since Simon was at the gym, I launched right in.

The first shaman on my list sounded dumbfounded the moment I asked about multiverses. After a pause that was a bit too long, she declared them "not possible," and lectured me sternly about "taking care of my own garden." I had to suppress a snort. I finally managed to interrupt and tell her she wasn't the shaman for me. If I hadn't hung up quickly, I'm sure she would have kept right on scolding.

Shaman Two was very suspicious. He demanded to know if I was a reporter, and acted as though my goal was to take down the entire "shaman industry" with a hit piece that exposed... what? What was there to expose? He was definitely not my guy.

My conversation with Shaman Three started out well, and I felt a sliver of hope. She listened to my abbreviated story, then went all therapist on me and I got off the call.

None of these shamans seemed nearly as open or informed as Mr. Angelus. Would Mr. Angelus have been as kind and available without the referral? No idea. Were shamans different in this world? No way of knowing. As I crossed out Shamans Four and Five—just as clueless as the first three—I began to lose heart. Luckily, I had made a fairly long list—twelve shamans in all.

I heard Simon come in the front door. I closed all the folders on my desktop, and began to play a solitaire game that other-Lexie seemed to like a lot (she was on Game Number 10,843). I hoped I wasn't screwing up her average scores.

Simon and I made dinner together and, as the evening went on, he was on better behavior. I'd even say we had a good time, though all we did was watch television. Had he listened to my lecture about his anger? I reminded myself there was no point getting my hopes up.

Of the shamans I reached the next morning (Simon having gone out for coffee with a friend) the first (Shaman Six) said I shouldn't believe my doctors because I was undoubtedly hallucinating. He recommended his own holistic physician and I pretended to write down the details before I crossed him off the list.

Shaman Seven said I should seek therapy. I tried to say that I was already in therapy (though not that my therapist existed in an alternate universe). She launched into a description of a known psychiatric disorder called Capgras syndrome where people believe their loved ones have been replaced by imposters. About three sentences into attempting to tell her that *I* was the imposter, I realized that I was tilting at an impenetrable windmill. It was all I could do to get off the phone without screaming.

I had tried to sound humble and reasonable during my previous calls, but if all these supposed shamans were more interested in jumping to conclusions than being open to the universe(s) (not to mention getting my business) what did that imply? It might be me. I must be going about it wrong. Maybe if I led with the "imposter" concept, it might make shamans less inclined to either lecture me, diagnose me, or dismiss me out of hand.

"This is Constance Abierto," said Shaman Eight as she answered the phone.

"Hi," I said, trying to put a little quaver in my voice. "I have a weird problem."

Ms. Abierto laughed. "Most people who call me do."

It made me feel better right away. I went on, "I've been to a doctor and had a whole check-up, I went to therapy when my doctor suggested it, and at this point, I don't know what to do."

"Okay," she said.

"This is going to sound absurd, but I think I'm an imposter." I continued quickly, "Not like what they call 'imposter syndrome;' I don't feel like a fraud or that I don't deserve the life I have, but more like I have wandered somehow into a life that's not mine. With people that don't exist in my life."

"Keep going," she said.

"It's almost like the part of me that is me—my soul, if you will— has found its way into the wrong me." I was kind of proud of myself for coming up with that one.

"Uh huh," she said, and I could hear the sound of a pen or pencil scratching on a pad.

"What do you know about the multiverse?" I asked.

Miracle of miracles, she knew about multiple universes! Though she hadn't ever heard of a situation like mine ("and I'm an old lady," she said), she suspected that people drift into the wrong universe more than we knew. She'd even read a few articles about the physics involved, though in no way did she claim to be an expert. Did I want to come see her?

I did! We made an appointment for two days later. I hung up feeling elated.

CHAPTER FORTY-THREE

Constance Abierto worked out of her house, a Spanish style one-story painted a rich saffrony yellow. A dense tangle of bougainvillea in full bloom arched over a gate into the front yard. A boy who looked at most fifteen perched on the roof atop a ladder, Christmas lights on his lap. He smiled and waved and I swallowed my "Be careful up there!" comment and waved back. I walked up the path, admiring the neat rows of herbs on one side of the front garden.

Another teenager who introduced herself as a granddaughter showed me into the office itself. Pillows on the floor, colorful children's artwork and the faded aroma of many flavors of incense made the space seem chaotic and cozy at the same time. A selection of drums cluttered the bookshelves, blocking haphazardly packed books on subjects from mythology and classic psychology (Freud, Jung) to a number of works by a swami I had never heard of. This was much more like what I had envisioned for a shaman than Mr. Angelus' sparsely decorated office.

A second look told me the desk doubled as a craft station. There was a landline phone and a closed laptop, but also a sewing machine, a small stack of fabric, a basket of yarn and a short pile of cookbooks. The room was warm and bright.

I sat down on an orange director's chair and waited a few moments, listening to the sounds of the house. I heard muffled Spanish—the teenager and Ms. Abierto?—and laughter. The door opened revealing a woman who must be my new shaman.

227

She was shorter than me by a lot, older than me by a little, and was chuckling, an oddly melodic sound. Her hair, like mine, was short and grey, and she wore jeans and a t-shirt that said "Grow Up." As she came into the room, she called over her shoulder to the house beyond, "Now everyone, be quiet and respectful." It made me smile.

I was momentarily silenced by the sheer number of questions I wanted to ask her. How many grandchildren did she have? How old were they? Should I be sitting on the floor on one of the comfy-looking pillows? How would I get up and down from the pillows?

Ms. Abierto shook my hand and settled herself across from me in the other director's chair. "Ask whatever you want," she said. It was an obvious thing to say, but it felt like she had read my mind.

I hesitated, trying not to let myself go off track and ask questions that were not relevant. That's when she *actually* read my mind.

"Lucy is my granddaughter," she said. "She helps me with my husband, whom you did not meet today." She swept an arm around the room and added, "No one has to sit on the floor who doesn't want to. But I think you could manage if you did want to. I think you're probably happier in the chair, though."

Answering my un-asked questions certainly upped my level of confidence.

"What else do you want to know?" She folded her hands in her lap.

I inhaled and began, "So, Ms. Abierto, my shaman in the other world seemed to feel I was an unusual case, and even a difficult one."

"First off, you can call me Connie," she said, and went on. "That makes sense. Not everyone has a penchant for traveling between universes." Her eyes swept over me. "But I can see you don't belong here."

"You can?" I asked, taken aback.

"This will sound strange, but when I look at you, there's an extra shimmer to your outline." She squinted, examining me from head to toe. "It's kind of like your colors are calibrated for the wrong monitor."

I grinned, though I wasn't sure why.

"You like that description?" she said.

"Yes, I do," I answered. "And, if you can help me, I'm fine if you see me in color in a black-and-white world or the other way around. But," curiosity made me ask "why hasn't anyone else noticed?"

She shrugged. "People have different capacities. Men see fewer colors than women—more rods or cones, I forget which one. Perception is personal. Mine has always been acute—I'm sure it's in my DNA. I wouldn't know how to experience the world without..." She smiled. "I was born in Argentina. My mother was a fortune teller and my father a physics professor. They were high school sweethearts who stayed married for 53 years. I'm the only one of my siblings who got our mother's gift, but it was impossible to grow up in that house and avoid either the supernatural or the science. That's why I've followed all the debates about multiple universes."

My questions kept piling up. When did she come here? How many kids did she have? Did she have special shaman training? But most importantly—

"Out with it," she said.

It was like she was inside my brain along with me while I tried to formulate questions. I tried not to shake my head in disbelief. "It seems silly now that you've said what you've said, but, why did you believe me?"

"I have a good relationship with the truth," she said, as if that explained it. "Obviously, I don't know everything. For example, you never said what you want me to do for you."

"Oh, I didn't," I said, realizing it was true. "I want to return to my home universe and stay there." I felt glad to be completely sure of myself. "What I don't know is if it can be done. Do you think it can? Do you think you can do it?"

"There are no ruby slippers, unfortunately," said Connie. "And I've never returned someone to their rightful universe before. I don't think you'd find a lot of shamans who have. But I do have an idea about what to do."

I felt immeasurable relief.

Connie outlined her plan. The common ritual for finding a wandering soul, she said, might be adapted for my special situation. She warned me that she had no idea if it would work, because doing the ritual here—in the universe I had unwittingly traveled to—might undermine the entire operation. I hadn't considered that. I put the thought on hold while she continued.

It was important that I understood the ritual wouldn't be done *to* me. Instead, we'd do it together. And, she said, I had to be one hundred percent on board. She paused, waiting pointedly for a response.

"I thought at first that my life would be better here," I said. "My husband—who died in that world—he's alive here, and my brother who died is too. Seeing them that afternoon when I woke up,"—as usual, my memory of that experience threatened tears—"I thought I was hallucinating, or dreaming, but it kept going and going."

Connie handed me a tissue.

I blew my nose and continued. "It's been amazing seeing Ben— my brother, I mean—growing old and happy and healthy, but—" I had to blow my nose again. "I don't belong here."

Connie nodded. "We belong where we belong," she said, with another shrug and a smile. I hadn't noticed her gold tooth before, an incisor. It gave her smile a sparkle. "But what an adventure, right?"

The comment threw me. I hadn't ever thought of it that way. Not once. "Huh," I said. I smiled back. "Yes. Kind of like a gift. I wish I could be more like you, more positive, glass half-full, whatever."

"But then you wouldn't be you," she said, then rather pointedly pulled a face. "Sorry. That was trite, even for spiritual talk."

I laughed, glad in the moment that this woman had a sense of humor about New Age catchphrases, especially after getting them by the earful from the other shamans I had called.

"I can't claim to know exactly how or why you came here," Connie gestured around the room as if it encompassed the entire alternate universe, "but your losses do seem a likely source. Probably something to think about…" She sat up straighter in the chair. "Alright then." She opened a drawer, selected some papers and a clipboard and started scribbling.

I could see that the papers were pre-printed handouts—the kind people get before a medical procedure—but these contained instructions about how to prepare for the soul finding ritual. When Connie finished annotating, she handed me two pages.

"Normally when I help someone find their soul," she said, "I have them bring items from their childhood like the ones listed on the first page. But I realize that nothing you can bring from your home here will be technically yours—it all belongs to your counterpart who comes from this universe. You might see if anything in your home here 'speaks' to you." She put air quotes around the word. "The second page is herbs. You probably have most of them already. Any natural foods market should carry whatever you don't have, but they occasionally run out of stock on some of the rarer ones."

"What if I can't find something?" I asked.

"Oh, I keep them on hand here, all of them," said Connie. "I ask my clients to bring some themselves because it involves them in the process."

I glanced down. I could see that a few items on each page were crossed off and a few were circled. There were notes. My insides began to churn.

"Also," she said. "I'd like you to bring a person, a person who is special to you. That's written down there, too. Your brother in this world, or your husband. Someone to be your guardian, in a way. And you should wear comfortable clothing like you would to a yoga class."

"Okay," I said, trying not to sound too nervous.

"Don't worry too much," she said. "I will be here. I will take care of you."

I couldn't remember the last time someone had said that to me.

"So," she continued, "You will come here—" She fished a small book from a pocket and leafed through it. "Is next Tuesday good for you?"

"Um, sure," I said. I had so many questions bubbling out of me that it was all I could do to not trip over my own sentences. "What will happen?" I asked. "Do I need to prepare? How should I prepare?"

Connie waved my questions away. "You will bring the items and the person. You will lie down and get comfortable. I will make music of several kinds, but I have to warn you that my voice isn't what it used to be." She laughed. "I will ask you to travel in your mind, to see people and places here and there. You may sleep, you may not. It's different with everyone." She looked back down at the book. "Eleven a.m. on Tuesday? That way you'll avoid some traffic. Be sure to call me if you decide not to come."

I had a horrid thought. "What happens if I'm not here?" My voice rose with anxiety. "I mean, if I go back to the other universe before Tuesday?"

"Then you won't show up for your appointment," said Connie, shrugging as if to say, *Not much we can do about that, is there?* "You seem like a responsible sort." She stood and brushed her hands together briskly.

I stood up too, clutching the papers. We shook hands and walked out of her office together.

"It was a pleasure to meet you, Lexie. You are giving me a gift too—a peek into the most fantastic depths of the universes. I don't say that lightly." She opened her front door and, before I could muster the words to answer, to thank her for her time, I found myself outside, dazed, and blinking in the harsh light of a clear December morning.

I was in my car before I could think, my assignment lists on the passenger seat. I was on the freeway before I realized that Connie hadn't charged me any money at all.

CHAPTER FORTY-FOUR

I parked in our underground garage and decided to look over the lists before I went upstairs where Simon might question me. Connie had crossed out most of the items on the first page, but the five that remained had their share of challenges.

The first and second items were photographs—me as an infant, and me as a child, ideally between five and ten years old. That would be doable, I thought, largely because other-Lexie kept such an orderly house. The photo albums were all lined up in the living room, and well-marked photo CDs were similarly stored in my office. I wondered if any of the images would look familiar and/or be evidence of a shared history.

The third item was something I had made as a child, and the fourth was something I had made as an adult. I'd have to look through other-Lexie's personal mementos which were, without a doubt, all neatly identified and stowed. Maybe she'd kept a few elementary school projects. In my own world, I had hung on to one or two of my favorite art works from childhood, but they were tucked away in boxes in Nora's garage. It would be interesting to check if I'd made similar creations in both worlds.

As an adult, most of my creations had been gardens. I could look through other-Lexie's work files to see if there were photographs or even brochures—technically, work done by other-Lexie, but it might fit the bill.

The fifth item was a length of thread (at least two feet, the list said) in a color that spoke to me. Connie suggested embroidery thread and said it was available at any craft store.

About half the items on the second list were circled. Another few had stars beside their descriptions. Reading the list took me back to a research paper I'd written years before about the historical uses of common herbs.

The first starred item was a fragrant sprig of pine. Pine, Connie's list said, was a harbinger of new beginnings; it helped to break with the past, offering strength and growth. Winter holidays were approaching, so it was the perfect time of year to find pine boughs.

Next up, rosemary, an all-purpose purifier, with its distinctive Southern California smell. Connie noted it as an aid to memory and clarity.

I wasn't surprised to see sage on the list either, as its purifying uses were widely known and frequently cited. It was also good for the acceptance of loss.

Cilantro was for peace and protection, ragwort for courage, and comfrey for safe travel. Connie had also included primrose, "to clear out secrets," and agrimony, which "unmasks hidden troubles."

Finally, there was myrrh, which tends to the spirit and "opens the mind to new beginnings." All in all, finding the herbs seemed manageable, and I resolved that once acquired, I'd leave them in the trunk of my car where Simon would not look for (or smell) them and ask questions.

Simon couldn't be my "person" at the ritual, because for one thing, he had no idea I wasn't his correct Lexie, and for another, who knew how he'd react to being asked to accompany me to a shaman? Well, I did know—and it would never work.

Ben was the only one I could ask, but he was on a business trip to the Bay Area. I decided to ask him anyway and sent an email. He wrote me back instantly:

A shaman, huh? Sounds strangely appealing. How could I refuse such a potentially fascinating offer? I'll change my schedule around and will look forward to being your "person."

Given the perversity of the universe(s) and my complete lack of control thereover, it seemed like a good idea to keep other-Lexie up to date. I emailed her too.

Tom and Matt got to our apartment around 4 p.m. on Saturday. From our phone call, I already knew this Tom's voice was nearly identical to my Tom's, and in person I could spot no visible differences from the son I had raised in my own universe. Like my Tom, this version of my son looked and dressed like his father, in an un-flashy button down shirt with black jeans. He seemed entirely unsuspicious about me.

As for my grandson, I was dismayed to see that this Gretel and this Matt didn't have the same bond they did in my universe. Gretel seemed to tolerate Matt, and he seemed indifferent. Also, this Matt seemed older, and not in an appealing way. He was less present, more distracted, more like a regular teenager. He was less attached to me, too, and I could feel it—though to be fair, I was on edge about Tom and Simon getting along. I had already decided that at the first hint of "tension" (cue the string section) I would make a proclamation along the lines of people treating each other with kindness and respect. I had no idea if that would work.

Simon couldn't resist bringing Thanksgiving up with Matt immediately, though he knew it would bother Tom. They had settled on the couch, Tom looking uncomfortable and Matt fiddling with his phone.

"How was the Wild Animal Park?" Simon asked.

I shot him a pointed look, but he chose not to see it.

"You've been there before, right?" Simon added.

"Yeah." Matt looked up from his phone briefly. "Remember? I went to camp for a week there when I was younger."

I jumped in, "Did you see different animals this time?"

Matt had looked back down at his phone and didn't answer right away.

"Not a big deal then, huh?" Simon put in.

"Matt?" I prodded. "Put the phone down and answer your grandfather."

"Oh, uh," he said, finishing up what might have been a text. "Sorry."

Tom said, "Matt, you know your grandmother isn't a big fan of you having a phone at your age. Don't make her take it away from you."

"I'll put it in my pocket, Matt," I said, "and you'll have to ask me if you want to use it. Call me old-fashioned, if you want." I smiled at him to lessen the blow. "I'd love to know how the tour was, if there were any new animals or things you didn't see before."

Matt gave his phone one more longing glance. Then he handed it to me.

"Um," he started, "I didn't remember much from my week at camp. I was a little kid. I think we just hung out around the petting zoo. We did that too, this time," he said, "but we also got to do a ton of other stuff."

"Like what?" I prompted.

"We took the train around, but I've done that before a bunch of times." He grinned at Tom. "But we also got to watch them prepare meals for all the animals. It's amazing what they all eat and how much there is!" His eyes grew wider—and there was the Matt I knew and adored. "We also got to see the nursery. That's what they call where the babies are. Though most of them aren't babies any more. I mean, not like our babies, people-babies I mean. The apes swing on swings and play with toys and there was a tiger whose mom had died and it had a giant stuffed tiger that it could cuddle with, but it was already like a hundred pounds and they said it plays sometimes with the bigger tigers to get used to being one of them."

It was my turn to be obvious. "So, it sounds like you were glad you went."

Matt nodded vigorously. "It was great."

"We missed you at Thanksgiving," said Simon.

"I missed you too," Matt said, "And I wished Dad could have been there 'cause I know how much he likes animals but…" He trailed off.

"We're glad you had fun," I said. "Okay, now what shall we do until it's time to go to dinner?"

The rest of the visit went fine, considering. We talked for a while longer, then headed for the restaurant where Matt gobbled down practically the entire plate of nachos, then managed to finish his burrito, too. He was definitely having a growth spurt.

I never had to use my "be nice" speech, and when Tom gave me a hug before they left, he thanked me for keeping his dad on the straight and narrow. I asked myself again if my Simon would have had a similar reaction to Denise changing plans at the last minute. There was no way to know. When my Simon died, Matt was a baby and Tom and Denise were still trying to make it work. In retrospect, Denise did her best to be kind to all of us. She stuck her own nonsense on the back burner and brought baby Matt over all the time. Back then I had some hope that their marriage would work, but in this universe, where

238

Simon had never been sick, it seemed there hadn't been an occasion for Denise to demonstrate a good side.

By the time Sunday rolled around, I felt almost ready for my appointment with Connie on Tuesday. I had discovered a photo of my/our 7th birthday party that looked roughly as I remembered it from my universe. There was a letter other-Lexie wrote from the exact same summer camp I had gone to. I had no memory of writing that specific letter, but other-Lexie's childhood handwriting looked indistinguishable from my own. I had found a printout of the first email I wrote to other-Lexie, and a brochure of her landscaping work which looked similar enough to mine to include. I tucked in a skein of a lovely soft green embroidery thread and put it with all the rest in the trunk of my car.

By Monday night I was counting the hours and worrying that I would be whisked back to my world before I could go to my appointment. But finally, it was Tuesday morning.

CHAPTER FORTY-FIVE

I would love to say that I functioned as an equal participant in the ritual Connie performed, but I remember very little about that morning. Even the drive to Connie's is hazy in my mind—picking up Ben at his house, greeting his dogs, swallowing my nerves, trying to chat on the way.

My only memories of the ritual itself are flashes—moments that made impressions, nothing more. The images that stuck in my brain may be real, or they may have been constructed out of whatever a brain uses when it fills in blanks.

A few of those moments:

Hugging Ben before it started. Dreading and hoping—simultaneously—that this would be our forever goodbye.

Adrenaline running amok when I lay down on the pillow-strewn floor and realized it was time.

Connie's voice—cracked and harsh—chanting words I didn't understand.

The pungent smell of pine and rosemary as Connie rubbed pieces between my hands.

When I opened my eyes, I was in my car and Ben was driving. He told me later that we'd stopped at his house for a cup of tea, but I don't remember being there at all. I must have been too muddled to protest when he insisted on driving me home.

Everything else I know about what happened came from Ben. He told me the ritual had lasted about two hours and most of the time I appeared to be sleeping—so much for being an active participant. Connie chanted, drummed, and sang, and he believed she was in a trance for a good part of the time, linked to "something intangible" he couldn't quite perceive. He said Connie tried multiple times to move me back to my proper universe, repeating a section of chanting, stopping and starting over sometimes in the middle. Ben's description was vague, but my disappointment—as I slowly realized I had not been miraculously transported back to my proper universe—overshadowed any need I had for further details.

Ben also said Connie refused payment because I was still me—the wrong Lexie. He thought I should talk to her about it later, when I felt clearer. I certainly couldn't have completed a sentence in that moment, let alone convinced Connie to take my money.

I do remember feeling apprehensive in the car on the way home—would Simon question me about where I'd been?

When we parked in my garage, Ben called upstairs. No one answered, so Ben accompanied me into the apartment before he ordered a ride home. By then, I was feeling physically better—more aware of my surroundings and reasonably coherent—but also thoroughly disheartened to remain in the wrong universe.

When Simon got home, I was sobbing on the couch.

He sat down beside me, alarmed at my inability to say what was wrong. And then, for whatever reason—probably because my defenses were low, or the ritual itself had altered my ability to make sensible choices—I finally stopped crying long enough to tell him precisely what was wrong.

CHAPTER FORTY-SIX

Simon was apoplectic. He was angry, he was afraid, he was every emotion I didn't want to deal with on top of my own distress. He didn't believe me, he didn't want to call Ben and check my story, he claimed I was having an "episode" and wanted to take me to the emergency room. When I finally managed to fully articulate where I had been and why, he threatened to report Connie to the police and take her to court (for what, I couldn't imagine).

That was it. I lost my temper. I shouted at Simon to sit down and "shut up"—a phrase I had never allowed in our home. It shocked him into silence. And, he sat down.

Gretel retreated to her safe space under the kitchen table.

"At this point, I don't give a shit if you believe me or not," I began, so angry that my own voice pierced through the leftover fog in my head. "But in order to not mess up a whole bunch of people's lives, you need to be quiet and listen. I am from another universe. I can't give you any proof—of course not!—but I can tell you it's different. For one thing, you're dead there."

At this, Simon sat up straighter. He opened his mouth to protest.

"Be quiet," I said. "Just listen. Ben is dead there too. You died of cancer twelve years ago and Ben OD'd in his early thirties. Heroin. We have the same kids and this apartment has one less bedroom." (I don't know what possessed me to include that triviality, but it made Simon's brow furrow, as if the idea that a physical space would be different in another universe was the sticking point.)

242

I continued, barreling through my pauses to keep Simon from interrupting. "Lily is alive. Married, divorced, married, divorced, and pretty much runs her country club and plays tennis." Simon's brow creased further. "I even have the same Gretel." I shook my head, realizing I was getting way too specific. "But none of that is the point. I don't actually care much if you believe me, but if you decide to start punishing people like Connie or even Ben, it will only make everyone's lives worse."

Simon shook his head, audibly sighing, but at least he didn't try to speak.

"No one can explain what's been going on with me," I said. "I even read a bunch of physics books trying to figure it out. But I am not losing my mind." Simon opened his mouth and I cut him off again. "No. Shush. There's more." I inhaled. "In both universes, doctors have assured me there's nothing wrong with my brain, and even the shamans can't say how this"—I gestured around the room with my hands—"happened. I have to get back to my proper universe and stay there. The ritual today was my last hope. And it didn't work."

That last came out as a wail, and then I was crying even harder and forcing words out between my gasps to keep Simon from interrupting.

"I don't like it any more than you do. I wish I could offer you proof, but it doesn't exist. I'm not supposed to have been able to fall into another universe, I know that. All I can do is try to point out the small discrepancies between me and the other me—your real wife."

I saw Simon's reaction and barked, "Don't roll your eyes—it's disrespectful!"

Simon swallowed and then raised a hand tentatively, as if it was the only way he could think of to be allowed to speak without sending me off on another tirade.

"Yes?" I asked, in schoolteacher tones.

"You do get that this is impossible?" Simon asked.

"I do. Of course I do." I answered. "But I promise you, my brain is fine. I remember everything. Well, everything except the ritual Connie did today."

"The ritual today…" Simon stopped and seemed to consider, absently pushing back the cuticle of his thumbnail with his index finger while he went on. "The ritual that Ben took you to, that you kept from me, that was with some quack of a person who calls themself a shaman?" I could hear his anger reignite as he spoke.

"I'm glad you have an open mind," I snapped, before I could stop myself. I made myself take a deep breath. "I'm sorry, that wasn't helpful. It makes perfect sense that you feel that way—I probably would too if you'd come to me with this story. And yes, I kept it all from you, and yes, I asked Ben to take me to the shaman's. Why? Because I didn't trust you. You're—" I stopped and shook my head, a few leftover tears trickling down my cheeks. "You're so suspicious. My Simon was never like that. You seem damaged."

I could see Simon gather himself up to protest, but I stopped him again. "When you died I didn't think I'd ever get over missing you. I thought this other universe was the answer to my prayers, and I didn't care if it was real or a hallucination. That first day when I woke up, and you and Ben were both here, I couldn't tell if I'd come from a nightmare in which you were dead, or whether I was having an amazing dream where you were alive. But now I've gone back and forth enough times to know for sure that this is not my universe. And you're not mine." I subsided into another bout of sobbing. Simon took a tissue from his pocket for me. I gave him a teary smile of thanks.

"Lexie," Simon spoke slowly, as if he didn't want to spook me back into crying or yelling. "I'm worried about you."

That made the tears flow faster, but I struggled to stop them so I could answer. "I know, Simon," I said. "I know it comes from a good place, and you do have every right to be concerned. I want to go back to my universe, to my Gretel, to my own kids, and let the other Lexie come back to her life. You and she are good together I'm sure. You've grown together, which you and I haven't."

Simon reached out and patted my hand. "Honestly, Lex, I don't know whether to take you to the emergency room or put you to bed with a cup of hot chocolate."

I almost laughed, and for the first time I sensed an inkling of the Simon I knew buried within this man. I tried to go with it. "Maybe a cup of tea?" I asked. "Let's sit down in the kitchen. You can ask me all the questions you want and I'll do my best to answer. What do you think?"

Simon nodded, but he looked deeply unhappy.

"And maybe you should call Ben," I said. "But not to yell at him, okay?"

Simon nodded again.

CHAPTER FORTY-SEVEN

I sat at the kitchen table. Simon lit the burner under the tea kettle and stood at the stove. "Just out of curiosity," he said, "what did I die of?"

I knew he was humoring me, but I answered anyway. "Cancer," I said. "Leukemia. We did treatments and they worked for a while until they didn't."

"And Ben OD'd?" he asked.

I nodded. "He did a lot of drugs. He started young, and never stopped. I always felt like I should have been able to stop him."

Simon seemed to be taking that in. He asked, "But Lily is alive?"

"Yes. What happened to her here—it never happened there."

Simon blinked. It meant he was listening, at least a little. I knew it had required a substantial inner concession for him to ask me questions.

"I think it changed you," I said. "I mean—and it's totally amateur psychology on my part—but I think in this universe, Lily's murder made you different than you were in my universe."

The kettle whistled and Simon turned it off. He poured the water out slowly, and when he finished, he folded his arms in a classic defensive posture. "Asking me to believe what you're saying" he said, "it's a huge leap. Bigger than huge! Gigantic! Why would I believe something as unlikely as my wife visiting alternate universes?"

"You wouldn't." I shook my head sadly. "I know that. I lived through all the steps that took me to this conclusion, but you didn't. I know it makes more sense that I'm crazy and hallucinating than that I've traded places with your actual wife who's stuck in my universe."

"What?" he said. This was a detail I hadn't fully spelled out yet, and it took Simon a minute to catch up. "How do you know that?"

"We write emails to each other," I said.

"What?" he repeated.

"We can't communicate between worlds," I said, "because when I come here, her consciousness seems to go to my world. It took a while to figure that out. So, we leave each other emails."

Simon's mouth hung open and he stared at me.

"Never mind," I said. "It doesn't matter. But it was the only way we could exchange information. Sending emails to ourselves. If you want, I can show you."

Simon let out a long sigh. "If this is a hallucination or brain tumor or some other type of dementia, it's extremely elaborate."

"Yes," I said. "Very complicated and specific for a hallucination, huh?"

Another sigh from Simon. "I'm still not buying it, you know that, right?"

"I didn't expect you to accept it right away," I said. "It isn't in your nature. For what it's worth, I think my Simon would have felt the same way."

"Well that's a relief," he said. It seemed that Simon had recovered his wits enough to be sarcastic.

"You should talk to Ben," I said.

"It can't hurt," he answered, "I guess."

Simon brought our tea over to the kitchen table and took out his phone. I tried to sit still while he dialed.

"Ben?"

I could just hear Ben's reply—indistinct words.

"Yes," Simon continued, "I don't want to lose my temper here, but what were you thinking taking Lexie to see a shaman? Without letting me know?"

I heard muffled speech, still indecipherable.

"I know, I get that," Simon responded, "But damn—you do understand," he paused, "that she thinks she is from another universe." He said the words slowly, enunciating each syllable as if the statement itself proved the absurdity of the proposition. "How could you possibly believe her?"

As the reassuring tenor of Ben's voice came through, unintelligible to me sitting across the table, I noticed my hands were clenched so tightly that my nails dug into my palms. I stretched out my fingers, one at a time, attempting to relax them while I tried and failed to make out Ben's side of the conversation.

Simon spoke again. "You believe her?" He shook his head. "Is this a family delusion?"

Ben answered and Simon let out a chuckle. "You wish you could do it too? What the hell, man?"

Ben and Simon had always gotten along. And whatever Ben said next made Simon outright laugh. "I'm plenty adventurous, but I have no desire to live in any world but my own, thank you very much."

I heard Ben reply, and watched Simon put his hands up in the universal *WTF* gesture. "Okay," said Simon. "I'll put it on speaker." He pushed a button and placed the phone in the middle of the table.

Ben's voice came through the phone. "Lexie?"

Relief washed over me. "I'm here," I said.

"Are you alright?" he asked.

"Yeah, I'm fine," I answered. "Just upset."

"Uh huh." Ben sounded wary. "Should I come over there?"

"Yes," said Simon, and at the same time I said, "No need. You've spent your whole day on me already."

"I'll be over in about an hour," he said, and hung up.

Simon and I looked at each other across the table.

"Before he gets here I need to email other-Lexie," I said. "She needs to know this is going on."

Simon blinked. "How often do you do that?" he asked.

"When something important happens. So, like when I broke up with my boyfriend in the other world during Thanksgiving dinner at Nora's." Simon's jaw visibly dropped. I let it pass. "And she wrote me about you and Tom arguing at your Thanksgiving dinner. That way, we're prepared."

Simon shook his head. "Well, she's going to need to be prepared for this."

"Yes," I said. "She is."

CHAPTER FORTY-EIGHT

Dear other-Lexie,

Quick note to catch you up. I found a shaman in your world (see link below) who agreed to try to send me back to my own universe. Ben drove us, and watched the ritual, but it didn't work, probably for reasons that either Ben or I will explain later.

I was miserable and crying when I got home, and Simon tried to figure out why, and well, I'm so sorry, but I ended up telling him I believe I'm from an alternate universe.

Ben is on his way back over to help Simon understand. I hope to send you more info later this evening.

Lexie.

The smell of roasting chicken wafted down the hall to my office. Simon must have decided cooking would help him cope. I was grateful we'd at least be able to feed Ben, who was on his second unexpected trip of the day to Santa Monica.

"Good idea," I said, walking into the kitchen. "The chicken, I mean. It smells great. Ben will appreciate it."

"We have to eat."

"Can I help?" I asked.

"Sure," Simon said, and handed me a colander full of newly washed tomatoes. I took out a knife and cutting board and started slicing.

"Did you feed Gretel?" I asked.

"Uh huh," he said. He began rummaging through the refrigerator, I assumed for a side dish.

"There's some broccoli in the crisper," I said.

It amazed me that we were having this normal dinner-making conversation when less than an hour before we'd been at odds about whether or not I was an imposter.

Food had to be prepared. Life goes on, even in the wrong universe.

"Thanks for listening to me and not totally freaking out," I said.

"Well, I am freaking out," he said.

"I know, but you're not dragging me to the hospital or the loony bin. I was genuinely worried about that."

"I still might."

"Not helpful!" I said with a goofy expression to mitigate the implied complaint.

I must be feeling better. Maybe it was having come clean with Simon. As long as he didn't do anything rash, my life in this universe would be the better for him knowing. Though the whole living together as man and wife part might get tricky all of a sudden. If he thought about it.

And now he *would* think about it. That stopped my humming, but food was prepared, the table was set, and we were just waiting for Ben.

"I should take Gretel out before Ben gets here," I offered.

"I'll do it," Simon answered. "I could use some air."

"Right," I said.

Probably a good idea. And it would lessen the awkward waiting period we were in, where we both apparently had decided independently to put off the whole Lexie-is-from-another-universe discussion until Ben arrived.

I heard the knock, and let Ben in. Straight away he asked how I'd ended up telling Simon.

We sat down in the living room and I described how I had divulged my secret. I also recounted the post-revelation conversation as accurately as I could—I had been in quite a state.

"On a lighter note," I continued, "We've been making dinner together without any kerfuffle at all. Domesticity wins out over weirdness."

Ben laughed, "We've all gotta eat."

"That's what I thought," I said.

A memory from Simon's funeral in my own universe came unbidden. After the burial, Tom and Anton had created a whole buffet of their dad's favorite foods, and Nora had written a description of each dish with a short memory of her father. He would have loved it.

I sighed and Ben took my hand.

"Even if you're not technically my sister," Ben said, "it's been a pleasure knowing you."

"Thanks," I said. "I think you said that earlier."

"It bears repeating," said Ben.

Simon and Gretel came into the apartment bringing the scent of our mild December chill with them. As soon as she heard Ben's voice, Gretel raced around the corner and tackled him on the couch. He pushed her down but allowed her to lick his face.

Simon stood at the edge of the room taking in the three of us— Ben, Gretel and me. He looked morose, beaten.

"Should we eat and talk?" I asked, hoping for a civilized veneer to our conversation. And my stomach was rumbling.

"Sure," Ben said. "Thanks, Simon for making dinner. It's been kind of a long day."

"Yeah, though—" Simon stopped himself in the middle of the sentence and shook his head. "Never mind."

We put the food on the table and started eating in silence. Ben said, "This is good." I chimed in, agreeing. Another few minutes passed, and Ben put down his fork. "Simon, what can I say to help you with this?"

Simon swallowed. "You can convince me," he paused and looked from Ben to me, then back again, "that you two aren't running some preposterous hoax on me—" he raised a hand to keep us from interrupting, "or—I dunno—you could tell me that scientists have certified travel between multiverses as possible, or—" he paused to take a hefty swig of his wine, all the while holding his other hand up to keep us quiet, "show me some research proving that shamans are the practitioners of choice for impending dementia." He downed another gulp.

Ben shook his head. "Well, bro, I can't do any of that. All I can do is promise you that Lexie does not have dementia."

"How do you know that?" Simon asked.

"Look at her," Ben said.

Simon focused on me and I looked back, wanting to encourage him to see me as a person who remained in full command of her brain.

Ben continued. "She's fine; her memory's fine. If she wasn't, she'd be slipping up way more. If anything, she's caught on to a different set of circumstances quickly and managed to only make a few mistakes."

"And you were oversensitive to my early mistakes because of your dad," I interrupted.

"How do you know about my dad if you're not my wife?" Simon asked, entirely reasonably.

"I looked through files," I said. "Do you remember? When I said I was de-cluttering? I was trying to get an idea of what was different here. Different besides you two, I mean." I said, gesturing at them.

"That's not a sign of someone who's losing it," said Ben, picking up on my point.

Simon shook his head. "Maybe she forgot what happened to my dad, and had to look it up."

Ben tilted his head. "I suppose if you wanted to, you could come to that conclusion, but have you ever heard of people with dementia being as systematic? And then keeping a handle on facts after learning them?"

"It might be more like amnesia," Simon offered.

"It could be," I said. "I have tried to rule out all the other options. But why do I have such clear and detailed memories of your deaths from my real life? Along with a ton of other differences?" I sipped from my water glass. No wine for me—this was too important. "Look, I know how illogical this sounds because I went through all the same questions and doubts. It is not explainable in terms we'll ever understand. It won't ever make sense."

Simon's face fell. "How can I choose to believe something that won't ever make sense?"

"Because it will cause the fewest number of heartbreaks in the long term," I said.

Ben nodded. "Suspend disbelief, and it all gets better."

Simon slumped further in his chair.

I stood up and went to put my arms around him. "I'm going to try my damnedest to get back to the right place, and then you can chalk this up to a couple ridiculous months. You can even talk to your real wife about it." I kissed his cheek. "Get her opinion."

Simon shook his head and seemed about to speak but Ben chimed in first. "That reminds me—I have an idea. It may be a clue to why Connie's ritual didn't work."

"What?" I asked.

"Maybe you need to be in a certain place to switch back and forth? Or asleep?" Ben smiled. In fact, he looked rather triumphant. "Think back," Ben continued, "Haven't you only switched when you're asleep here in this apartment?"

Ben's idea was exciting and painfully obvious, so much so that I was a bit annoyed with myself for not putting the pieces together before. My brain went back to all the times I'd woken up in a new place.

"I think you might be right," I said.

But what about Seattle? And the sleep study?

"Though there were a few times…" I said. "I was on a plane to see Anton and took a sleeping pill for the flight, and I didn't end up here, but in another way worse place. But mostly you're right… at least when I end up here."

I could see Simon struggling to not scoff as I spoke, but it didn't matter. Ben's epiphany gave me a little bit of hope. My mind whirled through new possibilities.

"You *are* right," I said. "I usually go back and forth from this apartment—in both worlds. Maybe I could get Connie…"

Simon shook his head. "No shamans in my house."

"You could leave when we're—"

Simon put his hands up as if to ward off the entire notion. "Lexie, you're asking too much."

"But Simon," Ben said, "If it bothers you, you don't have to be here. I'll make sure—"

"Like you did with the 'ritual' today?" Simon put air quotes around the word. "How can I trust either of you, or a shaman who says she—" He looked at me. "It's a she, right?"

"Yes."

"A person who takes money for this nonsense? How could I trust her in our apartment?"

"She didn't take any money," I said. "You can't say that."

"Unless she's in it for the long con," Simon retorted.

At this, Ben protested and I snorted.

"In any case," Simon continued, "I don't want her in my house."

"Okay," I said, deciding we could talk about it later. "I'm going to see another shaman the next time I switch back to my world. Connie told me ahead of time that it might only work from my universe of origin, but I had to try anyway."

Simon swallowed more wine, and seemed to be trying to keep his face neutral.

"Can you just trust us? For a little while more?" Ben asked.

"Not do anything rash?" I added.

Simon looked from me to Ben and back. He put his head in his hands and sighed. "Yeah, sure."

I sighed too, in relief.

"But if it gets scary," he went on, "I reserve the right to take you to a doctor."

CHAPTER FORTY-NINE

After dinner, and probably Simon's fourth glass of wine (I wasn't counting, but the bottle was nearly empty and he was the only one drinking,) Ben announced that he needed to get home. I hugged him, remembering how—in this very universe and this very apartment—I'd awoken to find him alive.

"Thank you," I said, as I drew back from his embrace for what might be a last look at him. "I couldn't ask for a better twin."

Ben laughed and smiled affectionately down at me. "I couldn't ask for a better twin either, whichever one of them you are!"

"Okay, Twin Appreciation Time is now over," I said, feeling the familiar knot in my chest. "I wish every single frickin' goodbye didn't feel like it might be the last one. Let's all get some sleep. Who knows where I'll be tomorrow?" I held Ben by the hand as he turned toward the door. "Ben," I said, "If this is forever..."

"You should be so lucky!" he said, then his face changed. "I know," he added. We hugged again.

"This is insane." I shook my head. "Every time I wonder if it's the last time, and when it isn't, I feel both happy and let down—and more than a little bit out of my mind."

Simon laughed, looking at me with a tinge of sympathy for the first time since I'd spilled the truth. "That sounds terrible," he said.

"Yeah, but at least I got to meet both of you."

Simon's sympathetic smile turned into a tiny head shake, as if he'd started the gesture then thought better of it.

Ben and Simon did the manly back-pat-hug thing. Ben joked "*I'll* still be me, whichever Lexie you get."

I headed toward the dining room to clean up.

Simon stopped me. "You're exhausted, Lex. Let's leave it 'til the morning."

"You're right." I turned around. "Good idea."

I splashed my face with cold water in the bathroom while Simon brushed his teeth. My reflection in the mirror looked exhausted, ghastly. Like someone who'd been through some cosmic version of a wringer and ended up with all her oomph pushed out. I brushed my teeth perfunctorily and put on my nightshirt—well, other-Lexie's.

Simon followed me into the bedroom and we pulled back the covers on the bed in unison as if we'd been doing it together that way for years. I caught Simon raising his eyebrows, possibly at how naturally that action came to me. He couldn't know that my Simon and I had perfected the same motion in our world.

I settled under the covers and turned on my side to face Simon, feeling guilty for what I had put him through. "I truly am sorry you got stuck in all this," I said.

"Me too." Simon turned his book right side up on his lap, opened it, then closed it. He leaned over and stroked my cheek gently. "I have so many questions," he said. "I want to believe you, I really do. But I'm scared—and I also feel taken in, as if by believing you, I'm allowing myself to be fooled. Like one of those old TV game shows where they get someone to act stupid for the audience to laugh at."

"I'm sorry," I said again. "If I had been able to figure out what was going on earlier, I might have told you right away. But you're different than my Simon was."

Simon considered this and we lay in silence for a moment.

"What's different?" he asked. "Between me and your Simon."

I couldn't answer right away. Asking this question meant Simon was buying in to my alternate universe story—if not completely, then at least enough to allow himself to be curious.

"My two cents is that because my Simon's dad didn't have Alzheimer's—which I gather went with a lot of secrecy and many denials—my Simon was more trusting. And because Lily was never attacked in my world, my Simon didn't take on guilt, or then feel a need to protect everyone," I said.

"But did you and, uh, the other me," he frowned as he said it, "ever live in that neighborhood in Hollywood, or have Lily over for dinner or anything like it?"

"We did, but it was a different apartment building altogether. I looked up your address in other-Lexie's files," I answered. "The building was all over the news reports from back then. My Simon and I, we never lived there." I paused, collecting my thoughts. "When I see you at your age brimming with health—my Simon didn't get that. With Ben, I never knew him anywhere near this age so I didn't have expectations. But you and I—I wish…"

I felt the tears coming, but tried to tough it out. Who was I crying for anyway? For my Simon, I supposed. The one who didn't get to have an old age. And for me—for not having had a chance to grow old with him.

I croaked out, "I wish you'd each had perfect long and healthy lives."

The tears were pouring by then. I was surprised I had any more left. And as I cried I clung to Simon. He kissed me, first brushing my face with his lips, then pulling me closer. I felt the beginnings of a newly familiar dismay wash over me. It was one thing to have had sex with Simon when I wasn't aware of the adultery factor. It was another when I realized that the person that Simon should be making love to was other-Lexie, and not me.

I pulled away as gently as I could.

"Too weird?" he asked.

"I think so. But I'm too tired to think it through," I answered.

"Yeah, I get that," he said and leaned back into the pillows.

I watched as he retrieved his book from under the covers and paged back to his place. "Thank you," I said.

I felt comforted in the knowledge that I'd done a lot to repair my (and other-Lexie's) relationship with this Simon. I was asleep before I even realized I was. And I dreamed.

I lay alone on a studio floor surrounded by pillows. Mirrors and a ballet barre enclosed the room. A corner of a book dug into my thigh and I struggled to pull it out from under me. It was big and heavy like a textbook, *Your Guide to Navigating the Dimensions* etched in gold on its rich blue leather cover. Wow, I thought, this could be super useful. I tried to open it to absorb every word of wisdom, but it was stuck shut as though its pages were glued together. No matter how I strained, even the cover didn't budge.

I wanted a sharp object to pry it open. The only remotely suitable item in the room was a stick of incense. It burned on a small wooden table that had materialized in the far corner. I picked up the incense, mindful of the still-burning tip, and jabbed the stick end into the tightly stuck pages. But it only tore off tiny fragments of paper from the book's edge which fluttered to the floor. The book remained tightly closed.

The studio door opened and Simon came in leading two EMTs in full uniform, complete with reflective vests. One held a defibrillator and the other a potted rosemary that had been trained to grow into a heart shape—the kind people buy at the grocery store as a quick gift. I said, "That rosemary should be in the ground," and laughed at my gardener's one-track mind.

"You see," said dream-Simon, "she thinks this is funny!"

The stiff white bow and elaborately calligraphed card on the rosemary plant was too far away for me to read. I squinted and patted my pocket for my glasses, which made me lose my hold on the book. It hit the floor with an enormous thud, which finally, somehow, jarred it open. But before I could make out a single word on its pages, dream-Simon and the EMTs came at me holding bungie cords. I backed myself right into the barre at the edge of the room trying to get away, but instead of stopping me, it triggered a switch. There was the whine of a motor, and the wall collapsed behind me. I screamed and fell backward.

CHAPTER FIFTY

I woke to find Simon leaning over me, and Gretel, chin on mattress, snuffling at both of us. The bright red numbers on the digital clock said 3:46 a.m.

"You may be right after all," said Simon, patting Gretel. "I don't think you can be my real wife. She has never had a dream that woke her up."

I blinked, confused. "She hasn't? How is that possible?"

"I don't know, maybe she does, but in all these years I've never heard her cry out in her sleep like you just did."

"Huh," I said. "Maybe that's a good thing?" I still felt frazzled from the dream.

Simon gave a chuckle. "Yeah. Enviable."

"Simon," I had to say it. "You've come a long way in the last twenty-four hours."

Simon slid back under the covers and said, "Don't push it."

We grinned at each other.

"Right," I agreed.

Simon did his little dance with the covers and pillows, pulling the sheet over his shoulder just so, pulling his knees up in the perfect curl of a fetal position. I watched as his breathing slowed. Whatever disappointment I felt about not waking up in my correct reality, I knew how much I missed sleeping with someone, sensing their movements through the night.

I wondered how other-Lexie was faring in my world. Was she sad? Angry? Lonely? It takes time to adjust to being alone. Was she still sleepwalking through my life? I wanted to talk to her, compare notes, meet the other me that might have been.

I should catch her up on what happened when Ben came over. I slipped out of bed and wrote a short paragraph describing the rest of yesterday, ending with,

Btw, Simon seems to be allowing himself to believe me at least a little bit. He's been very kind. I hope you can get back here and enjoy that.

Love,

Lexie.

The next day was thankfully drama-free, though Simon watched me much more intently than usual. I called Connie, who apologized up and down for the failure of her ritual. When I told her about Ben's idea—that I might only be able to return to my proper universe when I was asleep in my own bed—she asked if I wanted her to come over and try again, a "house call," as she said. I said that Simon wasn't at all happy about the idea, and that I didn't want to force the issue, at least not yet. I remembered to ask her about the money too, and basically insisted on sending her a check. After I hung up, it occurred to me that I would be paying with other-Lexie's (and this Simon's) money and not my own—How had I not thought of that before?—but there was no help for it.

I felt freer and lighter, as if a large burden I'd been carrying had dissolved into the ether. Not needing to pretend for Simon meant I could ask him, for example, where and when he and other-Lexie bought their Christmas tree. He could ask me questions about his life in my world, which felt strange, but also intimate. After lunch, I found him sitting in the living room, nose deep in one of the multiverse books

I'd left lying around. He was already on the chapter about other dimensions and branes.

He said, "I have no idea what I'm reading."

"I know," I said. "I didn't either. It only made sense while I read it. As soon as I put it down, all comprehension disappeared from my brain—the other type of brain, I mean."

Simon made an unappreciative face. "You were never a punster."

"I'm still not," I said. "Totally unintentional."

Simon and I had a good talk about Tom and Denise. I think he was more open to my point of view because it was me, not his real Lexie. We took Gretel for a walk together and planned a hike for the next day since the weather was mild. At dinner, I allowed myself two whole glasses of wine and tried to talk about why it was weird for me to have sex knowing that I wasn't the right person. At one point Simon was laughing so hard at me that he nearly choked on his (perfectly cooked) whitefish. I jumped up and thumped him on the back, but he just shook his head and kept laughing.

We pulled the covers down in unison again when we went to bed, and I think it was all we could do to keep our hands off each other.

Of course—of course!—I jolted awake the next morning in my own bed, my alone bed.

CHAPTER FIFTY-ONE

I sat up, breathless. This time, the sensation was palpable. Muscles I didn't know I had complained at me. It felt as if I had been physically squeezed sideways through the porous borders of the universes—and even though this cosmic journey had returned me to my home, all I could do was miss Ben, Simon and my other home where, after all the ups and downs, I'd finally become comfortable.

I sat in my still-dark bedroom, aware that I had to take Gretel out, and that now there was no one but me to take Gretel out. While I didn't burst out crying, I will admit to a short but sincere festival of self-pity. I tried to buck up by reminding myself that it was a testament to my resilience that I was still doing fine—persevering—and I should be proud of myself. Out with the wallowing and in with the self-congratulations! And besides, I might go back and forth who-knew-how-many-more times—I couldn't fall apart each time.

So, I did not fall apart. I made myself get up and take Gretel for her morning walk.

Maybe later I'd look online and see if by any chance Constance Abierto existed here too. If she was anything like other-Connie, I'd be thrilled to put myself in her hands—and never mind Mr. Angelus and his inconvenient-for-me retreat. I'd call the kids, hear their voices. Plus, there was probably an email from other-Lexie waiting.

When I got back from my walk with Gretel, I made breakfast and noted that other-Lexie had left the refrigerator well stocked. I went to my computer to get an idea what had been going on in this world.

Other-Lexie had written me two emails, but she hadn't been great about deleting the hundreds of others that had accumulated over the days I'd been gone. My inbox was inundated with pre-Christmas offers, sales, and "events."

It could all wait.

I opened the first of the emails from other-Lexie. It was written the day we switched.

> *Dear Lexie,*
>
> *I'm here, which means you're there. Or at least I hope you are there. If not there, where would you go when I come here?*
>
> *Sorry to have left you with such a mess about Simon and Tom. I hope it didn't make things harder for you. I did try to talk to Simon—help him give Tom a little leeway, but now it's all fallen in your lap and I hope you're up for handling it.*
>
> *All your kids left messages. If I'm here a while I'm going to have to call them back. Should I identify myself as not-you? What do you think?*
>
> *Oh, and I finally stuck my nose in one of those multiverse/physics book you left on the coffee table. Definitely hard to get my head around, yet helpful. Thanks.*
>
> *Gotta get the dog out.*
>
> *Lexie.*

I opened the next one.

> *Dear Lexie,*
>
> *It's been four days since I wrote you and I'm still here. I've talked to all three of your kids, fielded phone calls from Lily and, yes, Bill, and even talked to Matt.*

Before I get into the phone calls, though, you should know that I canceled your appointment with the therapist. Twice. I said I had a cold, and she seemed amenable both times. I really didn't think I could pretend to be you while talking to a therapist. I hope that's okay. I hope she doesn't charge you.

Have I already mentioned that every time I'm here I've felt a little clearer? Now I seem to have more of a sense of where I am and what to do with my days because it's become my life, too. That's why I started answering the phone instead of letting the machine get it.

The first time it was Matt, and I didn't think it would be useful to identify myself as not-you. I told him there was no need to apologize again for telling Bill, and also that grownups make mistakes too. I said I wasn't heartbroken or anything like that. Matt sounded very relieved.

Nora called next, and right away she seemed to know that I wasn't her correct mother. She was very kind—asked me if I was okay, did I need help with anything? etc. She must have informed Tom and Anton immediately, because they both called within the hour. Tom was solicitous, like Nora, but Anton seemed to want answers—ranging from exact details about events in my universe to how I felt being the unwitting victim of what he called "a hole in the fabric," or some such. It wasn't that he wasn't nice, though—don't worry about that. He was just inquisitive, as if my responses might help it all make some bigger kind of sense, or give him a better idea about how the universe worked. I was sorry to have to dash his hopes, though, since I know way less about this than you do.

The next person to call was Lily, and she knew right away that I was the "other," which is what she called me. She has a great sense of humor! She was so cheerful that it took about five minutes of talking for me to connect to the fact that she's my sister, my little sister who died horribly in my world. I'll admit that when I got off the phone I had a good cry. It gave me an inkling of what it's like for you when you see people you've lost.

And then Bill called. His name came up with his number and at first, I let the machine get it. Then I heard him say he felt bad for "leaving you in the lurch." I picked up the phone and tried to thank him. He was still very angry. I actually think his call was an excuse to berate you and try to get you to apologize again.

After a minute of being yelled at, I interrupted and said something like "I'll be sure to tell the real Lexie." He said, "Huh?" and I told him it was me. He got even angrier, and sputtered about you making fun of him by pretending to be me. I tried to listen calmly but finally I blurted out, "She deserves better than you," and hung up. A day later he left a few messages and I let voice mail get those. You may (or may not) want to listen to them.

That's what's been going on here.

I'll email again if anything new or different happens before we switch back. Gretel has been very good company.

I hope my little bit of meddling doesn't mess you up.

Lexie.

How funny that each of us had decided to solve personal problems for the other! Other-Lexie dealt with Bill's nonsense and I'd (eventually) helped Simon see that his anger wasn't helpful to Tom or Matt. Maybe, in the future, other-Lexie and I could arrange to do life's most dreaded tasks for each other—tackling other people's unpleasant errands, messes, and jobs is always much easier than tackling one's own.

I listened to Bill's messages just to get it over with.

"Lexie, I'm sorry I lost my temper yesterday. I did call to apologize but when you said it wasn't you, um... Anyway, it felt like you were laughing at me, setting me up for some stupid joke. How can you treat me that way? I was always straight with you." Click, dial tone.

The next message continued, "I stopped talking because I didn't know what to say next and got cut off, but I am expecting you to apologize for trying to gaslight me."

No apology would be forthcoming. I reminded myself that it had taken me a few months and some super weird experiences to figure out what was happening to me, much less to accept it.

Bill's third message, a day after the others, said: "Sorry to call again but I wanted to say don't bother with an apology. This is good-bye. I will try to think of our relationship as it was before Thanksgiving. I wish I knew what's going on with you. But never mind. That's all."

And that was indeed all, thank goodness. I'd leave it be. I certainly didn't want to wind him up again.

After that, I called and left messages for the kids. I assured them that all was well, I was home and that I was determined to stop the back-and-forth forever.

CHAPTER FIFTY-TWO

I checked Mr. Angelus' outgoing message—he would be away for another two weeks. With Anton and his family coming for the holidays, waiting seemed too risky. So, I googled "shamans," "Los Angeles area," and "Connie," on the off chance she existed in this universe too.

Once in a while, the workings of the internet are blissfully straightforward. Connie's website appeared—Connie Abierto, retired midwife, now birth educator and (under a different tab) shaman, specializing in rebirthing.

I picked up the phone and dialed the contact number.

"Hello," said a voice I recognized.

"Ms. Abierto?" I said. "I'd like to make an appointment. I'm hoping I can see you as soon as possible."

"Would you like to describe your issue?" asked this Connie. "It's usually a good idea to make sure you're dealing with the right shaman for the job. Were you recommended by someone I've seen before?"

"Well, kind of." I laughed, then stopped myself—it might give her the wrong idea. "It's a long story." I took a deep breath and jumped in. "You see, I met a version of you in—"

"Sorry?" said Connie. "I'm not sure I heard correctly."

"I said, 'a version of you,'" I repeated. "Honestly, it's hard to explain." I sat back in my chair thinking, *hell, I should be better at this by now.*

"Go on," said this Connie.

"So, I keep falling into an alternate universe. I know it's crazy. More than crazy, really. Extraordinary."

"Indeed," Connie's voice didn't betray a thing.

"And the last time I was in that other place, I found you——you're a shaman there too——and you tried to help."

"Hmmm," said Connie. "That certainly is intriguing." She paused, probably deciding if I was deranged.

"I have no control over my life, or lives, and I can't do it anymore. Do you think you could make it stop?"

Another pause. "Well, I'm definitely curious," she said. I heard riffling pages in the background. "I could see you in three days, but without having been recommended by a mutual acquaintance, I hope it's okay if my grandson sits in."

"Absolutely," I said. "It's great. What time should I be there?"

I hung up the phone feeling pleased with myself, like I'd made a baby step toward fixing my problems.

Two thankfully boring days later I headed off to meet this Connie. In making the appointment I had assumed I would like her because I genuinely liked the other Connie. But on the drive over, I fretted. People in different universes seemed to have different life experiences, which then seemed to make them different people. Other-Simon was a case in point. This Connie had been a midwife, while the other Connie had not. But would a background in birthing babies make her that different from the other Connie? I'd have to be patient, wait and see—not my finest skill.

The directions Connie gave me were to the same little house I'd visited a few days before in a universe far, far away. This Connie's house looked like its twin, but weathered, its yellow paint muted. The herb garden took up a section of the front yard, and around the path to the front door, succulents were mixed in with flowering California natives like poppies and yarrow. The Christmas lights were already hung—no ladders or young men perched on the roof.

Connie's grandson opened the front door before I made it all the way up the path. He introduced himself as Gabriel and guided me into the office. In this Connie's workspace, the floor was pillow-free, but there was a familiar sense of comfortable clutter, some of which came from overflowing baskets of brightly colored baby toys. The desk was piled high with cookbooks and books about early childhood and pregnancy. An educational model of a pregnant woman (with removable baby) sat on a bookshelf. There were many chairs—padded, comfortable, and mismatched in style and fabric. A bulletin board held flyers for all kinds of local events and "take one" printed schedules. No incense smell, though—I guessed new mothers wouldn't want their babies to inhale smoke, even the leftover kind.

Connie came through the door a few moments later. She looked almost the same, down to the shiny tooth that gave her a sparkly smile. We shook hands, Connie sat behind her desk and I sat opposite. Gabriel found a seat on the periphery of the room. Connie motioned for me to pull my chair closer and carved an opening between the piles of books and papers on her desk so we could see each other.

"Alright, dear," she said. "It's time for your story."

It took me a while to center myself. Having experienced so much with other-Connie made explaining my situation again slightly surreal. "I'm sorry," I said. "I'm having a hard time because it feels like we already know each other."

"It's a unique situation," said Connie. "Why don't you start at the beginning?"

I took a (cleansing) breath and began my recitation—how I'd found myself in other versions of my apartment, spent time with my supposedly dead husband and brother, and ultimately felt trapped by my complete lack of control over—for lack of a better description—which world I woke up in.

"Are you saying you want to be able to move between the universes at will?" asked Connie. I had to hand it to her—she didn't reveal if she was at all put off by such an unusual (loony-tunes?) request.

"Oh, no," I answered. "Well, at least not anymore. I want to stop all the traveling and stay here."

I told her about Lily's suggestion that a shaman was the person to fix me. I also reported as much as I could about the ritual that other-Connie had done, and Ben's idea that other-Lexie and I needed to be asleep in our respective beds for us to switch between our universes.

I finished my tale of supernatural woe with, "So I'm here now, and I found you, and all I want is to stay put once and for all."

"That's certainly more possible than what I thought you wanted. I don't know a lot about this, but then again, I don't know many shamans who might. Anchoring you to this world seems feasible. Giving you power to travel at will—that's a lot less likely. It's difficult when a client wants the impossible."

"I'm amazed you think any of this can be done."

"That's not what I said, dear," Connie said. "I don't know if it will work," she shrugged, "but it never hurts to try." She took some notes, then added, "As it happens, I have some understanding of alternate universe theories—the basics anyway." Connie sat back in her chair. "Actual scientists are very careful about theories that can't be proven. My father was an astronomer. But that didn't mean he lacked imagination. He read me *A Wrinkle in Time* when I was nine and had chicken pox. Ordinarily my mother read to me. But he insisted. We talked about the other dimensions that were in the book—but mostly I remember that he did wonderful voices for the helpers, Mrs. Whatsit, Mrs. Which, and Mrs. Who—one was deep and croaky, and another was high and squeaky, and for one of them he whispered."

"I loved that book too," I said, feeling grateful that this Connie seemed as unflappable as the Connie I met in the other world.

"If you can give me some time, I'd like to think it over." Connie continued. "We'll make an appointment. In the meantime, Gabriel will do some research for me. He's in training."

"Wow," I said. "As a shaman?"

Connie smiled proudly. "I think he shows enormous promise."

"That's terrific," I said. "I'm curious, how long were you a midwife?"

"About forty years—it's what I went to school for. Catching babies—" She grinned. "It's the best. But you're always on call. It helped that I was part of a practice so it wasn't only me. Then I finally got tired of the all-nighters. Now I do childbirth education and run a baby and toddler group."

Ah, I thought. The toys. "What fun!" I said, smiling myself.

"Mostly it is," she said, "though some of the parents are very hard on themselves. It was easier when we had kids, right?" She looked at me.

I wondered how she knew I had kids, but I nodded. Maybe I had started looking like a grandmother at some point.

"You have how many?" she asked.

"Three kids and four grandkids," I answered. "How did you know?"

"I didn't become a shaman for nothing." She laughed. "I have good intuition. It was especially useful with women in labor—it's sometimes hard to articulate when you're in pain."

"Right," I said. "Of course."

"We should make a plan for about a week from now, does that sound okay?" Connie said, picking up her desk calendar.

"Sure," I said, and sighed. "I really want to be here for Christmas with my own kids."

Connie looked up at that. "I'll put Gabriel on it right away."

"Thank you. And thanks also for believing me. I know it's not a given. But I do have a few more questions, if that's okay."

"Of course."

"Do you have any idea yet what you're planning to do? Should I bring anything with me? The other you gave me a list of items—herbs, photos, souvenirs. And a person. Even though technically none of it was mine." I shook my head trying to banish that particular complication from my brain.

"I'm not entirely sure yet, but you won't need to bring any herbs," she answered. "I have them already. I do think it's a good precaution to have a friend or relative around when experiencing a ritual trance. So yes, think about who you want to bring with you."

"I will."

"Great," I said. I stood up and reached across the desk to shake her hand. "It was nice to meet you, Ms. Abierto," I said.

"Connie. Call me Connie," she said. "It was nice to meet you, too."

CHAPTER FIFTY-THREE

When I got back home I wanted to talk to my kids but I didn't want to repeat my story three different times. I sent them an email and Anton set up a Zoom.

There were the usual delays as we signed on. Tom was having trouble with the video, which meant that Anton could tease him about his tech skills. Nora tried to mediate—her life's role in miniature—and I sat back waiting for my kids to get it together and stop their playful sniping.

"We should do this more often!" I laughed when all the little rectangles on my computer screen were filled and we could all hear each other.

Anton shook his head, "Mom, you can't honestly say you miss this."

"I do!" I said. "Sure, it's nice to be able to hear the car radio these days, but your squabbling makes me nostalgic for when I had you all in the back seat."

"You aren't serious," said Nora. "When Audrey and Ruby fight in the car, all I want is earplugs."

"Now you may want earplugs," I told her, "but when they grow up and decide they like each other and eventually move away—I'm here to say you'll even miss the fighting."

Nora rolled her eyes.

"What's going on, Mom?" Anton asked, always the one to get to the point.

"Yeah," said Tom.

"I wanted to catch you up," I said. "I heard that you all talked to the other version of me while I was wherever I was."

"Yep, that was seriously whacked," said Anton. "She sounds almost exactly like you. I was surprised I could tell. I still can't put my finger on what the difference was…"

"You're more confident," said Nora.

"But she was in the wrong world so it makes sense that she wasn't as confident," said Tom.

Nora and Anton both started talking at once about their theories of what had been different about other-me. Between the occasional missing word caused by a random digital glitch and all three of them talking at once, I stopped listening. After a few minutes, I considered whistling to get their attention, but I was a lousy whistler. "Okay, kids, enough already!" I said, finally.

"Not so fun, is it?" said Nora. She stuck her tongue out and that started all three of them making faces.

"Do you remember Fish Face?" asked Tom.

"Yes!" We all chimed in.

Every family has peculiar little traditions. Fish Face involved sucking in your cheeks (like a fish) for as long as you could. It was impossible to hold a fish face and laugh at the same time, which meant that whoever was "out" would torment the finalists by trying to make them laugh. My cheeks always hurt afterward.

"Dad was the champ!" said Anton.

"He was!" I said. "But if we don't want to stay on this call all day, I have something to tell you."

Silence.

"Don't worry," I said, "It's good."

"What is it?" Tom asked.

"Well," I began, "I had some experiences with a shaman in the other universe and though it didn't work there, I'm going to try it again here. I'd like one of you to come with me when the shaman... does her thing," I said. "Anton, it's silly for you to fly down now. You're coming in two weeks for Christmas anyway. Don't feel guilty."

"I wish I could be there, Mom," he said, "I'm super curious. But I've also got a project at work to finish up before I leave."

"I know," I said, "No biggie."

"I'll come, whenever it is," said Tom. "I'll say you're having an operation. Which you are. Kind of."

"Good plan," I said.

Nora said, "I'll try, Mom, but it depends on finishing my grading, and child care. Jack has some business parties he wanted to go to and I can skip... Sorry, just thinking out loud. If you want me to be there, I'll work it out."

"I think one of you will suffice," I said. "And no one loses points for not being able to do it. Especially at this time of year."

Their faces had become serious.

"It will be fine," I said. "*I* will be fine. Having one of you there is only a precaution. When I did it last time I was out of it and it was good that I had Ben there to drive me home."

That kicked off questions about Ben, and then their father. I reminded them that neither were precisely the people that had lived and died in this universe, which was tricky and sad, and at the same time fascinating for each of them in a different way. Tom was the only one who could remember Ben, and they all had their own questions about Simon. I didn't want to get into the differences between that Simon and our Simon—it seemed too much for one conversation.

Nora asked to see baby Edie. Anton sat her on his lap where we could all admire her. Irina stood smiling in the background. It felt lovely. Not the same as hearing them argue in the back seat, but lovely.

CHAPTER FIFTY-FOUR

The next afternoon I had an appointment with Dr. Stewart, and if other-Lexie hadn't already canceled twice, I would have been tempted to do so myself. The list of things I didn't want to talk about had now expanded to include interactions with shamans in two universes.

First, I thanked Dr. Stewart for allowing me to cancel.

"But you're alright now," she said. "You definitely sounded ill on the phone. Not even quite yourself."

I was beginning to think that other-Lexie's voice might be different from mine.

"I was extra bleary," I agreed. "I walked the dog a couple times a day but other than that I didn't leave the apartment."

"Can't you find someone else to do that when you're sick?"

I was also beginning to suspect that Dr. Stewart wasn't a dog person.

"It was fine. I appreciated the fresh air. And Gretel doesn't need a lot of exercise. If I were in my old house, I'd just have opened the back door for her."

"You must miss that. The house I mean," said Dr. Stewart. "It's where you raised your kids, right?"

"It was," I nodded. "I loved our house. But there was no point in rattling around it by myself. It was full of good memories, which is how you want to leave a home, right? The kids expected me to sell it, which meant I didn't have to win them over."

"Do you want to tell me about it?"

Absolutely! This was an easy subject—far from shamans and alternate universes and all the topics I wanted to avoid. I started by describing my yard and my extraordinary lemon tree. The lemons had thick rinds, often misshapen, but their taste was as near ideal as I've ever had. I admitted to Dr. Stewart that I frequently contemplated putting a step ladder in my car and sneaking over in the dark of night to steal lemons. I even shared my fantasy court case, wherein I argued that I had nurtured the lemon tree from a two-foot tall sapling to its two-story plus height, and therefore should have lifetime access to the lemons.

Dr. Stewart seemed content to let me natter on. I told her about the house itself—the boys in their shared bedroom, Nora in her own, Simon's study full of movie memorabilia, and my own library of books about plants. I described the family room where we usually kept a jigsaw puzzle in progress, the quirky antique stove, and the remnants of paint, markers, and crayons on the big kitchen table where my kids did their homework and art projects.

"It sounds very warm and comfortable," said Dr. Stewart.

"It was. Leaving was like letting go of a part of myself," I said. "Every so often I find myself driving there by mistake—it didn't happen at all for the first couple years after I moved, but then it happened a few times in a row and I wondered how my brain was doing." I laughed to show her that it wasn't a huge concern, more of a funny story.

"Pathways," she said. "Sometimes it's like the pathways in our brain only need a moment of inattention to reassert themselves. About once a month, I reach for a knife in a drawer where I haven't kept the knives since we redid our kitchen." She looked at her watch. "I'm sorry, but our time is up and we should discuss our schedule over the holidays."

I tried not to show my relief when Dr. Stewart said she'd be on vacation from the end of December through early January. One less thing to worry about. We set a date for the week after New Year's.

Connie had a small list of items I should bring to the ritual with me.

"Honestly, Lexie," she said, "I have no idea if this is going to work. I don't think it's been tried before—and I asked around. However, I think I have a game plan now. And I'm up for it if you are."

"Is there a downside to trying?" I asked.

"Of course—there's always a downside," she answered.

That was logical, but not particularly hopeful. "What should I worry about? Worst-case scenario."

I heard Connie sigh through the phone. "The best 'worst case' is that it doesn't work," she said. "The worst is a worse version of what you said happened when you tried before. You said you didn't have any memories from the ritual. That might have been for a lot of reasons—the trance of the ritual can be profound for some people. But the other possibility is that you might have trouble fully coming back into yourself. Your grief, as you've explained it, is what took you to that other place. But your grief is also a part of you. That's something you have to contend with. If we try to eliminate it—even as a means of keeping you here—then you aren't who you are anymore. It's tricky."

That sounded complicated and scary. "Are you saying that afterwards I might not be me anymore?"

"Sort of," she said. "Though I doubt it would be permanent."

"Huh," I said. "I have to think about that."

"What I want to do is allow you to focus on your grief—give you some peace with it—which then should enable you to move forward. Afterwards, I'll see if I can anchor you here. If that makes sense."

"It does," I said.

"It's not an exact science," she said.

"I know."

I did know. A year earlier it had never occurred to me that a shamanistic ritual might touch my life in any way. By choosing this method to fix my problem (and was there another?) I had also chosen a completely unscientific path with no guarantees. But I was ready. I had to try.

"Are you there?" Connie asked.

"Yes," I answered. "I'm ready."

CHAPTER FIFTY-FIVE

Connie's email said she would provide the "shaman stuff"—herbs, crystals, and some aromatherapy oils. She also told me I would drink a tea she made from common herbs (she included the recipe in case I had obscure allergies). It was supposed to relax me.

My contributions would be entirely personal—photos of Ben, Simon, my children and grandchildren, and any keepsakes such as childhood locks of hair or baby teeth. Had I kept or buried any portions of their placentas? (I had not, which was a relief when I thought about it.) She also suggested I look through my jewelry for any pieces with black stones, which are "grounding"—as are hematite, various quartzes, moss agate, turquoise, black tourmaline, and magnetite. Even small bits would be helpful, especially on jewelry I had had for a long time.

I began with the photos. That part was easy—my favorites were framed and ready to go. Then, I rummaged through my "keepsake" box and took out the envelopes with locks of hair from my children's first haircuts, and the old prescription bottles in which I had stored their baby teeth, each tooth washed carefully, and the child's name scrawled in sharpie over the label.

As for jewelry, I had buried my wedding ring with Simon and I didn't wear anything else anymore, not even earrings. I hadn't opened my old jewelry boxes since I moved into my apartment. Even if I found no pieces with black stones, I should see what was in there—after all, I did have granddaughters.

I got out the step ladder and headed for the hall closet. On the top shelf, among containers of miscellany that defied any filing system, were three old jewelry boxes. One was rectangular, made of maroon pebbled leather, another was treasure-chest shaped and covered in a padded and worn pink velvet. There was also a smaller tarnished tin box with a simple lid. One by one I turned them upside down on the kitchen table.

There was the necklace my mother gave me when I graduated high school. It was a Navajo piece, turquoise, an attempt by my mother to give me a "cool" gift. (She had also given Ben a beaded leather and turquoise bracelet. What had happened to it?) There was my father's class ring and some chipped coral earrings that had been my mother's. There were old leather watch straps, a few actual watches (one with a rose on its face) and more than a few enameled pins in the shape of flowers. There was an unsurprisingly large number of peace signs as pendants, rings, bracelets and pins, some of which looked like I'd made them in summer camp. There were so many loose beads—some made of seeds, some of glass and stones, and a lot only partially strung—that I knew I'd be finding them in the corners of the kitchen for weeks. I remembered Nora and Tom going through my jewelry when they were little, heaping the necklaces around their chubby necks and twisting them many times around their arms for bracelets.

It's amazing how memories fade and re-emerge. I hadn't seen these things for years, and I didn't remember all of them, but the ones I did took me right back to the days when they had been among my most important possessions. Even the ones I didn't remember set off tiny sparks in my brain that suggested the impressions still existed somewhere in my mind's recesses.

Only a few items seemed right for the ritual, but these (including the Navajo necklace and the pieces that had been my parents') I put into a bag with the photos. I put the "good" jewelry for Nora and my granddaughters back in the in the velvet box, and the costume jewelry into the leather box which I could take out for grandchildren to play with.

Finally, I swaddled the cut-glass bottle of my mother's perfume in bubble wrap. It seemed an important part of my journey through sadness and memory into that other universe. It should definitely accompany me on this, the next part of my journey.

The days passed more quickly than I expected. Every day I felt more anxious, but I assured myself it would be like an annoying-but-necessary medical procedure. What other options did I have? If I chickened out, I might keep going back and forth, and I didn't want that. The ritual itself was daunting—it might be psychologically painful, and it might do nothing whatsoever, but I had to try. I had to show up.

By the night before my appointment I was very nervous. When I finally fell asleep, I dreamt I woke up with Simon next to me. I was in the wrong universe again! I tried to move, to sit up, but I couldn't. I was paralyzed, stuck in my own head, and there was no way I could even cry out. Simon pushed the covers off us both and now he was my Simon, as emaciated as he had been in the weeks before he died. He turned his skeletal face toward me, and said, "Oh, honey it's all right," and I wanted to scream that it wasn't all right—it would never be all right—but no words came out. He patted my arm and said, "Don't worry, sweetheart, you get used to it." Tears trickled from my eyes. All I could do was blink.

I felt Gretel licking my hand and knew I was awake.

I lay in the dark, grateful to be able to move my body, grateful to have not been transported to the other universe. I didn't need a therapist to tell me what my subconscious was up to. I was scared.

I decided to not try to go back to sleep. I went into the living room to distract my brain with television until Tom came to pick me up.

CHAPTER FIFTY-SIX

Tom came in and found me dozing on the couch, the television droning in the background. I hadn't even walked Gretel yet. I showered and dressed while Tom took Gretel out, and when they got back, I made him promise to take care of Gretel if I didn't make it through the ritual.

"Of course I will," Tom said. He patted my hand, "You're more anxious than I expected. You already did this once."

"Yeah, I know," I said. "I'm definitely on edge, and it feels way worse this time. I don't know why."

"I do," said Tom. "You have a better idea what might go wrong. And you're where you want to be and you don't want to mess with that."

"You're right," I said. "You are a very smart person."

Tom laughed. "You raised me that way!"

"We did our best," I said, taking his hand. "But nothing prepared me for this—and I don't mean only how out-there my life has been recently, or that I'm on my way to see a shaman." I shook my head. "I'm still not over the fact that my children are trustworthy, kind adults now. That's the best measure of success your dad and I could have had. It definitely seems like a lot to lose."

We drove east to Connie's, and parked across the street from her house. Tom put his arm through mine as we walked. It took everything I had not to lean my full weight on him.

"You're nervous," Connie said, when she answered the door. "But right on time. Thank you for that." I introduced her to Tom ("You have such a special mother," she said) and she introduced her grandson Gabriel.

Most of the chairs in Connie's office had been cleared to the edges of the room, as had the desk. There were three extra-large blue yoga mats spread across the floor. Gabriel took Tom to a chair on the sidelines. My heart beat faster.

"I'm going to go get that tea," Connie said, and headed out the door.

"Are you okay, Mom?" Tom asked from his perch across the room.

"Kind of," I said.

"My grandmother knows what she's doing," said Gabriel, with an encouraging smile. "You shouldn't worry."

"I know," I said—though I didn't. "It's just pre-performance jitters."

"You won't have to do a thing," Gabriel said. "And the tea will calm you down."

"What's in it?" asked Tom.

"It's herbal," I said.

Gabriel answered too, "Rose petals, motherwort, and violet, mostly—though I think she also uses hawthorn berries. Nothing dangerous, just calming, grounding herbs so your mom can settle in before we start."

Connie came back in with the tea in a mug that said *Keep Calm and Call your Grandmother.*

"I have the same mug!" I said.

"Yes," she laughed, "I think it's a popular gift."

I blew on the steaming liquid and ventured a tiny sip. The tea was tasty, in an acrid herbal way. You either like the flavor of rose petals or you don't, and I happen to like it. Between careful sips I told Connie what I'd brought with me, and she began to tell me what we'd do—I'd lie down, my items would be placed around me, the photos where I could see them, the kids' keepsakes, the jewelry and Connie's crystals touching my skin.

"I haven't opened the bottles with the baby teeth probably since they went in there," I said. "If we take them out, how will I know which is which?" Now I was micromanaging.

"We'll mark them in some way, okay?" Connie said. She sat down next to me and described how we'd begin. She told me I should try to concentrate on the sound of her chanting, which would help ease me into a trance. Then she would "do her magic."

"Magic?" I asked. "Do you want to be any more specific?"

"I could give you a play-by-play in advance," she said, "but it probably won't mean much. It will also postpone starting—which is only going to make you more antsy."

"Good point," I said and took another draft of my tea.

Connie came over and held out her hands to mine. I took them—they were warm and strong and soothed me. This was a woman who had been a midwife. Her hands and voice were the tools with which she resisted fear and pain. I made myself inhale and exhale more slowly.

I finished my tea while Connie and Gabriel placed items around the yoga mats. Connie gave me a small and extremely fragrant pillow—I could detect rosemary and sage, plus a jumble of other herbs in smaller quantities. I lay down and she balanced several crystals and a few pieces of the jewelry I'd brought on my torso and limbs. The perfume bottle nestled in the space between my neck and right shoulder. Connie moved in closer, holding what looked like a gourd. There was another small drum in her lap as well.

"Ready?" she asked.

I nodded.

CHAPTER FIFTY-SEVEN

Connie struck the drum. She began to chant, syllables I could barely untangle under the layers of her complex drumbeat.

It took time for me to relax. I tried to shut out the rest of the room—to push all my cares into the background. Finally, I noticed my thoughts and fears, my sense of myself in my body, fade.

It felt like a narcotic. Uncomfortable.

I flashed back to when, as a child, I had been playing in our overfull garage (where I had been told not to play) and unwittingly stepped on a pitchfork. It punctured the sole of my lightweight tennis shoe, went on through my foot and out the top of the shoe. It took a moment for my brain to register the pain. At the hospital, my mom held my hand while they gave me shots—tetanus and a strong "pain killer," an opiate. The sensation in my impaled foot receded to the deepest part of my brain and became just one thought amongst many. I fell asleep while they cleaned the wound, and when I woke up I was horribly nauseous. For some reason, that was the association I formed—opiates equal nausea. I hated that feeling. It could have been an early difference between Ben and I.

Thoughts of Ben brought me back to the present. I became aware of my body again—a twitch in my toe, the weight of a crystal, the scent and faint prickle of pine needles—but then I was outside looking in, the tableau of the room below me. I saw Tom sitting forward, elbows on his knees, chin on his hands, restlessly tapping his foot. Gabriel was perched forward too, whistling in time with Connie who sat cross legged at my side.

The tableau disappeared.

I re-emerged standing in the rain at Ben's open grave, the walls of dark wet earth before me, the coffin already nestled in its new home. I stood with my parents, Lily, Simon, and a very young Tom—so small among all the adults around the grave. Other mourners formed a blur of faces and rain gear behind us. Tom leaned into Simon. My father held an improbably orange umbrella over my mother. Lily flanked my mother's other side. They both cried.

I sobbed from my gut. I could no longer stand under the weight of my grief. My knees buckled and landed on the sopping grass. I was heaving, almost vomiting. I felt Simon's hands and my father's support me as I maneuvered to try to stand up again. My boots slipped on the slick ground. Grass clippings clung to me. My hands, knees, coat, it was all wet from rain or tears or snot.

As I regained my feet, my father became Tom, now a grown man by my side. It was a dry day, the Santa Ana winds blowing, the sharp smell of fall in the air, grass crunchy underfoot. Anton's arm was around my shoulder; Nora held his hand, Jack beside her. Denise held baby Matt. Simon's coffin was lowered, his grave a few feet from Ben's. I read a passage from the poem Simon had chosen and my eyes filled with all the tears I'd thought I'd already shed during my husband's final days. Words on the page swam but I knew them by heart:

For most of us, there is only the unattended
Moment, the moment in and out of time,
The distraction fit, lost in a shaft of sunlight,
The wild thyme unseen, or the winter lightning

Or the waterfall, or music heard so deeply
That it is not heard at all, but you are the music
While the music lasts. *
(*Eliot, The Dry Salvages, ll, 206-212)

Sun sparkled on dust motes and I was back in my body, gazing up to the ceiling. Connie's chant seemed loud and raspy and Tom now stood behind his chair, nervously bouncing in time with Connie's rhythm. I could feel that both sides of my face were wet from tears. I tried to wipe them off but my hand felt too heavy—gravity pulled it back to the floor.

I sank further. I sank through the earth. I opened my eyes in what might have been a tunnel. Misshapen mirrors lined the walls from ceiling to floor, their reflections distorted, carnival funhouse style. I shivered. It was freezing cold. A dim light ahead of me reflected from mirror to mirror. I tried to walk toward that light, but my feet were bare and the mirrored floor was so frigid that my toes curled in protest. I stepped back, but everywhere was cold.

I tried to think logically—if this was some kind of maze, I should be methodical about trying to find my way out. I stretched my hands forward and turned slowly in a circle. One hand touched a wall. The chill shot through my fingers and up my arm as fast as I pulled it back. I pulled a stretchy sleeve down over my hand to protect it while I inched myself forward, following the wall. When one hand got too numb, I switched to the other. The chill circulated up through my feet making me stiff, my movements jerky and painful, a wind-up toy winding down.

Whatever I was doing, it wasn't working.

I stopped.

Walls opened and closed before me in perfect silence, my infinite reflections moving with them. I was turning pointlessly, stuck trying to find a way out. I saw another source of light in a corner of a mirror—a candle burning?—and for a moment I thought I could outsmart the place. I inched my feet forward again. My toe caught something I couldn't see and in spite of the numbing cold, it hurt. I cried out. My voice echoed sharply through the space, repeating my "Ow!" over and over. I felt a rush of anger. I yelled, "I'm not a bat!" then "Or a dolphin!" and finally—proud that I remembered the word—I screamed, "I don't echolocate!"

I sat down in a fit of irrational giggles. The freezing floor burned through my thin yoga pants and I curled into a fetal position shivering, utterly depleted.

My brain whirled, ramping up as my body shut down. I reminded myself that this was a hallucination brought on by a ceremony. I was in an elaborate construction of my own making, my multiplying reflections all the lives I wasn't leading. By trying to wrench myself away from my sadness, I had surrounded myself with only myself. No living creature would ever grow in this place: no trees, no roots, no leaves. No person. I would die. So be it.

"Nothing grows here!" I called, even knowing no one could hear me. My voice came back, "Not here."

I answered myself, declaring, "I know that," and heard, "Know that," come back to me.

But if I was going to die, I wanted to be in the real ground, the living ground, the ground with plants, earthworms, the disintegrating bones of the dead like me.

The strength of the thought made me sink further. When I forced my eyes open there was nothing. Darkness. But not quite as cold. I sensed insects, and ropy tenacious roots, and small shards of stone around me.

I tried to breathe, but the weight of earth crushed down on me. My lungs struggled to take in air. Dirt forced my eyelids closed. I opened my mouth to scream and soil rushed in. I could hear Tom's voice as I tried to spit, push out the dirt, inhale again. He whispered, "It's okay, Mom," but I couldn't respond. When I finally wrenched my eyelids open the dark was still there. I was buried. I wailed.

I came back into a body suddenly lightened. Connie must have removed the heavy crystal from where it pressed on the bone between my breasts. I felt the slight give of the mat under my body and the hard floor underneath the mat. I sucked in air as completely as I could. My lungs expanded. My back arched away from the floor. Someone's hands ran from each shoulder to hip to encourage me to relax back down. I still couldn't see. The scent of cedar and cypress and the faint whiff of the old perfume surrounded me and I felt the percussion of drum beats from my toes to the tops of my ears. I may have slept. The drumbeat continued but there were no more dreams, no more visions.

CHAPTER FIFTY-EIGHT

I don't know how long it lasted. At some point I tried to sit up, felt blood drain back into my body, got dizzy and lowered myself slowly back to the mat. I heard Connie's voice say, "Don't move until you're ready."

I tried to speak but it came out as a croak. "I'm thirsty."

I opened my eyes and saw Connie kneeling beside me, a sheen of sweat on her face. She smiled and stroked my forehead. I saw Tom standing behind her, anxiety plain on his face.

"Mom?" he said.

I tried to say "thirsty" again.

Connie motioned Gabriel. He left the room.

I tried to sit up, and Tom knelt down and supported me with an arm around my back.

"Are you okay?" he asked.

"Let's give her some water before she tries to answer," Connie said.

Gabriel came back and handed Tom a glass with a bendy paper straw.

"Not too much," said Connie.

Tom put the straw to my lips. The water was blissfully cold. I tried a sip and then I wanted more, but Tom parceled it out slowly, as if it were ice chips and I was in the hospital.

I wasn't in the hospital, was I?

I looked around wildly, caught my chin on the glass and spilled the cold water all over myself. I gasped.

"Sorry," said Tom.

I shivered once, a big shiver, and shook my head. "It's fine," I rasped, "just startled."

"Stay there for a few minutes," said Connie, "or lie back down if you feel like it."

I tried to ask how long it had been but couldn't formulate the sentence. I pulled up my legs and hugged my knees. I concentrated on my breath. I didn't want to scare Tom—it was the downside of having brought him with me. At the same time, what I had experienced was too frightening and too intimate for anyone not family to witness.

"Thanks, sweetie," I whispered.

"It's okay," he said.

Somehow Tom got me into the car, where I believe I fell asleep trying to describe my visions. When I woke up he was talking to Nora on the car speaker. "Connie said not to leave her alone. I'm going to spend the night."

I tried to protest, but my words came out mumbled.

"Hang on," said Tom. "She's awake."

Nora's voice came through, "Mom? How are you?"

I tried to say that I was fine, but my voice wasn't loud enough for the car microphone to pick up.

"Mom?" Nora sounded as if she was going to cry and I rallied my strength to answer her.

"Fine!" It felt like I yelled it but the word came out softly. "Tired. Talk when home."

"Okay," she said, holding back a sob.

"Don't cry," I said. "Not necessary."

"Right," said Nora, a hint of sarcasm perceptible.

Tom took over. "She's tired. It was intense."

"Call me when you get her home."

"'Kay," said Tom.

I sank back into sleep and when I came to, I heard Anton's voice through the car speaker telling Tom to call him after he got me home. I didn't wake up again until Tom pulled us into the garage.

I was home.

EPILOGUE

Christmas and New Year have come and gone and I'm still here, in my own universe. Whatever happened—and superstitious person that I am, I'm not inclined to look too deeply—I feel surprisingly content in the here and now. My experiences in that other universe are memories, existing alongside my memories of all the people I have ever loved.

I've been to Ben's grave a few times. It felt strange at first, because my perception of my Ben was influenced by my time with other-Ben. I talk to them both when I am at the cemetery—the Ben who died so many years ago, and the Ben who got to live long enough to have a daughter, and befriend me when I needed him. I am grateful to have met him, to have been lucky enough to encounter another, better future for my brother.

I still go to sleep with a certain amount of trepidation, and there's an adrenaline rush when I wake up in the middle of the night—though it does seem to be getting incrementally better. Connie calls regularly to check on me, and my kids call or text nearly every day. Gretel seems slightly less vigilant, which is interesting, but I may be organizing my reality around what I wish for—a trait that's not necessarily new for me. At the same time, if Gretel thinks all is well, maybe I *am* okay now.

We had a lovely Christmas. Anton and Irina flew in a few days before. I had to take everything off the coffee table and substitute safe items— toys and books and plastic containers from the kitchen—because the baby was beginning to crawl and pull herself up. She bumped her head a few times on tables and corners, and the Christmas tree had to be surrounded with furniture to keep her from pulling it down, but all in all, it was a success.

Anton and I talked the day before Christmas while Irina and Edie were napping. I could see that he wanted to have a moment with me. I made us tea and we sat at the kitchen table. Gretel put her head on his lap and he played with her silky ears absentmindedly.

"You do seem better, Mom," he said.

"I think I am," I said.

"Do you think that ceremony made a difference?"

"Probably," I answered. Connie had suggested including "grounding" herbs in my tea recipe at home, and I had made up a big batch.

"What if it was all in your head?" he asked.

I choked on my tea and spluttered a little. Gretel picked up her head to check on me.

"I mean," he continued, looking a little sheepish, "what if you had like a fugue state going and—"

"Really?" I said, trying not to sound overly outraged. I wasn't, actually, outraged, but I was taken aback.

"Uh huh."

I put my cup down. "Have all you kids been wondering about that?"

"Well, I have," he said. "Maybe it's all been a giant illusion and the ceremony got you over it."

I sighed. No point in arguing. "I guess it's possible," I said. "All I have to go on is that it seemed real."

"It's not exactly evidence," said Anton.

"Right." I nodded and hazarded another sip. "Though I do remember it all perfectly, which feels like evidence to me."

Anton shrugged. "I suppose."

"But, as far as you're concerned, the jury's still out?" I asked.

He nodded, almost apologetically.

I looked at my son thinking, *why not?* There were all kinds of ways to fit my experience into what I had learned about the multiverse, but there would never be any proof. "I can live with that," I said.

Anton smiled and stood up. He took a step, leaned down and kissed the top of my head, just like I used to do when he was a small child. "Glad you're back, Mom," he said.

Nora and Jack showed up with the girls early on Christmas morning. Audrey and Ruby cooed over the baby, their little cousin, and tried to carry her around with them while they waited for it to be time to open presents. Watching Edie try to wriggle out of her cousins' arms I had to stop myself from shrieking, "Don't drop her!" No tragedies ensued. If anything, Edie was delighted by her cousins. She pulled Audrey's hair a few times, which made Audrey cry, which then made Edie cry, and Irina had to intervene, untangling the baby's little fingers one at a time. Irina then won Audrey's heart by braiding her hair to keep it out of the way.

"Will you do mine?" Ruby asked.

Irina beamed.

After the presents had been opened and Irina took the baby off for a nap, Nora and I sat down on the couch. Audrey and Ruby were playing with one of the craft kits they'd received, and the boys—well, they weren't *boys*, were they? They were men—Tom, Jack, and Anton had taken Gretel for a walk.

Nora patted my hand. "How are you doing, Mom?" she asked.

I looked around me. There was wrapping paper detritus on the floor where we'd left it for the baby to crumple and squish and hopefully not put in her mouth, there were piles of children's books and gifts on the floor too—my favorite sort of chaos. "I could be happy forever like this," I said.

Nora smiled. "Yeah, I get that." She looked down at her hands. "Any more waking up in the wrong place?"

I shook my head. "No. Not once."

"That's great," she said, then asked, "Do you miss it?"

I had to think about that. "I don't think so," I said eventually. "You know, your brother Anton isn't sure that anything happened to me. He thinks it might have been all in my head."

Nora's expression didn't change.

"You too?" I said. "Et tu?"

"It's not a betrayal," Nora said huffily. "It's not like we ever had any proof one way or another."

"Fine." I shook my head. "But what do you really think?"

"Now that it's over?" she asked.

"Yeah," I said, "Now that it's over."

My daughter looked into my eyes. She took my hand. "I'm just glad you're okay and we can have this Christmas together—and yes— I want it to stay this way always."

I hugged her.

Tom didn't have Matt this year but in a burst of inspiration, I invited Denise and Matt to join us for Christmas dinner. I was pleasantly surprised when she accepted the invitation.

"Matt seems worried about you," she said, after everyone had greeted everyone and Matt went off to play with his cousins. "He wouldn't say why. I checked with Tom to see if you'd been sick and he said not exactly. I don't know what that means—you seem fine now?"

"I am," I said. Telling her more wasn't a good idea. "You know," I said, "I've been thinking a lot about when Simon was sick."

Denise blinked, not understanding.

"It was very kind of you to bring Matt around back then, and I'm not sure I ever said that to you."

She smiled. "You did. And then you did all that babysitting for me."

"That was a pleasure," I said. "The offer remains open, though I'm sure Matt'll be babysitting me soon."

We laughed and I was gratified that she appreciated my little joke.

After dinner, Denise gave me a hug and told Matt it was time to go.

"Can I take Gretel on her walk first?" he asked.

"Fine by me," I said.

Denise shook her head. "It's late and I'm not sure about you going on a walk by yourself.

Gretel was a pretty good deterrent for random crime in Santa Monica, I thought, but I didn't say it. Instead I offered to go with them, promising Denise, "We'll make a quick trip around the block."

Matt and I took Gretel downstairs. Gretel kept looking up at him as if to say, "Is it you?" and then turning her head toward me, "Wait, you're here too?"

As soon as we were out of sight of my building Matt said, "I wanted to ask you a question."

"Sure."

"Dad says you're all better now. That you won't be going to that other place anymore."

"That's true," I said. "At least it seems so."

"I asked him if he believed you'd been in an alternate universe, and he asked me if I thought it mattered."

"Huh," I said. I hadn't expected that. After all, Tom had been there for the ritual. "What did you answer?"

"I had to think about it. I guess I'm still thinking about it."

"That makes sense," I said. "I'm still thinking about it too."

"And I decided that Dad's right. It probably doesn't matter."

I made a skeptical face and Matt continued, "But maybe it matters for physicists? I mean what if it totally happened and we could figure it out and control it?"

"Do you mean people should study me?"

"Uh huh."

"I'm not sure I want to be studied," I said. "But you could be the guy who learns all about dimensions and universes and understands them. And then we'll learn about it from you. Maybe you could be an astronaut *and* a physicist."

Matt rolled his eyes. "I don't know if I want to be an astronaut any more. Or a physicist. Right now I think I want to be an architect like Dad."

"That would be great," I said. "But on the off chance that you find out anything about the multiverse, you'll tell people, right?"

Matt laughed. "Yeah, duh!"

We got back to the apartment and I thanked Denise again for being with us. Anton and Irina had already gone to put the exhausted and over stimulated baby to bed. Jack and Nora were rounding up the kids and all their presents. A load of dishes was running in the dishwasher and the kids had disassembled the table and put away as much as they could. We said our goodnights and goodbyes.

I asked Tom to wait a moment—there was something I wanted to ask him. We stood in the little hall by the door listening to the rest of the family make their way down the stairs.

"What's going on?" Tom asked.

"Don't take this the wrong way," I said, "but I've heard from your siblings that there's some debate on whether that alternate universe place—whether it was all in my head."

Tom didn't seem at all perturbed by the question. "Makes sense," he said.

"What does that mean?" I asked. "Do you think it was all in my head?"

"Does it matter?" he said.

"Come sit down for a sec," I said and walked into the living room. "Yes, that's what Matt said you told him."

"Some of that was because I didn't want him to talk about it, especially at school."

"But you could have—"

"I know, Mom," he interrupted me. "I could have said, 'If you tell anyone they might not believe you,' or 'You might get your grandmother in trouble.' But that wasn't the whole reason."

"What was the whole reason?" I tried to look stern, but it had been a long day and I probably just looked exhausted and a little cranky.

"Don't be mad. Remember, it was your experience, not ours. We only know what you told us," Tom said.

"But—" I started.

Tom cut me off. "Hang on, let me finish. Yes, I went with you, and whatever Connie did seemed to work. But we don't know definitively what took place, do we? I wanted Matt to realize that we don't know everything. Tolerate ambiguity and all that. I wanted it to be an open question."

I looked at my son. My son who had seemingly accepted my wild stories and held my hand—and more—while I tried to fix myself. My open-minded child, my first-born. A man in his own right who gets to think whatever he wants.

"Huh," I said. "That seems fair."

"Good." He nodded. "Then I'm going to head home. I'm tired." He stood up. "Are you going to be okay? I could stay here if you want."

"You're sweet, but I'm fine," I said. "Go home. And you're right, it doesn't matter. Whether it was real or not, it changed me, and I think for the better. I'm…" I thought for a long moment, "I'm happier."

Tom smiled, one of those smiles that looks like it just covers up tears, and we hugged goodbye. Gretel and I stood at the door looking mournful together.

"It's okay," I said, as my excellent dog and I walked down the hall toward my bedroom. "He's right, it doesn't matter. Real or not, it was quite an adventure."

Gretel nosed my hand and I realized I had been talking out loud.

That night, in my dream, I saw Ben and Simon again.

I was on the deck of an ocean liner and Ben and Simon stood on the dock waving. It was an old-fashioned scene like in a movie where a huge boat leaves for a trip and there's bunting and confetti falling and low-pitched ship's horns and smoke blowing out of a giant smoke stack. I watched Ben and Simon get smaller and smaller as the crowd on the quay became more amorphous, a jumble of colors as my ship pulled away from shore. When the crowd became a tiny smudge on the horizon, I turned around to find that I was alone and my boat wasn't so big after all. More like the size of a rowboat, but there were no oars, just a bottle of water and a little wooden seat across a rickety bow.

Gretel and I were the only passengers, and I had to get her to sit and stay because otherwise her weight would capsize our little boat. We sat together, looking out over an ocean that soon took over the horizon in every direction. I wasn't scared. I leaned back on Gretel and she licked my face, almost tipping us. I laughed.

I woke up.

END

ACKNOWLEDGMENTS

Thanks to my teacher, Eve Lasalle Caram, and my writing group: Katherine Easer, Mary Marca, Linda Overman and Susan Ware, and my dear friends and first readers Linda Whittlesey, Sandy Bieler, Kate Nason, Gaili Schoen, Nancy Grant, and Jan Minium. Special thanks to my sons Nico and Jakob Brugge for their thoughtful readings and suggestions.

Special thanks to Kathryn Gerhardt for her fabulous cover design, and to Amanda Jane Getty and Coryn Pettigrew for their excellent editorial skills.

Heartfelt appreciation to my publisher, Summer Stewart, for her support and flexibility during this difficult year.

And finally, thanks to my beloved John Archibald Getty III, who enriches my life immeasurably.

ABOUT THE AUTHOR

Anna Boorstin cut sound on many classic films of the 1980's, including *Real Genius*, *Clue* and *Beaches*. She raised three sons, each taller than the last, volunteered in several capacities at their schools, and tended to dogs, lizards, hamsters and a sainted cat. Since her nest emptied, she has traveled extensively. Books have been a constant in her life ever since she was old enough to check out ten at a time from her local library.

ABOUT THE PRESS

Unsolicited Press is based out of Portland, Oregon and focuses on the works of the unsung and underrepresented. As a womxn-owned, all-volunteer small publisher that doesn't worry about profits as much as championing exceptional literature, we have the privilege of partnering with authors skirting the fringes of the lit world. We've worked with emerging and award-winning authors such as Amy Shimshon-Santo, Brook Bhagat, Elisa Carlsen, Tara Stillions Whitehead, and Gabriella D'Italia.

Learn more at unsolicitedpress.com. Find us on Instagram, X, Facebook, Pinterest, Bsky, Threads, YouTube, and LinkedIn. Unsolicited Press also writes a snarky newsletter on Substack.